D0915786

Concerning The Matter of
The King of Craw

A Story
RON RHODY

Outer Banks Publishing Group
Outer Banks • Raleigh

Dedication

To
Joyce Hudson
and
Russ Hatter

Who felt this story needed to be told.
And whose help and encouragement made sure it was.
They are golden.

Author's Note

This is a story.

It is not a history or a biography.

It is based on a real person, but it is fiction.

This John Fallis is not the real John Fallis. This is the one I have imagined. As are the others whose real names are used in this book.

I have tried to stay as true to the record that exists as I can.

But I repeat, this a story.

The real John Fallis deserves a proper biography. He was a remarkable man.

Until then, there is this.

"The essence of good and evil is a certain disposition of the mind."

Epictetus

PROLOGUE

I have been able to reconstruct most of the facts of his life, but I still cannot explain the man.

The sudden explosions of violence.

Like the cutting of Semonis.

The surprising acts of compassion.

Like the burial of the mountain child.

What drove him?

He and Semonis were friends. At a dance. A woman. A remark by Semonis that John Fallis thought insulting? The knife was out and in Semonis' side before anyone could move.

Some spark, some circuit in his mind connected and he reacted violently and without thinking.

That happened often.

Ted Bates.

Not serious. The bullet missed the bone and the leg healed.

Tubba Dixon had a pool cue broken over his head and would have had the jagged stump shoved down his throat if he hadn't been pulled out of Fallis's reach.

There were other shooting and cuttings.

Anger? Surely.

Self defense? Perhaps.

For the Semonis knifing, he was arrested, charged with cutting and wounding with intent to kill without killing, and jailed.

But nothing came of it.

From his bed, Semonis petitioned the Judge to set John Fallis free. John is my good friend, he declared. It was a simple misunderstanding, as much my fault as John's. Please let him go.

The battered and the wounded often petitioned the court to let him go.

Because of acts like the burial of the mountain child?

A stranger, a man from the mountains, had come to town to find work and feed his family.

No work could be found.

While the man searched, his baby son caught the river fever and died.

The man knew no one. Had no friends or family to call on. No job. No money. No way to bury his baby son, his only son. For a man like him, a man from the prideful culture he came from, the shame of it was damning, the despair of the loss of his son crippling.

Then someone told him about a man who might help.

No need to belabor the story.

The stranger came to the grocery. Stood before the counter. Humble. Humiliated. Told his story. Promised somehow, someday, if only Mr. Fallis could see his way clear to lend him enough money to bury his son, he'd pay it all back, swear to God.

John Fallis listened quietly. Took the measure of the man. Didn't lend him the money. Gave it to him. More than was needed. And stood with the man and his wife at the burial so that they didn't have to endure it alone.

Like the spark that set off the violence, there was a spark that triggered compassion.

I doubt he was aware of either.

Whatever the case, to most of those in that section near the river where the poor lived, that section where the bad-ass bars and the honkey-tonks and the cat-houses huddled, to most of the people in that part of town where John Fallis had his grocery, and to many others all over town that were poor and powerless, he was revered. He stood up for them.

To the proper folk of the city, though, he was Lucifer unleashed. He was a lawless, thuggish, un-intimidated insult to decency and the Powers-That-Be.

They wanted him gone.

John Fallis was ten when he began to carry a knife.

The older boys, the bigger boys, picked on him. He fought back. They thought it was funny.

Until he got the knife.

When he became a man, no one thought it would be funny to pick on John Fallis. He brooked no insult, would not be cheated, would not be pushed around.

He bent a knee to no man.

He was the King of Craw and Lucas Deane was his acolyte.

I came to know Mister Fallis through Lucas.

That's how I thought of him—as Mister Fallis.

He was strikingly handsome. He had a charm that was almost magnetic. When he chose to use it, which was not always, he won friends easily and women became willing prey. Being around him was like being swept up in a vortex of energy where something exciting, something dangerous, something unexpected could happen, would probably happen, at any second. I fell gladly into his orbit. I was only a boy then.

We were in the seventh grade, Lucas Deane and I, when we met. I was transferring in from a distant school. Lucas was already there.

That year was nineteen-twenty. The Great War was over. The country was opening the door to the Roaring Twenties. The Big Shoot-Out was a year in the future.

The Big Shoot-Out.

The day John Fallis took on the entire city police force.

You've heard of it. Everyone's heard of it. Even the *New York Times* was appalled.

But John Fallis was special to Lucas Deane long before that.

Lucas and his mother would have starved but for John Fallis.

Lucas's mother was ill and couldn't work. They were penniless. No money for food, no money for rent. Lucas was only seven at the time. John Fallis heard of it. He found Lucas and gave him a job ... things he could do, sweep up at the grocery after school, stock the shelves ... and paid him enough that they could get by.

Later, Mr. Fallis kept Lucas on. He liked the boy. Lucas's gratitude was endless, his admiration boundless.

I could understand that. I came to admire John Fallis, too. But not to the point of blind devotion.

Lord, save us from our heroes.

JOHN FALLIS

ONE
Stranger

The morning is too warm for September and the setting isn't right. The hills that ring the town are full of oak and maple. No pine. No aspen. There is no bite to the air. No patches of snow on the peaks. No mountains at all.

I'm twelve years old in a strange place among people unfamiliar to me and faced with making my way into and among them. I've not been in this predicament before.

I wait on the fringe until the others start in.

I've been assigned to Miss Thompson's homeroom. The others laugh and talk as they jostle for seats. I take one at the end of a row in the back of the room that no one else seems attracted to.

The teacher starts the roll call. When she gets to my spot in the alphabet, she stops.

"Owen Edwards," she calls, and pauses. Then says, "Please stand."

No one else had been asked to stand. I do so, uneasily.

She smiles, "Welcome, Mr. Edwards. Class, this is Owen Edwards. He is new to town. He and his family have just moved here from Colorado, from a town called Estes Park, which is way up in the Rocky Mountains on the other side of Denver. His father is with the U. S. Forest Service and is going to help our foresters work up plans for the big new forest the state hopes to establish down in the Cumberland Mountains."

She smiles again. "You can sit now."

All eyes are on me, curious, sizing me up, deciding whether to be interested or not. Not exactly indifferent, but not enthusiastic. They all know each other. They have their own little cliques. Who needs a stranger thrust upon them?

"Don't worry," my mother said, "you're a friendly boy. You make friends easily. You'll fit in."

I guess.

But in the meantime I'm nervous and uneasy and would just as soon be back where I already fit in, where I already have friends.

Miss Thompson speaks again. "Lucas Deane."

A boy in the front row straightens up.

"You are just the boy to get Owen settled. Show him where things are. Explain how we do things."

Lucas Deane doesn't look pleased. He has curly blond hair and a frown.

"Owen is your charge now, Lucas. Don't let him get lost." She smiles again at this and a few in the class laugh. She continues the roll call.

Lucas Deane turns to look back at me, holds my gaze, then nods, and turns back to the front.

There was nothing to suggest that Lucas and I would become friends.

We had almost nothing in common.

Except the chemistry.

This is not a dynamic I can explain. You may have felt it, an affinity that springs from a quality in another person that draws you, a chord struck deep that resonates with you. Nothing that you can command or summon. It's there spontaneously, unconsciously. Or not at all.

Lucas and I had that between us.

My mother, at supper that first evening after school, asked me about how it went that day...what did I do, who did I meet?

I told her about Lucas Deane.

"Did you like him?"

"I think so," I said.

"Where does he live?"

When I told her he said he lived somewhere down Wilkinson Street, she frowned and looked to my father.

"Where down Wilkinson Street?"

"I don't know. Just down Wilkinson near something called the Bottom."

She put her fork down and, looking again at my father, reached across the table to put her hand on mine.

"I am sure this Lucas Deane is a very nice boy and I think it is fine that you might become friends. But under no circumstance are you to go where he lives. You understand, Owen? Under no circumstance are you to go home with him or to his neighborhood. He is perfectly welcome here. But you are not to go there. Understand?"

No, I didn't understand at all.

In Estes Park, I'd never been told to stay out of a friend's neighborhood. There was no place in town we couldn't go.

"Why?"

My mother and my father exchanged glances. My father took over. "The section of town where your friend lives is not a place for children."

"But Lucas lives there."

He frowned, thinking about how to respond to that, then decided to take the parent's way out. "We just moved here, son. We're getting settled, finding our way around. The people I work with say the Bottom is a place to stay out of. They wouldn't say that without good reason. Do what your mother says."

With that phrase I knew the matter was closed.

"Yes, sir," I said, and sat there wondering where the Bottom was and what was there that had the adults so on guard.

This town I'm in is the Capital City of the Grand & Glorious Commonwealth of Kentucky. It's much larger than Estes Park—three, maybe four times larger. The streets seem full of people night and day.

It has factories and sawmills and distilleries. Two movie theatres. Two! And a prison and a railroad and a J.C. Penny store and a baseball field. And its own newspaper. And two capitol buildings. Two!

The one they call the New Capitol, the one where the work of the people is done, overlooks the town from a hill in the residential area on the south side of the river. It is more grand than the one in Washington. The other capitol, the Old State House, is on the north side of the river. It sits in the center of town in what was the village square in olden times. It's made of Kentucky River marble and was built in the style of an ancient Greek temple. At night when there's moonlight, you can imagine Apollo might be nearby, or Bacchus laughing somewhere in the shadows.

Outside of town the land is soft and green. Little creeks run through picture-book meadows and sycamores lean over them, so gentle and peaceful you just want to stand and look.

There are no mountains and no forests. Corn and tobacco fields are everywhere. The most beautiful horses I've ever seen graze in white-fenced pastures of bluegrass and clover.

A river winds through the middle of town. But there are no trout in it.

And no one I know anywhere in sight.

The school is bigger, too.

And Lucas Deane is my shepherd.

I ponder all this, lying abed in my new home in this new town waiting for daylight to come.

Yesterday was not bad.

The class work will not be a problem. I'm up with it. Even a little ahead. Fitting in probably won't be either. None of the kids were unfriendly. A couple of guys looked eager to show me that they were the kings of this particular hill, though they didn't seem to want to try to make that point with Lucas around.

He was with me the full day. Ushered me from class to class. Introduced me to the teachers. Showed me where the lunchroom and the toilet and the gym and the music room were.

We didn't talk much. He got me where I needed to be, told me what I needed to know. He was polite, but was otherwise remote.

I am more neighborly. All I reap, though, is that scant bit of information about where he lives and the surprising news that he has a job and can't hang around for after-school games.

A job?

Lucas Deane is a mystery.

Yeah, I'm gonna like him.

TWO
There Are Rules

The would be Kings-Of-The Hill caught up with me the third day. After school.
As I was crossing the playground on my way home.

"Hold up there, pretty boy."

There were three of them. Two about my size. The third one was bigger, a
head taller ... and tubby. Neat, though. Nattily dressed and preening.

"Pretty boy. Pretty boy. How do you do. The girls think you're cute. How
nice to be you."

It was the tubby one chanting. He gave a little flourish of a bow.

There was just enough arrogance in his voice to know this was not a we-
want-to-get-to-know-you-better gathering.

He clapped me on the shoulder.

"We haven't had a chance to tell you how glad we are you're here." He
glanced around to his buddies, smiling. "And to make sure you know the rule."

A pleasant September afternoon. Kids walking slowly across the lawn. No
clouds in the sky. A choose-up touch game getting underway at the far end of
the playground.

"What rule?"

He stepped closer, tapped me on the chest—an overbearing fat boy
wearing knickers and a tie.

"Why pretty boy, there's only one rule. My rule. And that rule is...." He pointed to each of his buddies and then back to himself. "We," poked a finger in my chest, "rule!" Poked me again, more forcefully.

The other two moved close, forming a menacing little circle.

I gathered I was going to have to give up on my mother's reminder to be nice. Just then I heard a voice from across the playground.

"Owen. Wait up."

Over Tubby Boy's shoulder I could see Lucas coming.

Tubby turned and saw him too.

"The Crawbat."

Turning back to me he said, "The rule is that the rulers get a nickel a week from the peons to keep them safe. We collect on Mondays. Don't forget. Don't be late."

"Safe from what?"

"Safe from us, pretty boy!"

And he and his little cohort hurried away.

I stood there winding down my temper while Lucas caught up.

"What did those guys want?"

"A nickel a week," I said.

"For what?"

"To keep from getting beat up."

He watched them, frowning, as they left.

"You gonna pay it?"

"I'm going to tell Tubby Boy what he can do with his rule and make sure he understands."

"Tubby Boy," he smiled.

"Who is he?"

"Jay Overby. His dad's one of the big lawyers in town. He thinks he's something."

"Is he?"

"He's a big bellied bully trying to lord it over anybody who'll let him."

"Not me," I said.

"There are three of them."

"Fine."

At that, Lucas laughed, "An honest to god mountain man."

"He was calling me pretty boy. Where did that come from?"

He stepped back then and made as if to study me carefully.

"You are kinda pretty."

"Come on, Lucas, don't play around," I spluttered.

He laughed again. He hadn't laughed much before. Hadn't found anything to laugh about, I suppose. He turned and started to leave. "If you need help, yell," he said.

"They're getting a game started," I said.

Lucas looked down the field to where the game was about to get underway. I wanted him to stay. But what he said was, "I've got to get to work. See you tomorrow."

As I watched him leave, I remembered what Tubby had said.

"What's a Crawbat?" I called out.

He spun around, a look on his face like I'd hit him.

"That's what Tubby said when he saw you coming."

Lucas stared at me for the longest time, then turned and walked away.

Understand that all this is foreign to me and I am trying to find my way in. I don't know the drill, don't know the place. I don't know the players or how they play.

All my life I've lived in a small town where people know each other.

The year round population in Estes Park where we moved here from was less than five hundred. More in the summer when people from the cities down below came up to cool off and play in the mountains. But year round, just enough people to make it cozy.

The only places we needed to be careful of going were into the high country alone in winter or into the forests in the spring when the bears are cubbing.

I had a bike and snowshoes and a sled and a .22. The .22 was only for learning, I was to get a proper deer rifle when the season opened but I don't know if that's still the plan now that we're here. I had a compass and a 6-weight Heddon bamboo fly-rod. I knew the trails, could find trout, and knew the names of all the trees and most of the wildflowers.

And I had friends, Jimmy D., whose dad had a ranch up Chin Valley where they ran black angus and grew alfalfa; and Andy, whose dad was the best elk guide in the mountains; and Winston, son of Kerry Jensen of Kerry Jensen & Son Hardware. Winston was the son so mentioned.

No friends here.

Not yet.

Except Lucas?

If I haven't bent him out of shape with that question about Crawbat.

Even before I asked the question, I knew the word was an insult. The way Tubby spat it out made that clear.

My mother says I need to be more, her word, circumspect, need to control my curiosity.

"Ask any question you want of your father or me, but with others, give some thought to how your question might be taken. Think, Owen, think before you rush in."

Even so, I still want to know what Crawbat means.

And I still want to know what there is about the Bottom that makes it a place I am to stay out of.

I'd gone into the mountains in winter alone.

I'd hiked through the forests in the spring when the bears are cubbing.

I wasn't dumb about it. I had my compass and my .22 and my snowshoes. And in the spring I made sure to whistle while I hiked so the momma bear would know I was coming.

I could do the Bottom.

I wouldn't be dumb about it.

This town I'm in lies in a wide valley cut by the Kentucky River deep down into the limestone plain that underlies the Bluegrass region.

The valley is wide. The walls are steep. You come on the town unexpectedly.

The river defines the town. It makes a big S-curve through the center of it.

Most of the businesses and the Old State House are on the north side. That's where the town began just after the Revolutionary War, on land being developed by General James Wilkinson.

The street bearing his name, Wilkinson Street, starts at the bend where the river makes the second curve of the S then straightens out. This is where the aristocracy lived. Their mansions are still there. The street runs north beside the river for almost a mile, crossing the railroad tracks past a sawmill and a hemp factory on the west side of a big hill called Fort Hill. There is a big dam across the river near the street's end and a famous distillery sits beside it.

The Bottom is off to the town side of Wilkinson.

At the last census, the town's population was 16,206, not counting my mother, my father, and me.

The distance by road from here back to Estes Park is 1,220 miles. You have to cross the Mississippi and the Great Plains and climb the eastern flank of the Rockies to get there. I know this from the library. My mother is a teacher. She showed me how to look things up.

The main road, Highway 60, runs east to west. East is Lexington. The university is there. It's about thirty miles. West is Louisville. All that gold at Ft. Knox. Fifty miles or so.

There were no specific references to a place called "The Bottom" that I could find. So I asked the librarian.

"Why do you want to know?"

"A boy I know lives there. I'm new. I don't know where it is."

So she found a city street map and ran a little circle with her finger over a section of town to show me.

A motherly lady looking concerned, she said, "don't go there."

"Yes, ma'am," I said and thanked her.

THREE
If I Was You Boy, I'd Stay Uptown

Exploring unmapped country that you've been warned away from is a temptation too strong to be resisted.

What's there?

I could hardly wait to find out.

Saturday there'd be no school.

"What are your plans?" my mother asked at breakfast that morning.

"Exploring," I said. "I'm going to take my bike and explore around."

"Be careful," she said. "You're not used to so much traffic."

I'd gotten a copy of the city street map from Mrs. Anderson, the lady at the library, and had already marked out my route.

I wanted to see the capitol and the prison and go downtown and check out the movie theatres and maybe walk around the Old Capitol grounds, but my main target was the Bottom.

The area the librarian traced for me on the street map, the area called the Bottom, was about a third of the way down Wilkinson Street.

"In the early days it was not much more than a swamp," she told me. "As the town grew, people began building and filling it in. It flooded every time the river rose and when the high water went down, the streets were full of stranded crawfish. So they started calling the area Crawfish Bottom, which in time got shortened to the Bottom. Or sometimes, just Craw. It is a bad place. Gambling and drinking and fighting, and other things too raw for decent people to even consider, go on there. You stay away from that place, you hear me," she said.

"Yes, ma'am," I said.

I chose Wilkinson Street for the reconnaissance.

Saturday.

Mid-morning.

Cool enough for a sweater, but the sky was clear and I knew I'd shuck it before noon.

Wilkinson is a wide street and very busy—horse drawn wagons and delivery trucks constantly chugging up and down the roadway.

The land between the street and the river was given over to factories and shops. There was a big saw mill and further down a factory where hemp is made into rope and twine. Scattered around were repair shops and supply stores.

The houses were on the side of the street opposite the river—a lot of them. There were several big ones with outside stairs, boarding houses probably. The rest were plain one and two story frame houses, a few with brick fronts, many with upstairs balconies overlooking the street. Most could have used paint or a screen door fixed. The houses that weren't squeezed between Fort Hill and the street had front yards.

Once past Fort Hill, the land opened up and the houses were further apart and larger. I saw vegetable gardens in back yards, and chickens. Not many people. A few sitting on their porches in the afternoon sun. No one waved.

Off Wilkinson, looking down the tunnel of cross streets as I passed, there was a different feel. I made out places that seemed to be little more than weathered shacks. Not everywhere. There were some nice houses, but they were interspersed among run-down shanties and dilapidated two-floor structures with washing drying on clothes lines strung across upper floor porches.

These were only flashes of what lay there, fast glances down corridors as I rode by.

I'm not sure what I expected. Something surely to explain why this was stay-away-from territory. Bandits and magicians and gun fights in the streets.

Harem ladies and trolls lying in wait to gobble up the innocent. But I felt no sense of menace. I did, though, have the sense of danger lurking. Not threatening exactly, but something to be wary of, the sense that comes when you are alone in high country and night is coming on and there is movement in the bush that can't be the wind because there is no wind.

On the way down I'd passed a big grocery store on the corner where Wilkinson cuts the edge of Fort Hill. I stopped there on the way back.

"John Fallis" the sign read. "Grocer." It seemed friendly enough. The day had heated up and I was thirsty and I had seen a Coca-Cola ad on the side of the store.

There were men standing around outside talking and women shopping. The men eyed me curiously as I leaned my bike up against a post. There were a couple of benches on either side of the entrance door. Several sat there. Two were standing at the curb. They looked like working men, sturdy high top shoes, heavy pants, long-sleeved work shirts. One had red suspenders. That one called to me as I started inside.

"You from around here, boy?"

"No, sir," I said.

"What're you doing down here then?"

"Nothing, sir. Just riding around."

He frowned.

"Riding around?"

"I just moved here. I wanted to see the dam and the distillery."

He leaned back and stared hard at me

"This ain't a tourist place, boy." He was frowning. He looked me over a longer moment. He nodded toward the grocery door.

"Go get whatever you were going to get then."

There were boys hanging around off to the side of the grocery. He glanced at them and said loud enough for them to hear. "I'll watch your bike while you're inside."

He stood up. I'm sure he wasn't as big as he looked, but he looked awfully big to me.

"If I was you boy, I'd stay uptown."

12

FOUR
Rise Peon

Monday came.

Collection day.

The day Tubby and his merry men would be expecting to collect their tribute, the day that would mark the start of my second full week of school in this town still strange to me, the day that would set the way my peers would think of me.

I knew they knew of Tubby's shakedowns. They must have talked of it. The word must have gotten around. Not that they were likely to ostracize the timid and the weak among them. They'd just have no respect for them.

I understood that. If you don't respect yourself, no one else will. To prove that you do, you can't let others push you around.

While I was a boy, the only instruction I ever had in fighting came the afternoon Andy Charbonneau got beat up.

Jigger Swinson beat hell out of him. Jigger was the biggest and meanest boy in class.

We were playing marbles after school behind the swings. Jigger said Andy cheated. He grabbed Andy's taw and wouldn't give it back. Andy called him a liar.

"Don't call me a liar you little bastard." He took Andy apart.

When Andy couldn't stand up any longer, Jigger kicked him in the side and walked away with Andy's taw.

Jimmy D. and Winston and me helped him home. Andy's dad, the guide, the elk hunter, was there. "What happened, boys" he said as he washed the blood from Andy's face.

Mr. Charbonneau, Baptiste Charbonneau, was a cheerful man with an easy way and the build of a bear. His face was wind-burned and sunburned and his eyes crinkled at the sides when he smiled. No smiles now.

When we finished, Mr. Charbonneau said, "Did anybody help this Jigger Swinson beat on Andrew?"

"No, sir."

He waited a moment or two, considering, then said, "I'm not for fighting, boys. But some things you can't let pass."

He looked around to each of us. "I want all you boys to pay attention to this."

Another long pause, waiting to be sure we were listening.

"I don't expect you to fight unless you have to. But from time to time you'll have to. Life works that way." He seemed saddened by that, but continued.

"If there's going to be a fight, don't stand around jawing. Don't waste time pushing or shoving. Knock the sonofabitch down and stomp on him. Hit him as hard as you can! Go for the stomach. Knock his wind out. When he bends over to try to get a breath, hit him behind the head with both your hands locked together. When he falls, stomp on his hands so he won't be able to hit again for a long time. Don't give him any quarter. Don't give him time to collect himself."

Mr. Charbonneau was a respected man. He had to master the mountains. Sometimes had to master the egos of the swells who could afford his skills but who drank too much or wanted to take a calf for the meat when it was bulls only season and he wouldn't permit it.

We listened.

"Beat him so bad he'll never want to fight you again," he said. "Blow through him like a Maria and then stand over him and tell him if he ever sees you coming he damn well better get out of the way."

We were gathered in his kitchen when he told us this. Andy was sitting on a stool by the sink with the bloodstained washcloth floating in the basin and we were ringed around him. Mr. Charbonneau was standing behind Andy with his hand on Andy's shoulder.

"Understand, boys? Understand what I'm telling you? Don't get caught up in ideas about fair fights. There are no fair fights. You hit first! Hit with as much force as you've got. Drop him down and stomp on him before he knows what's happening. Make him never dare mess with you again."

He ran his gaze over each of us, satisfying himself that we understood.

"Now, Andrew," he said, moving around to stand in front of Andy. "I want you to go find this boy Jigger Swinson. I want you to give him that message. And I want you to get your taw back."

He walked to the corner by the fireplace where he kept a staff that he used when he was scouting in the mountains, a long wooden staff of fire-hardened oak that had been shaved into round and varnished slick. He hefted it, swung it, slapped it against his open palm a couple of times, walked to the window and looked out. The afternoon was fading but there was still an hour or two to sunset. He walked back across the room to stand in front of Andy.

"This boy's bigger than you. Take this to even that up. When you find him, don't say anything."

Mr. Carbonneau raised the staff above his head and swung it down in a sweeping arc.

"Smash him! Hit down, like you're chopping a log. Hold the staff in both hands. Hit hard. Aim for a spot between the shoulder blade and the neck. Then switch your hold and swing like you're hitting a baseball and hit him across the upper arm."

He drew back, pivoted and stepped into the swing as if he expected to drive it out of the park.

"Then swing it down and bark his shins. Then stab it into his gut. When he falls, stand over him and jam the stick into his neck where the Adam's Apple is. Not too hard. You'll kill him if you press too hard."

Mr. Charbonneau stood there, legs apart with the staff's point shoved into the floor at his feet and him leaning into it, steel in his tone.

"Tell him give me back my taw. Tell him don't you dare come at me again."

He handed the staff to Andy. "Go now."

15

And turned to us. We were breathless at what we'd seen, shocked at what we'd heard. "You boys go with him," he said. "See that no one interferes."

No one did.

Andy got his taw back.

Jigger Swinson didn't mess with any of us again.

I remembered.

Tubby and his three merry men circled me when class let out for morning recess.

"Pretty boy, pretty boy, we're waiting for you. It's Monday morning and tribute is due."

They were standing by the outside water fountain. You had to pass it on the way to the playground. Tubby made his little sing-song chant loud enough to be heard by those who were passing. Most of the class knew what to expect. They didn't stop as they passed but began to gather in little groups just far enough away to be close enough to watch.

The morning was chilly. Tubby had on knickers again and a neatly knotted tie and a button- up sweater, with hair slicked back and an arrogant smile. He stood hands on hips, looking big and threatening. The three merry men grinned at each other.

He held out his right hand, palm up, smirking. I smiled right back and drove my fist into his gut with all the force I had. Tubby's eyes widened. He folded over, gasping, and I hit him behind the neck with my interlocked hands. He splayed out flat, almost bouncing off the concrete pavement at the base of the fountain. I let him lay gasping for a minute, then rolled him over and knelt down with my knee in his chest. I grabbed his tie and forced his gagging face up to look me in the eyes. The surprise on his face was deeper than the pain.

"Wha...." he tried say but he was fighting too hard to breathe.

I tightened my grip on his tie. "Tubby, the peons have risen," I said.

I dropped him down then and rose to deal with the merry men. But there was no need. Lucas was standing behind me, protecting my back.

Across the schoolyard kids were running in to get closer.

Tubby was still on his back gasping for breath. The merry men seemed dazed. Lucas nodded his head toward Tubby and said to them, "Your little shakedown is over, boys. I wouldn't try it again or pretty boy might get mad. Now pick your friend up, clean him up, and get out of here."

Then he turned to me laughing and shaking his head said, "Where'd you learn that!"

FIVE
Hats Off To You, Baptiste Carbonneau

Lucas Deane's particulars remained a mystery to me for quite a while.

Early on I learned that he lived in the Bottom, that he was a year older than me and had a job, and that his mother worked. There was no mention of his father so I assumed his father was dead or had left.

No one else in school seemed to know much about Lucas either.

There were three other boys from the Bottom in the class and two girls. They walked softly around him. All the boys walked softly around him.

There was nothing overtly intimidating about Lucas. He was a bit taller than the rest of us, a little more agile, a little quicker maybe, but he was not arrogant or overbearing. He was polite. There was no apparent reason that he should have generated the deference he did among our classmates. I suppose it was the way he carried himself. There was an air of singularity about him, the throb of intensity. You got the sense he was a person best not to challenge.

Though the kids were careful around him, I think he would have been very popular had he been more sociable ... and had he not lived where he did. The Bottom was the wrong side of the tracks. Most of the privileged folk in town looked down on it and on the people who lived there. Lucas resented that. He resented that people look down on people because they're poor. It wasn't fair. That resentment put an edge on his personality and made him standoffish. He wasn't part of any of the little cliques. He kept to himself. But he was always the first boy picked in the choose-up games at recess and he was always the captain.

My little session with Tubby turned me into a celebrity of sorts. No one had stood up to him before. Tubby was smart about his game. He didn't try to shake down the boys as big as he. And certainly not the girls. They'd tell their mothers. That left him the timid and the weak to prey on.

The others knew what he was doing, but as long as he wasn't doing it to them, they looked the other way.

So my act became the talk of the school.

The violence of it had as much to do with the attention it got as did the act itself.

School fights, such as they were, were mostly pushing and shoving and a wild swing or two. No one had seen, or expected, the kind of onslaught I made on Tubby.

Tubby didn't give me up to the teachers. He would have too much explaining to do. He and his boys sulked, but they behaved. I knew I'd made an enemy. I didn't care. I got slapped on the back and grinned at and had thumbs-up flashed as I passed. A pretty red-haired girl brought me cookies one day, and another asked if I knew how to dance and, if I didn't, said she'd be happy to teach me if I wanted. I was golden.

Lucas shared the attention, but it embarrassed him.

I liked it.

I thought fighting bad guys might turn out to be a very good thing.

Anyway, I was now in with the in-crowd at Second Street School in the Capital City of the Commonwealth of Kentucky.

I had a friend.

The school year was just beginning.

The Bottom was waiting.

And I had Baptiste Charbonneau's wisdom to gird me.

SIX
Moonbow

The work that brought us to this town was my father's work, which concerned itself with the care and nurturing of wilderness. It was a mission for him, not a job.

All the foresters I ever met who worked with my father at the U.S. Forest Service felt that way. "In wilderness is the preservation of the world," Thoreau said. They believed it. They could imagine no higher calling to which a man might devote himself.

My father was assigned here to help the Kentucky state forestry people work up their plans for a magnificent stretch of wilderness that angled through the mountains of the Cumberland plateau which they hoped one day to make a state forest—a region of trees and meadows on the southern border with Tennessee where bear and cougar prowled and deer and elk grazed. Hawks and eagles held the sky and quail and grouse hid in the brambles and worked the cornfield edges. In the spring, wildflowers carpeted the slopes and in the fall the turning leaves of the hardwoods painted the mountains bright.

My father hadn't seen it yet. He needed to walk it, scan it, get its feel. He decided to make his first inspection one that would include Mom and me. We'd headquarter in a cabin on the Cumberland River just outside the town of Corbin. While he had his talks and made his walks, Mom and me we'd see the sights.

The Cumberland River is a grand river that snakes along below the southern border of Kentucky through Tennessee past Nashville, then bends north back up into Kentucky to join the Ohio river near Paducah. I could take a friend. We could hike in the woods and fish.

"And you," he said to my mother, "I'll show you the Moonbow."

"The what bow?" she laughed.

"A rainbow of moonlight over the great falls of the Cumberland. It's close by."

"Be serious."

"Truly. When the moon is full, a rainbow forms in the river mists. A rainbow of moonlight." He gave a sly smile. "Romantic."

"Ha," she said.

"People come from long distances to see it. There is only one other like it in the world," he said, "at Victoria Falls in Africa."

She seemed amused. "I wouldn't want to go that far."

The friend I chose was Lucas.

John Fallis brought him to us, delivered him to us at exactly the appointed time the afternoon we were to leave.

The courthouse clock was striking five when my father opened the door. Lucas was clutching a duffle that looked brand new and he seemed uneasy. Mr. Fallis was smiling. At the curb was his car, a car liked none I'd ever seen before. It was sleek and shiny, midnight blue with white sidewalls and a black convertible top. Later, as we drove through the night and they thought Lucas and I were asleep, I overhead my father tell my mother that it was a Packard Phaeton. "The fastest car on the road. The grocery business must be very good."

They talked about Mr. Fallis as we drove that night. We'd left Frankfort just after my father finished work. He wanted to get to the cabin by ten or so and have two full days before heading back on Monday. The full moon of that September, the Harvest Moon, would rise on Sunday night. Mom would have her moonbow.

Lucas had been conflicted about coming. He had never spent a night away from his home. Had never ventured further outside town than to the creek to fish. He wasn't sure he'd know how to act around my parents, wasn't sure he'd know how to act at meals or bedtime, or whether he'd have the right clothes and know the right things to say. He was afraid he'd be embarrassed.

Yet the thrill of the adventure, the delight of traveling all that distance, of exploring the forest, of seeing things he'd never seen before, all that pulled at him.

I'm not sure what tipped the balance. I think it was Mr. Fallis. I think Mr. Fallis thought it would be good for Lucas.

"So that was the King of Craw," my father said. He was talking softly under the wind noise from the open windows.

"He has a certain charm about him, doesn't he," my mother said, "and handsome,"—a pause, then teasingly, "almost as handsome as you." I couldn't hear the laugh, but I knew they both were.

It was pleasant there in the back of the car, Lucas asleep on the seat beside me, Mom and Dad talking quietly up front. The hum of the tires on the road, full dark outside rushing by, me warm and safe in a little cocoon moving through the night.

I could hear only snatches of their conversation.

"Lucas works for him?"

"Yes."

"There is just the two of them then? Lucas and his mother?"

"So I understand."

"It must be hard."

"What must be hard?"

"Having to try to live like that."

They rode in silence for a while.

"Did you see a gun?" my father said.

"A gun? No. Why?"

"They say he carries two forty-fives."

Silence again.

"He can't be as bad as they say."

That was my mother in a soft, musing voice.

I couldn't hear my father's reply. It was blurred by the wind.

I eased back down into my own drowsy thoughts.

"I am pleased to meet you, Owen Edwards," Mister Fallis had said to me, reaching out his hand as he came through door. He had on a dark blue suit and white shirt with a red tie knotted neatly below the high starched collar.

"Lucas says good things about you. Tells me of some of the adventures you two have been having. I am impressed."

He had a mischievous smile as he said this, standing in the doorway with Lucas beside him.

He had already introduced himself to my mother and father.

"It's a long walk for Lucas up here. I thought I'd give him a lift and take the opportunity to meet you."

He turned to Lucas, smiling, "Lucas is one of my best. I didn't want him getting here late. It's very nice of you to invite him along."

Mr. Fallis was about my father's size, a little taller. The way he stood, the way he moved, reminded me of a cougar—graceful like a cougar, watchful like a cougar, full of compressed intensity ... like a cougar. He had dark wavy hair, a neat mustache, and eyes black as coal. I thought of Douglas Fairbanks in the Mark of Zorro.

"Adventures?" My mother shot me a questioning glance. "You'll have to tell me about those, Owen, dear," she said, smiling that inquisitorially sweet smile that meant I better not have been up to something she wouldn't be happy with.

Oh, damn, I thought.

"He's an impressive boy, Mrs. Edwards. You should be proud of him."

There really was a moonbow.

Late.

Almost midnight.

Suddenly there it was, a perfect arc of color curving through the mist like a fairy bridge rising from the water and disappearing into the forest.

If there is a pot of gold at the foot of the rainbow, what greater treasure must lie at the foot of the moonbow?

Lucas and I considered this and had no answer. My mother thought the sight of it treasure enough.

"Now you two get along to bed. Your Dad and I will be here for a little while." She looked pretty in the moonlight.

Lucas and I walked sleepily back to the cabin through moon shadows, still conjuring up the treasures that might lie at the end of the moonbow.

Lucas was three when his father, Thomas Deane, was sent to the State Penitentiary at Frankfort.

Thomas Deane killed a man. Or if he didn't actually do it himself, he was thought to be one of the men involved in the ambush of Brad Stiles. Stiles lived long enough to say he thought he saw the Deane boy running. The Deane boy was Tommy. Tommy Deane was Winston kin.

That was enough for the jury, which was made up mostly of Stiles. The Winstons and the Stiles had been feuding since before Tommy Deane was born. Feuds are something I was unfamiliar with. We didn't have them in our mountains, this craziness of families fighting for generations to defend their sense of honor or redress a wrong, real or imagined.

A knifing in a bar in the county seat town of Harlan on court day started this particular one. Hoss Stiles, big and mean, slapped Abner Winston, small and half drunk, in the face with an open hand.

To have struck Abner with his fist would have been acceptable and would probably have led to nothing more than a simple brawl and a broken head or two. But a slap? With his open hand? That was an insult not to be endured. Insults were erased with blood. Abner responding by running his knife through Hoss Stiles' heart.

Two days later, just before dark as he made his way home from the fields, some unnamed members of the Stiles clan shot Abner dead. It was the way things were done. Honor, you know. That was almost forty years ago. One killing led to another, which justified the next, which insured the following, until the practice became automatic. Brad Stiles was just the latest in the cycle.

After the trial, his mother had bundled Lucas up and followed young Tommy Deane down out of the mountains to be near him while he served his time in the penitentiary in Frankfort. She was sixteen, had never been beyond the county line, and, as the sixth child in a string of nine, had never been out of sight or sound of people she knew and loved.

24

She could read and write. She could sew and wash and cook and clean and she was strong and surely she could find a way to make a living in a town as large as the state's Capital City while she waited for Tommy to serve his time.

When I think about it now, I marvel at the courage it took for her to come alone and friendless to this frightening place some 200 miles from her home.

Her family, hard scrabble farmers on unforgiving land, sold a calf to get enough money to get her to Frankfort. The money wasn't much and it didn't last long. One room in a shanty in the Bottom was the only place she could afford, and that just barely. It had no running water. Only a small coal stove to cook on. Coal-oil lamps for light. No bed. They slept on a pallet on the floor. Lucas didn't notice. He was too young.

Lucas was told his father died of a sickness in the prison. That wasn't true. Tommy Deane, age 24, Lord have mercy on his soul, died coughing up blood from the beating he'd taken from a prison guard. Tommy wouldn't kowtow the way the guards thought prisoners ought to do. His honor wouldn't let him.

After the funeral, Lucas's mother decided to stay where she was. There was nothing to go back to. Even if there had been, she hadn't the money to get them there.

She had her job at the hemp factory. It was deafening work in the roar of the spinning machines but they were getting by. Then she got ill and couldn't work. It seemed they might starve.

That was when Mr. Fallis came and found him.

I didn't get all this in one telling. It came out haltingly, sometimes painfully, while we were there on the Cumberland.

My mother's gentleness and my father's patience overwhelmed the sense of not belonging that Lucas brought with him. After that first tense day, he began to ease. He began to trust that we wouldn't let him be embarrassed. If he wasn't sure of the protocol or the drill, we gave it no notice while he waited and watched and then imitated.

Let loose to run, Lucas and I explored the forest, hiking up over the ridges and climbing down into the canyons. Mom packed us lunches and we sat on high granite outcroppings looking out over the mountains of the southern

Appalachians. Lucas had never seen so far before. He had never seen so many trees or so much sky, never heard so much silence or felt so much peace.

Wilderness.

At night, though the light of the full moon brightened half the sky, the rest was full of stars and my father found the visible constellations and told us their stories. I'd heard them, but Lucas hadn't. He was mesmerized.

The time went too fast.

Odd the things that seal a friendship.

There is the chemistry I mentioned, but more than chemistry -- a shared enthusiasm, an action, a skill, a mind that engages. Respect most certainly. And trust.

Lucas and I had not spent enough time together to know what enthusiasms we shared or what mysteries we burned to solve. But in that morning interlude with Tubby and his boys and the time we spent together in the forests of the Cumberland, our friendship was sealed. Lucas knew he could trust me. He'd put himself in an exposed position, not a physically exposed position, but an emotional one, which is where he was most vulnerable, and I had seen him safely through it.

Trust was not easily earned from Lucas. He trusted his mother. He trusted Mr. Fallis. Now he trusted me. I already knew I could trust him.

We left the mountains fast friends. In time we would become best friends.

My mother liked Lucas.

She sensed in him a strength of character that reassured her. She thought he was sweet and steady and, despite the circumstances in which he had to live, a good boy. He would be a good friend to me, she was sure of that.

Lucas was welcome at our house anytime, and she hoped that would be frequently because it made her uneasy to realize that in order to visit him I'd have to venture into the Bottom. Her rationale for finally letting me, I think, was to reason that since Lucas was a favorite of John Fallis and John Fallis was King of Craw, I'd have not only Lucas's shield to protect me, but by extension the cloak of the King as well.

Which reasoning I happily accepted. She had overlooked a basic fact of kingship, though, and one I had not yet learned. Someone is always after the king's head.

More than a few wanted John Fallis's head. His rivals in Craw. The police. Most of the city establishment. The women who couldn't hold him. The men whose women he'd had. The hotshot gamblers he'd bested. The blowhards he'd deflated. The bullies he'd beat hell out of.

And even a small cabal in the governor's office who were convinced his escapades were bad for the reputation of the state's Capital City.

And let us not forget, for they are formidable, the church ladies in their righteousness.

Heavy weighs the crown.

SEVEN
The Day Of The Bike

Mr. Fallis did business from his grocery store on Wilkinson Street. It wasn't in Craw and was just on the edge the Bottom.

The distinction didn't reassure my mother.

"It's close enough. You be careful."

She didn't know, nor did I at the time but was soon to find out, that the Fallis Grocery was probably the safest place in town.

There had been a robbery attempt once.

Two of the three men who tried it were shot dead on the spot. A double barreled sawed-off 12-gauge shotgun was kept under the counter by the cash register. Mr. Fallis wasn't there but the clerk knew what to do.

The third man, attempting to hide in a shanty near the river, was tracked down, dragged back to a corner in the heart of Craw, and beaten. With a baseball bat. While a crowd looked on. John Fallis was at the plate. The would-be robber didn't die but he limped around terrified ever after.

There had been one try at a purse snatching.

The lady, Mrs. Struthers, was old, black, and a regular customer of Mr. Fallis. She'd come after a loaf of white bread and a quart of milk. It was twilight, a little before suppertime. She was alone. No one else was in the store. She was just making the turn onto Wilkinson for her walk back to her home in the Bottom when a young white man darted past her, grabbed the purse hanging from her shoulder, wrenched it free, and sped off. The force of the grab caused her to drop her groceries and dislocated her shoulder. Later that night, after Mrs. Struthers had been treated and taken home, John Fallis appeared at her door with a fresh loaf of bread, a quart of milk, and her purse. He'd found the snatcher and broken both his arms.

Word got around.

No one made trouble for anyone at John Fallis's store.

"It's gone."

"Where did you leave it?"

"Leaning against a post out front."

"You sure?"

I had ridden my bike down and parked it out front as I always did. When I went out it wasn't there. Yeah, I was sure.

Lucas was at the flour barrel serving a young white girl with a baby asleep on her shoulder. The store was full of women shopping. There was a young clerk behind the counter by the cash register and an older man, Yancey, a man who worked there, at the rear of the store.

Saturday afternoon. Warm for October. Skies clear. Some of the trees on Fort Hill already taking on their autumn colors. People up and down on the street outside running errands, getting ready for tomorrow, for Sunday. Sunday was a looked-forward-to-day. Any Sunday. Every Sunday. No work. A day off.

Lucas finished with the young woman and turned to the older man at the rear of the store.

"I heard," the man said. "JF won't like that."

Lucas scrunched his shoulders and made a face. "Damn, damn, and damn again," he said, then grabbed my arm and hustled me toward the door calling to the clerk behind the counter, "Cover for me."

The usual small group of men were around the benches out front. Whatever had happened they'd seen. No one spoke as we came out but they seemed to be expecting something.

Lucas rushed past them and headed for a band of small boys playing tag on the corner. He called to them, asked something, frowned at their answer, closed his eyes and shook his head. He looked at me, then looked around and then back at me as if deciding, then said, "I need something," and rushed back into the store.

When he came out he said, "Let's go get it back."

Several blocks away there was a large area of hard-packed sand on the riverbank, a stretch almost as long as a football field and dotted with driftwood and small bushes. I'd noticed it before. Kids played there. That's where we were headed.

When we got there, on the far end, underneath an old sycamore back up the bank, a little knot of kids was gathered. There were six or eight, a few whose clothes made it look like they'd been wrestling in mud, all of them crowded around a boy sitting on a bike, holding court.

Lucas headed for it.

The boy waved when he saw us coming. "Well, I'll be damned. It's Lucas Deane. Heard about my new bike, did you? Come to see it, did you? It's a beaut, ain't it?"

I'd never seen this boy before. He looked older than us. And even sitting on the bike seat he was monumentally bigger.

The boys around him stopped giggling and shoving as we walked up. They began to back out into a wide semi-circle, not sure what was about the happen but certain something was.

Lucas stepped toward him. The boy stood up astride the bike. He dwarfed it. He was a full head taller than Lucas, heavier and brawny.

I'd seen elk circling to fight for dominance, a hush falling over the mountain meadow, the air becoming charged with tension. It felt like that. I didn't know what there was between them, but whatever it was it was incendiary.

Made no difference. It was my bike. My problem. Before either could move, I started forward. "That's my bike," I said. "I'll take it."

The bigger boy, his concentration on Lucas broken, looked over at me surprised. Then laughed.

"Pretty Boy. I heard about you." He glanced to Lucas then back to me. "Yeah, I heard about you. You're an uptown boy. You're a tough cookie."

He dismounted the bike slowly, made a show of looking it over carefully, looked back at me to make sure I was watching. "Don't see your name anywhere." He was standing there taunting. "Your bike? Prove it!"

Oh, damn, I thought. Mr. Charbonneau, don't desert me now.

With no other alternative available, I started toward him.

Lucas grabbed my arm.

"Not your fight. Mine," he whispered.

"What are you...?"

"Shut up."

The little semi-circle of boys had broken apart. They moved up the bank, nearer the street, ready to run but eager to watch.

The big boy waited beside the bike, legs apart, arms akimbo, smiling.

I tried to pull free but Lucas held on.

"Stay out of this."

The big boy waited while Lucas came to him.

"What's wrong with you, Vik." Lucas sounded almost sorry for him.

"The bike? I don't have one. I wanted this one."

"You know you can't bother anybody or bother anybody's things at the grocery. You know that, Vik. Anybody's. What's wrong with you?"

"Things change."

"This doesn't."

"Screw you, Lucas."

"So what you're going to do," Lucas said in a soft and reasoning voice, "is wheel the bike back where you got it, lean it up against the same post, apologize to Owen, and never dare take anything from anyone at the grocery again."

The big boy threw back his head and laughed.

"The hell I am. How you gonna make me? Sic John Fallis on me?"

"I'm taking care of it."

"You? You're taking care of it? Why you dumb little Crawbat, I'll..."

Lucas's fist shot out. Vik's head shot back. Blood spurted. Vik dropped to the ground, Lucas on top of him, hit him again, stood up, looked around, then back down at Vik squirming on the ground, kicked him hard in the ribs, hard enough to break one or two, slowly removed something from his fist and said to me, "Let's stand him up and get back."

I couldn't have been more surprised if trumpets had sounded and doves rose into the sky.

I wonder what the people passing made of us as we progressed up Wilkinson ... a boy with his face bashed in pushing a bicycle up the street with two smaller boys flanking him on either side and looking triumphant.

At the grocery everything was normal ... shoppers in and out, a few kids still playing on the corner, the small group of men still there. Waiting as if they expected us.

They stopped their talk as we approached. The kids quit playing. Two women coming out the door with bags of groceries in their arms stepped back at the sight of Vik. He did look awful. Bloody. Pain in his eyes at every breath. The ribs, I suppose. And the way his jaw hung askew.

Haltingly, Vik made his way to the post where my bike had been. The men who were sitting rose. The kids stood motionless. Everything seemed to stop and everyone seemed to turn to watch as Vik leaned my bike against the post. He leaned against the post himself for a moment, trying to gather himself, trying to find some armor against the scowls of the men and the disbelieving silence of the kids.

Lucas put a hand on his shoulder and, almost gently, turned him to me.

"Now apologize."

But Vik couldn't. He couldn't talk. His jaw was broken.

He shifted his weight and turned away from me as if were only incidental to the proceedings. Breathing painfully, Vik pulled himself up a little straighter to face Lucas. He was beaten and humiliated and everybody in his world would know it soon. Shame and hate radiated from him. He tried to speak but could get nothing past his bleeding lips. He didn't need words. The message in his glare was clear enough. *I'll get you, you sonofabitch.*

Lucas nodded. Understood. Accepted without letting his eyes stray.

"Go find a doctor, Vik," he said. "Don't come back."

Inside the store, the older man, Yancey, the man who had told Lucas "JF won't like that," Yancey, was waiting. He said nothing, only nodded his head in approval and went back to work.

Lucas exchanged glances with the other man, the one at the counter. There were people in the grocery but no more than those two could handle.

Lucas got us a couple of Cokes and led me to the back of the store where a door opened onto a small outside yard that butted up against Fort Hill. He and the others who worked there sometimes used it for lunch or breaks. It was cool and quiet out there. There were some wooden chairs and a long pine picnic table with benches on either side. That's where we sat.

Behind us Fort Hill was beginning to slip into shadow. I'd have to leave soon.

Lucas sipped at his Coke, turning the bottle slowly in his hands, watching the motion, occasionally staring off into space, subdued. I was still high— adrenalin pumping, excited, eager to replay what had happened.

I couldn't figure Lucas's mood, but I capped my own and waited, marveling at how Lucas knew exactly where to go, marveling that we walked away from that encounter unscathed, marveling that we'd recovered my bike. Marveling most of all, that Lucas had taken that big hulk down with a single punch.

Finally, Lucas looked across at me. He was still subdued and seemed exhausted. He sighed, took the last sip of Coke, set the bottle down hard on the table.

"Hope Vik's got his jaw fixed by now."

"My god," I said, "his head exploded. I didn't think anyone could do that much damage with one punch."

Lucas reached into his pants pocket and came out with a small metal bar with holes in it. He slipped it over his fingers, made a fist, held his hand up for me to see.

"Brass knuckles."

He slammed his fist against the table.

"You can drop a bull with one of these."

There were indentations in the wood where he'd smashed his fist into it.

"That's what you went back to get?"

"I might have been able to take Vik. Might have. I was sure of it with this."

"That was my fight," I said.

33

"Your bike was just the prod. Vik was looking to make it happen. He told the boys on the corner to tell me where he would be waiting. It was my fight."

Viktor Aloysius Braun.

He considered himself the toughest boy in the Bottom and thought John Fallis ought to think so, too. Viktor had wanted a job with Mr. Fallis. Mr. Fallis took him on for a while then let him go. No explanation. Just let him go.

"I'm better than Lucas Deane," Vik argued. "Tougher. Smarter."

John Fallis wasn't given to argument.

From that day on Viktor Aloysius Braun detested Lucas Deane. He'd never liked Lucas. Pity got Lucas his job. Charity kept him in it. John Fallis's favor gave Lucas a status in the Bottom he hadn't earned and didn't deserve. To be discarded and Lucas Deane kept! No way. He'd show them. Beat Lucas Deane's ass. Show the mighty Mr. John Fallis that Vik Braun wasn't afraid to take what he wanted.

Give Vik his due. He was, as he claimed, tough and smart, though trying to pull off the stunt he tried at the grocery was idiotic. It only underscored his arrogance and conceit. Vik was older by several years than either Lucas or me, brutishly large, proudly unscrupulous. He might have made a decent recruit to the Fallis band. Mr. Fallis, I guess, just didn't like the tune he played.

"So what happens now?"

"Nothing happens now. You go home. I go back to work."

"You're done with Vik?"

Lucas stood up from the bench, gathered his Coke bottle, took mine. "It's getting dark," was all he said as he led me back inside.

Mr. Fallis was there, dressed as proper as an uptown banker in dark blue suit and bowler hat, standing at the end of the counter in a serious conversation with the older man, Yancey.

He saw us, broke off his conversation, and motioned us to follow him to the back of the store.

He looked us over silently for a few moments, studying Lucas's face, running his eyes carefully over mine. Our hands. Our clothes.

"You both okay?"

"Yes sir," Lucas said.

"Nobody bloody? Nobody bruised?"

Lucas glanced at me, then back to Mr. Fallis.

"We're okay."

"Yancey said it was one-on-one. Just you and Vik. Odds were long against it."

"Yes, sir."

"So?"

Lucas reached in his pocket and held up the brass knuckles.

Mr. Fallis began grinning, then laughed out loud.

He said. "Vik got the message?"

"Busted jaw, I think," Lucas said. "Maybe a busted rib."

Turning to me, "There is no need to tell your mother about this. I don't imagine she would approve."

"Yes, sir," I stammered. "I mean, no sir. I mean Lucas was great."

He nodded, smiling again, "Yes he is. I'm proud of him."

Even in the excitement of the moment, I caught the significance of that.

Is. Lucas *is* great.

I glanced at Lucas.

Then I understood. Simply recovering my bike wasn't enough. There had to be punishment, punishment so severe that the particular sinner would never try again, so severe that it would serve as a reminder to all others that Fallis ground is inviolate.

While it was happening Lucas had seemed almost regretful at what he was doing to Vik. There was no remorse now. He'd been given the highest praise he could receive. He glowed.

I left them talking—Lucas the center of attention, Mr. Fallis standing, arms folded, beaming at him, Yancey stepping forward to shake his hand, the clerk at the counter nodding and smiling, and customers still coming in and out unaware of the little coronation that had just occurred at the back of the store.

Looking back, I am certain that if there was a pivotal event in Lucas's life, the Day of the Bike was close to it. He'd experienced how force can lead to power and how power can lead to respect. I think respect was more important to Lucas than money. I think it was to Mr. Fallis, too.

EIGHT
A Bit Much

Lucas was better looking than I am but no one would dare call him "pretty boy." He was taller by a few inches, lean and muscular, and the best athlete in our class. He was as popular as he would let himself be.

With the boys he was a natural leader, respected and liked by most.

With the girls, since he wasn't on the teams or in the clubs, he was mysterious, and being mysterious, was exciting ... a boy from the other side of the tracks, a little dangerous, a favorite of the King of Craw, handsome, polite, probably experienced in some of the things of Craw their mothers warned them about. Yes, he was as popular as he would let himself be.

Another trait that set him apart from all the other young males who were trying to assert their machismo in those early teen years, Lucas had a gentle disposition.

My mother felt that about him and it was one of the characteristics that made him dear to her. I sensed it, too ... in the way he was polite with the girls and respectful of his elders and watchful of the young kids at the street crossings when we walked to school in the mornings.

So I couldn't fathom that he'd inflicted so much hurt on Vik when violence seemed so contrary to his nature. He hadn't seemed angry. Anger could explain it. And he wasn't afraid, as fear sometimes triggers a savage response. He was simply doing something that had to be done and was his to do.

He was always so. If he felt a thing was his to do, he did it. Regardless.

I admit to being of not so strong a character. If I faced a matter I thought not worth the effort or beneath my fine opinion of myself, I could usually manage to rationalize it away.

I admired that Lucas didn't.

And because of that, and because I owed him a better thank-you than the hurried one I'd offered in all the excitement, and because my curiosity about the brass knuckles kept picking at me, I mounted my trusty bike the next day, the day after the Day of the Bike, a fine fall morning, a Saturday, and headed down to the grocery.

Lucas worked afternoons after school and on Saturday mornings. He was stocking shelves when I got there.

He paused when he saw me, gave a little half grin and nodded his head toward the door that led to the small outside yard where we'd talked yesterday. He followed in a few minutes with Cokes.

"Everything okay? Your Mom guess anything?"

"She was a little concerned that I was late for dinner was all."

"So?"

"I didn't say a proper thank-you yesterday."

"You rode all the way down here to...."

"Say thank you. See how polite I am."

He laughed then.

"It's your curiosity, isn't it? You wanted to see if I'm still in one piece."

Then it was my turn to laugh.

"I wasn't worried about you being in one piece. But those brass knuckles."

Here it is a normal Saturday morning and I'm sitting in the sun in a secluded little space at the back of a grocery in an unfamiliar town with a boy I'm just beginning to know drinking Coca Cola and talking in a normal way about a shocking display of mayhem I'd witnessed just the day before. I'm not quite two months out of the cold, sweet air of the high Rockies into this river valley town on the northern rim of the Old South where people speak with an odd accent and do very strange things and I'm talking about an act of violence I couldn't, in my wildest conjurings, imagine a boy performing.

"The brass knuckles?"

I nodded eagerly. "I've never heard of them. Never seen anything like that."

Lucas handed me a Coke, set his down, held his right hand out in front of him, turned if over slowly, inspecting it.

"Yancey showed me. They're what the guards used in prison."

He sat down, motioned me to do the same, then, staring down at his hand, said,

"Vik will have to get his food through a straw for the next six weeks. His jaw's wired shut. They'll have to puree his food, make it like baby food. He has two busted ribs. Can breathe, but it hurts. Take four to six weeks for that to heal. Gonna be hell to eat ... to sleep." He paused, looked up at me, "Seems a little much for a stolen bike."

I wasn't sure whether he was asking a question or making a statement.

NINE
Fortress Fallis

The Fallis Grocery sat on a corner about halfway down Wilkinson where it intersected with Hill Street, which snaked east along the base of Fort Hill to the prison. There was a trolley stop right in front, so it was easy to reach and it drew from a wide area.

Almost anything could be had at the Fallis Grocery. In fact, almost everything. Even and especially, Prohibition be damned, booze and beer from a nondescript building in the rear if you behaved yourself. Or perhaps it should be Prohibition be praised, for nothing so contributed to the Fallis coffers as the gift of Prohibition. I didn't know about that until later, of course.

The grocery building itself was large and solid. Its walls were interlocking blocks of the stately grey limestone called Kentucky River marble.

There always seemed to be people around, mingling on the sidewalk outside or talking quietly on the benches under the big front windows.

In a way the store seemed as much a place for socializing as for shopping. Most who came there were regulars and had at least a nodding acquaintance with the others.

The I-heard-it-at-the-grocery grapevine that originated there spread news rapidly and was believed with far more credibility than what appeared in the newspapers.

Mr. Fallis liked this.

He liked his grocery being a center of things. He liked that, through casual talk or even a whispered remark let intentionally be overheard, ideas and conclusions he favored could be sown widely throughout the community.

After the Day of the Bike I came to think of the grocery and the space around it as Fortress Fallis. Not in the sense of a citadel to which the good folk of the community repaired for defense against attack, but rather as a gathering place where people came to conduct their business and trade their tales and were assured they were protected and safe—inviolate space which the brigands out raping and pillaging around the countryside knew better than to trespass. John Fallis was Lord of the Fortress and the punishments were severe.

I realize this is a bit overblown, but that was the feel of the place to me at the time and my explanation to myself for the hurt Lucas laid on Viktor Herbert Braun.

Vik had trespassed. Lucas felt it his duty to respond. I don't think he wanted to do it. I think the brutality repulsed him. I think he steeled himself and did it because he thought it was what Mr. Fallis would want done. I think he agonized over it later.

I had no frame of reference for his world.

Lucas knew about beautiful ladies and gambling men. I'd never been around them, but Lucas had. He knew about things I didn't even know existed like cathouses and speakeasies and sawed-off shotguns. He knew about danger. He knew about retribution. He knew how to do things I didn't. He knew how to use brass knuckles.

Alien world. Fascinating world.

I slipped into it whenever I could.

When I went to see him, the grocery is where we met. Always. In all the time we were friends, I never saw where he lived.

In all the time I knew him, I never met his mother. I never learned her name. We were best friends, yet I never met his mother.

As I think back on Lucas, I wish I had. It might have explained so much.

She was only sixteen when she came to what must have seemed to her the city at the gates of Hell.

All her life she had been surrounded by family, by people she could count on, people who knew her and loved her. She had come to this town alone. With only a baby in her arms. The courage that must have taken. The determination.

In many ways Lucas and I were as different as two people can be. I'd never gone hungry. I'd always lived in a nice house. I never had to dress in clothes from church charities or had to work after school to help pay the rent. I'd never had to bear the humiliation of being looked down on. I was never poor.

In the local working class hierarchy, the poor were at the bottom -- destitute, hungry, beaten down, and despairing. Next came the just-barely-making- it -- poor but hanging on. At the top were the doing-well-enough-to-get-by-thank-you-kindly-but- mind-your-own-business brigade.

That's where Lucas and his mother were when I came to know him -- doing well enough to get by, thank you kindly, but mind your own business.

I think it was this feeling, this pride, that was at the root of the reason Lucas never invited me to his home. He'd seen where I lived and how I lived. Where he lived made no difference to me. It did to him.

He never mentioned his mother to me.

To have kept herself and Lucas alive and pulled them up through the maelstrom of the Bottom during all those years, a girl alone, to have done that in that town in those times ... that took a person, it seemed to me, of rare character and strength.

The toll that must have taken on her, the price she'd had to pay physically and emotionally, maybe that's what Lucas didn't want me to see. All the same, and even though I never knew her name, I honored her.

My mother found it strange that I didn't know her name.

"You forgot it?"

"No ma'am. Lucas doesn't talk about her."

"Ever?"

"No ma'am."

She frowned quizzically at me.

"Let's invite them for Thanksgiving dinner and get to know her. That would be nice wouldn't it?'

Lucas said they couldn't come.

No explanation. No excuse.

"Some other time?"

Lucas, ever polite, said only, "We appreciate being invited. Thank your mother."

Some other time never came.

I'm not very good with numbers. Lucas is. He's not very good with words. I am. So we collaborated on homework. He helped me with the math assignments. I helped him with the reports and the book reviews we had to write.

We'd meet at the grocery. I'd catch the trolley down after dinner and we'd do our homework in the small office in the back which Mr. Fallis used. Mr. Fallis came in every day. Always in the mornings, sometimes at night around closing time.

There was more to running a grocery than I imagined -- inventories to be checked and kept current, suppliers to be dealt with, prices negotiated, deliveries scheduled, money to be counted and bills paid and books to be kept. And the fruits of each day's labor locked in the safe each night. Yancey usually did that.

Sometimes Mr. Fallis would drop by while Lucas and I were there doing homework.

He seemed pleased when he saw us. He'd nod and smile, be curious about what we were working on, talk with us a bit. Mr. Fallis himself had made it only through sixth grade. He'd had to leave school when he was thirteen and go work. He hadn't the chance we had. He wanted us to take full advantage of it and liked that we were using his space to do it in.

The principal attraction of the study time at the grocery for me was that it gave me a reason to be out at night ... and an excuse to be on the edge of Craw.

TEN
Craw

As fall slipped away I began to settle into a comfortable routine.

School was going well. I'd made friends, joined the History Club and the Junior Conservation Club, had been chosen by Miss Lucy, our music teacher, to sing in the school chorus (Lucas had as well, he had a fine baritone voice and practices were during the school day so he could be there for them), and with the help of a friend of my father who knew the publisher, I had gotten a paper route.

I'd be up each day before daylight to deliver the State Journal, our local newspaper, to the porches of the subscribers on my route (ironclad rule: put the paper on the porch, not in the yard or on the walkway and definitely not in the bushes), make it home for breakfast in time to meet Lucas at the bridge for the walk to school, then do school.

In the afternoons I'd hike to football practice (the high school had a junior varsity team and I'd gone out for that) then back home for dinner and, afterwards, homework.

Wednesday nights were for choir practice. My mother is of Methodist stock, rock solid followers of the faith the way the Wesley brothers proclaimed it, with its emphasis on helping the poor and seeing to the needy. Which may have been one of the reasons she was drawn to Lucas, though I think the fact that she simply liked him was stronger. She was a contralto with a tone as rich as the finest cello. I sang tenor.

Look out for the poor and the needy and be in church on Sunday. That was the Wesley brothers' creed. Come hell or high water, we didn't miss church on Sundays.

I'd set Thursday nights as my study-with-Lucas night and would head down to the grocery for that. My mother liked the disciplined way I seemed to be approaching my school work and approved. Often, though, Lucas and I only played chess or listened to Yancey's stories about his early days or, if he was in the mood, about prison.

On Friday nights there were home football games, or after the season ended in November, basketball games in the high school gym.

I was learning my way around.

The girl who offered to teach me to dance did. On rainy afternoons after school in the hall off the living room of her house where we could shove the rug aside and get our feet to slide on the hardwood floor.

Blue and yellow flame would be flickering from the coal fire in the grate and music pulsing from the Victrola ... snug and warm against the dismal drizzle outside. We practiced the waltz and a respectable fox trot when her mother was there. When she wasn't, out came ragtime. The girl, Mary Jane, kept the records ... Scott Joplin, Jellyroll Morton ... hidden in the closet in her bedroom.

Ragtime was all the talk. None of the mothers would let their daughters learn the ragtime dances ... the Baltimore Buzz, the Cake Walk, the Black Bottom ... much less dance them. They were decadent, sinful, coming, as they did, from the black musicians in the red light districts of New Orleans and St, Louis ... for loose women in skirts too short making spectacles of themselves

But of course the girls learned it, the bold ones did, and taught the others. I doubt there was a girl in school who didn't know how to dance ragtime by the time the Christmas dance came. They made it a point to corral enough of us to be their partners.

To no avail. The school wouldn't allow the dance and the parents would have been scandalized that their daughters had sunk so low. Which was fine with me. I was good at the waltz, passable with the fox trot, but a spastic at ragtime.

44

Oddly, Tubby ... Jay Overby, the one-time king of the late but not lamented Kings Of The Hill gang ... Tubby danced them well. You wouldn't think a boy of his dimensions and lack of coordination could manage the moves.

Tubby would have other surprises for me later.

The lessons were fun, but rain in December, especially as we neared Christmas, was depressing.

Decembers in Estes Park were blue-skyed and full-sunned with ice crystals sparkling like diamonds in the snow on the mountain crests. It was too cold to rain, so it snowed, and snow was allowed only at night.

We skied and snowshoed and, when twilight came, drank hot chocolate around big stone fireplaces where logs, not coal, gave off the scent of spruce and so much heat we shed our sweaters. Decembers there were bright, not grey. Gay, not somber.

Though I was settling into a pleasant enough routine, I was still adjusting to the strangeness of this town. To the size and pace of it. To the look and the feel of the place. And to these people and their practices.

All of it fascinated me.

What fascinated me most was Craw. It pulled on me as strongly as the song the Sirens sang to poor Odysseus that day in the Aegean.

Craw.

The place was mythic. Storyville on the Kentucky. The Barbary Coast in the Bluegrass. Gambling. Women. Booze. Knife fights and fist fights and gun fights in the streets. Party until the lights go out and the sun comes up and keep right on as long as you can still stand and walk unaided.

Anything you want. Anytime. All the time. Nothing but pleasure, man. Nothing but excitement.

Craw.

No place like it anywhere between here and the Big Easy. Escape. Partake. Be a man, man.

The mountain men started it.

Every spring when the rains came and they could get the timber they'd been felling all year down river to the sawmills in Frankfort, they started it. Hordes of them. They'd survived the dangers and the hardships of the hundred mile ride down the flooding Kentucky river on their rafts of logs. Some always drowned and some always got maimed. Those that managed to arrive intact descended on the town, wildly thankful, cruising the streets in the hundreds, money in hand, raising hell and looking for release. The locals saw opportunity. The joints to accommodate them sprang up just across the road from the sawmills in what the locals called Crawfish Bottom. That got shortened to Craw right away.

Word of the special pleasures experienced there rapidly spread throughout the area and were soon on offer all year long.

The National Guard had a training camp full of farm boys and small town Lotharios brimming with hormones just across the river. They couldn't wait to get there. Regular army troops from Fort Knox came rushing in on the weekends.

College boys from nearby campuses in the Bluegrass found the place, too. And deal makers and favor seekers from all over the state and even from out of state, drawn by the power and riches the Capital City held.

And of course the locals, high class and low, escaping for a night into the carnival of Craw.

White or black, monied or humble, cocksman or virgin, hustler or mark, they came.

The place was wide open.

That was in the early days.

By the time I got there, Craw had coalesced into a four or five block stronghold in the center of the Bottom and had quieted down just a bit.

There was still unbridled debauchery and high times abundant. And fights and knifings and shootings. The saloons and brothels, the drinking and the gambling, the music and dancing, it all ran full out. And the police still largely kept their distance. But a certain discipline was beginning to emerge. Brawls and the gun-play were bad for business. The men providing the fun and making the money from it were trying to crack down on that.

And there was John Fallis.

Also, across the wider span of the Bottom itself a fragile community was growing.

The Bottom had its start when newly free slaves at the end of the Civil War began to settle in the cheap shanties that opportunistic landlords were building on the low, marshy ground off to the side of Wilkinson Street. Then families of convicts trickled in, squeezing out a living while their men did their time in the state penitentiary just blocks away, and often staying once the sentence was served because there was no place better to go to.

As the town grew, Irish and German immigrants looking for work found the Bottom. Others followed. In time the area became a magnet for the out-of-work and just-barely-making-it.

Some of the lucky ones managed to get jobs in the factories along the river and in the sawmills and the distillery. Others found work uptown in the stores and bars and hotels. Many of the women took care of the chores for the well-to-do folk -- the washing and ironing and cooking, or took care of their children. In all cases the pay was low and the hours long.

True to its roots, the Bottom remained predominately black.

It had churches and stores, a clinic and an undertaker, and places to eat and fraternal clubs to socialize in, and a school, a good one, for the kids. Comfortable and well-kept houses lined many of the streets. Families were being raised and decent lives lived.

Strangely, for this wasn't the practice anywhere at the time, blacks and whites lived fairly peacefully side by side on some blocks. Their kids played together. They talked across porches on summer nights. They got mad sometimes and that could lead to fights, particularly if one or the other had too much to drink, but nothing too big, nothing major, nothing that festered and polluted. There were some rabid racists of course, but in general, people were too wrapped up trying to make a living to make much fuss about skin color.

Though it was a coalescing neighborhood, slum-like pockets still clustered in the back alleys and around the low-lying blocks that flooded first. The poorest of the poor huddled in these—miserable for those who wanted work but couldn't find it, infuriating for those no one would hire because they were weak or couldn't read or were Irish or black, hopeless for the bums, the deadbeats, the drunkards and the dregs ... desperate for the hookers past their time.

After a while, as I got familiar with it and liking to have places firmly fixed in my mind as on a map or in a picture so I could find my way around, I began to think of the Bottom as a large, black, irregular circle with a narrow band of white around the outer rim.

This circle was bounded by Wilkinson Street and the river on the west. On the eastern rim were the stately grounds of the Old State House. The northern rim was Fort Hill's mass of cliffs and trees. The railroad tracks that ran down the center of Broadway was the southern.

In the center of that circle, there was a pulsating red dot. That was Craw.

The upstanding folk in town said stay away.

I was not bold enough to invade it by myself.

ELEVEN
Don't You Worry, Maisie

Christmas week came. A cold, miserable, drizzly rain came with it. Little droplets collected on the greenery on the lampposts downtown. The red ribbons hung limp and forlorn. Lights in the shop windows tried but could barley manage to twinkle through the mist.

We went caroling anyway. A small a group of us. On the night before Christmas Eve. A tradition of Miss Lucy, our music teacher. Two mixed quartets selected from the school choir. She chose a different neighborhood each year. That year South Frankfort. Up Shelby Street all the way to the Capitol. Lucas and me among those chosen. The girls holding candles while we sang. The soft light softer still in the mist. The girls' eyes glistening, little jewels of water sparkling in their hair. We sounded so good, sang so melodiously. You can shed the world when you're singing that way, in close harmony, pulling the richness of the sound around you, becoming a part of. I forgot the wet, forgot the cold. Forgot I didn't care much for this place.

Afterwards, Lucas came home with me and we had yeast doughnuts and coffee in front of the fire while we dried. As we sat there, my mother started a carol, a simple one, about a baby asleep in a manger, one I'd been singing since I was little more than a baby myself.

She nodded to us to join. Lucas was hesitant, unsure of his place, but his hesitancy disappeared as she smiled and encouraged us with her eyes.

Her voice carrying the melody, Lucas's baritone and my tenor blending in, the room in shadows except for the glow from the fireplace, the three of us singing together ... ah, damn that felt good. I could see that Lucas felt it, too, actually felt it. The harmony. Of us. I think it was something he hadn't experienced before.

Later, my father loaded us in his new Model T and we drove Lucas home through the cold, drizzly mist. To the grocery. Lucas insisted. It was almost ten o'clock. Yancey would be closing up.

The next afternoon, Christmas Eve afternoon, I went back down to help Lucas at the store for a while.

Mr. Fallis was there, grinning and talking and patting people on the back.

He'd had a big Christmas tree put up in the middle space and had hot cider on a table behind for anyone who wanted a cup. Men came up to shake his hand. Women to brush a kiss on his cheek or touch his sleeve. I couldn't hear their talks distinctly but I heard enough thank-yous and bless-yous to think this must have been what it was like in olden times when the people came to pay homage to the lord of the realm.

I overhead him tell one woman, "Now Maizie, don't worry. Get what you want. Pay when you're able."

I turned to Lucas, questioning.

"He lets them take what they need and pay when they can."

"A Christmas thing?"

"All the time."

Later, as it began to get dark, I saw Mr. Fallis out back with Yancey loading bags of coal in the delivery wagon.

Again I turned to Lucas.

"He's taking it to some of the poor families down in Craw. Doesn't want them freezing."

"I don't understand," I said.

Lucas stopped what he was doing.

"He looks out for people."

"Why?" I said.

"He's John Fallis."

I told my mother the story as I dried the dishes after supper that night. My dad was in the living room putting the finishing touches on our Christmas tree. She listened without interrupting, listened intently, quietly. When I finished, she said, "Lucas must really admire that man."

I didn't have to think about how to respond to that.

"Do you?"

I hesitated.

"He's like the main character in a book I'm reading that's puzzling and exciting and maybe a little above my reading level but that I don't want to put down."

She nodded her head and smiled to herself and said no more. We finished and went into the living room to enjoy the tree and have eggnog around the fire.

The tree was another of those things I needed to get used to. It was an eastern red cedar. Large. Beautifully shaped. We'd cut it ourselves, my dad and me, a Christmas ritual, but in the past it was always a Douglass fir we'd bring back from the mountain. There were no Douglas firs here.

No trout either.

And rain at Christmas.

In time my mother told my father the story I'd told her.

"What do you make of him," she said.

My father didn't answer right away. He sipped his eggnog, gazed into the fire, shifted his look to me, then to my mother.

At last he said, "Everyone seems to know him, or know of him. The people who run the town don't seem to like him much. He gets in the way of some of the things they want to do. They say he controls the Third Ward which covers a large part of town north of Broadway and includes the Bottom and Craw. If they want to get elected, they've got to carry it."

He paused then and told us he could vouch for none of this, only that this is what the talk was.

"I don't know what to think of him. He is a legitimate businessman who is said to be a high stakes gambler and a brawler. Can be wildly violent at times. Has been arrested for assault. Carries a pair of ivory-handled Colt forty-fives and a Schrade switchblade. A proper businessman walking around packing two forty-fives and a switchblade knife? I don't know what to think of that.

"The church ladies think him an unrepentant sinner. But he's generous. He helps the poor and the needy. The blue bloods don't turn down his contributions to their causes. But they don't like him. They think him an insult to decency."

He closed his eyes and tilted his head back, concentrating to ransack his memory for more.

"What else? Well, he's successful. His grocery is one of the largest in town. He runs two sternwheelers pushing lumber up river to factories near the intersection with the Ohio. And he has other," he smiled to himself, "interests. Lucrative interests."

"Lucrative interests," my mother frowned. "Like?"

"Well, bootlegging for one. He's said to be the area's biggest bootlegger."

"Oh, come now, Eddie. That's against the law."

"I'm only telling you what others say," my father said, but with no tone of disapproval in his voice.

He took a long sip of eggnog. His had brandy, mine just the eggs and cream and vanilla and cinnamon. "No one, not any of the businessmen or the professionals or any of that crew up at the Capitol, dresses better. He has one of the finest baritone singing voices in the county. And to top it off, he is undeniably likeable. People are drawn to him. Now what do you make of a man like that, a man with that many sides to him? I don't know. You tell me."

She stared at him for a long moment, eyes crinkled, thinking, then gave that little impatient flick of her head. "Do you like him?"

"I've only met him once. Here. When he brought Lucas before our trip to Cumberland. You were with me."

"But did you like him?"

A grimace, a long look into the fire, a glance up to the star at the top of the tree, then back to her curious eyes.

With an almost apologetic smile he answered, "It's hard not to, isn't it?"

That night, in that safe, warm room in the firelight and the scent of cedar, that night it seemed so.

The dreary December segued into a drizzly January. The hills were seared by frost. The trees were bare. The days were bleak and the nights forlorn. When February arrived, the groundhog saw his shadow so the skies remained leaden and the wind was full of misty rain.

I longed for the clear, crisp days of my mountains.

My mother came from the Willamette Valley in Oregon, my father from the little town of Opportunity in the forests of Washington state. We'd lived in a world different from this one.

We spent that winter, my mother and father and me, getting used to it.

Then on an April morning when I wasn't expecting it, spring slipped in. A glorious spring of dogwoods and redbud and wildflower-sprinkled meadows. Of lazy cumulous in pale blue skies. Of caressing breezes and the call of whippoorwills at dusk.

I began to think this country was teasing me, flirting with me. I became even more suspicious of it as May wrapped me in its arms. This gentle, mellow, remarkable country seemed to be reaching out to me, seemed to want me.

By the time June came, I was in danger of becoming unfaithful to my mountains. The perfect days the poet said June would bring came as promised. School was out. I was free to explore wherever my interests took me. Lucas had changed his work schedule to mornings so we had afternoons for baseball and fishing.

Great days ahead.

Then the carnival came to town.

TWELVE
Paris Nights

I'd never been to a carnival.

Estes Park was too small and too far off the beaten path to be worthwhile for a carnival to make the journey up the mountain.

But here we were in the Capitol City of Kentucky and the Miller Brothers Carnival was coming and this marked the unofficial start of summer and this was a very big event.

I ached to go.

My father was off in the Cumberlands that week working on the plans for the proposed new forest. My mother wasn't sure about the carnival, wasn't sure a carnival was an entirely proper place for an unsupervised thirteen-year-old still finding his way in a new environment, wasn't sure about giving permission for such an adventure without talking it over with my father. But swayed by my excitement and the fact that Lucas would be with me, she said okay.

"You'll meet Lucas there?"

"Yes, ma'am."

"You won't go into the Bottom. You'll meet Lucas at the carnival and stay with him and then come straight home."

"Yes, ma'am."

"And you'll be careful."

"Yes, ma'am."

"You'll be careful. You won't let your curiosity get you carried away. You'll stay by Lucas and be careful."

"Yes, ma'am."

"All right, then."

Which is how I came to be there on the night of Wednesday, June 15, 1921, when the Big Shoot-Out began. I note the date on purpose. It is not to be forgotten.

The carnival had been set up, as it was every year, behind the Old State House. Lucas and I met there right after supper.

Music was playing and lights were flashing and hordes of people were streaming through the main gate, laughing and talking and pointing to the attractions There were freaks and fortune tellers and games of skill and tests of strength, marvels waiting behind every tent flap There was so much sound and color and churning movement that it took my breath.

The Ferris wheel was turning and the merry-go-round circling and I had just decided which amazement I wanted to see first when Lucas jerked my arm and pointed to the rear of the grounds. There, just outside the back fence, a policeman and a boy were scuffling. They were at the foot of a shed that overlooked one of the big pavilions. The banner above the pavilion proclaimed it "Paris Nights."

The policeman was pushing at the boy. The boy was pushing back.

Suddenly they were fighting. The policeman had his nightstick out and was hitting the boy, but the boy was dodging. The policeman lurched back, pulled his gun. The boy closed in, grabbed for it, knocked it away, and was starting to step away when two other policemen materialized. Clubs out and swinging, they beat the boy to the ground, held him while the officer he'd disarmed handcuffed him, and then jerked him to his feet and started yelling at him and swinging his club again. We couldn't hear what they were saying above the noise of the calliope, but we could see that the boy's head was bloody.

"This is real trouble," Lucas said. "Stay with them." He motioned toward the cops. "Make a lot of noise if they beat him to the ground."

"Who is he? Where you going?"

"To get Mr. Fallis," he called back, racing through the crowd to the gate. "That's Carlos, his son."

THIRTEEN
The Big Shoot-Out

Jarred by the way the boy was being jerked around and trying to grasp what might be about to happen, I followed.

No one noticed at first.

With all that was going on inside the carnival grounds, the scuffle outside the fence attracted no attention, but people began to notice as the police shoved and pushed the boy across the Old State House grounds and out onto Broadway. There they turned left and started toward a street I knew would lead to Main Street. The police station was there.

The police were moving slowly and seeming to enjoy the commotion they were creating. As they neared the corner at Main, a man called out, "Who you got there, Scotty?" The policeman looked around, nodded to the man who had called, laughed and gave Carlos a swat across the top of his head. "The Fallis kid. Caught him on a roof of a shed trying to get a peep in at the girly show at the carnival."

The man seemed startled. "Fallis? The Fallis kid? John Fallis's kid? Oh, hell."

I'd been holding back, staying on the opposite sidewalk out of their line of sight but close enough. The police didn't know me, so there was no reason to expect they'd react to a kid tagging along behind them even if they saw me.

I had no plan. No idea of what Lucas expected me to do, but I was there and I was determined I'd do something. It was still only twilight. The evening was warm and clear. Enough people were on the streets to attract a crowd if I yelled loud enough.

The little group reached the corner.

Carlos had stopped struggling. He slumped weakly between the two policemen who were jostling him forward. The one called Scotty was bringing up the rear.

They were just starting onto Main when behind me I heard someone shouting.

"Let him go, damn you!"

I turned. Everyone turned.

"Don't you hit him again, damn you! Let him go!"

John Fallis was in the middle of the street, rushing like fury unleashed toward the boy and the knot of policemen. He had a forty-five in his hand and more anger in his eyes than I had ever seen before and have never seen since.

The policeman called Scotty snapped his head up. He recognized the voice. He spun rapidly around. The two that were holding Carlos threw a startled look at each other.

Scott had his own pistol out by then and was raising his arm.

There was a report. And then another.

Scott staggered, dropped his weapon, clutched his side, fell forward onto the street.

The policemen that was holding Carlos fell next. My ears rang from the sound of the shots.

The other let go of Carlos and started to run. A shot sounded again. He staggered, then stumbled to a nearby doorway.

Carlos stood there, dazed and weaving, two bodies at his feet, another slumping in a doorway near him. Mr. Fallis ran to Carlos, took him by an arm. Lucas ran up to take the other. Together, half carrying him, they rushed away.

Lucas yelled to me as they left. "Go home. Stay there."

It happened so fast I could barely comprehend what happened.

The silence was paralyzing.

Then all hell broke loose.

People who had dropped to the sidewalk were beginning to get back up, dazed and unbelieving. Others were scrambling toward cars they'd abandoned in the street. Traffic was blocked both ways on Main. Voices were yelling for doctors. Police were scrambling out of the station up the street, running toward the sound of the shots.

As word blazed through downtown, the crowd ballooned. Diners in the restaurants put down their forks and headed for the streets. The bars and the poolrooms emptied. Soon hordes of frantic people surrounded the police station, clamoring, jabbering. No one was quite clear on exactly what had happened—but something had, dammit.

It was about eight-thirty then. Still light in the sky. The air electric with tension, charged with excitement.

Three men down. Right in the center of town.

Three policemen.

That was John Fallis, wasn't it? John Fallis? The King of Craw.

A gunfight right in the center of town?

Night coming on and John Fallis on the rampage.

Oh, lordy, lordy, lordy, do deliver us.

FOURTEEN
Sirens In The Night

By the time I got home it was full dark.

"Tell me you're okay."

My mother was almost beside herself, waiting at the window, watching for me to come up the street and be safely home.

"What's happening? Has John Fallis has gone crazy? Is he shooting up the town? Is Lucas all right? Was he with Mr. Fallis? Were you? Are you both all right?

I told her the evening's events as well as I could recall them. Some things take a hold on your mind you can never shake. Some vanish to be seen again only in dreams. The look on the face of the policeman called Scott, I'll never forget that. Not pain. Contempt. Or Lucas calling to me in a voice so full of concern and despair. That wakes me still sometimes.

"You saw those men shot? Oh, how dreadful. I shouldn't have let you go. I shouldn't have let you be in a place where you could be exposed to such an awful thing. Those poor men. You're all right? You're sure you're all right?"

Until she started fussing over me, I'd given it no thought. It happened so fast, was so unexpected. There was so much rant and confusion afterwards. I saw it. It didn't upset me. Maybe it should have. Maybe it would later, when the dreams came at night. But for then my concern was for Carlos and Mr. Fallis. And for Lucas. Not for the policemen. They were beating the boy. It was a rescue. Mr. Fallis came to the rescue. Like a knight. Like Harry Carey in one of his movies. You had to see it to understand.

She kissed me again, smoothed my hair, led me into the kitchen. "A nice warm slice of apple pie and a cold glass of milk. You'll feel better."

There was no sleep for either my mother or me that night. I replayed the events over and over in my mind, watching the little caravan of Carlos and the police struggling up to that fateful corner, feeling again and again the surprise of John Fallis behind me and the physical shock of the shots by my ear and then the bodies falling, an endless loop of disbelief rolling through my mind.

Lying in the dark not knowing what happened was maddening. Worse was imagining what might happen. My god, what might happen? Three policemen shot. Practically in sight of the police station. Were they dead? How was there a way out of this? Would Lucas be a part of whatever the retribution was to be?

Unexpected sounds keep me anxious. Around midnight the wail of police sirens rushing somewhere. Later, well after midnight but long before dawn, the clang of fire trucks loud then receding.

I dozed fitfully. By five I was wide awake, dressed and slipping out the back door when she called sleepily, "Where...?"

"My paper route, Mom."

"You come straight back. I'll have your breakfast ready."

"I've got to check on Lucas."

'Owen..."

"I have to, Mom."

They'd held the presses as long as they could. We carriers milled around in a stew of excitement waiting for the papers to be ready.

We all had heard something, though none of us knew anything for certain. We all wanted to get our routes out of the way and make it down Wilkinson before it was all over. But the press run didn't finish until almost six. On a normal day I would have been half done by then.

Everyone on my route seemed to be up. Waiting. Whether because they'd been part of it, or heard about it from others, or simply felt the uneasiness that hung in the air, lights in all the houses were on. A few men were even standing in their yards looking up the street for me.

My route was Taylor Avenue in South Frankfort. Taylor ran north along a curve of the river and melded into River Road. The fastest way would be on down River Road, cross the river on the railroad bridge onto Broadway and turn left onto Wilkinson to the grocery.

FIFTEEN
The Night Of The Posse

The crowd that was festering when I left the scene that night had erupted into a mob. The violence that the good people of the city thought was confined to Craw had crept uptown. They were seething with outrage and nipped at by fear at this. John Fallis, damn him.

Don't let him get away with this. Form a posse. Get him.

A posse!

This ain't Dodge City for chrissake!

But for that night it was.

There were righteous men in that crowd. The Chief of Police started deputizing the ones that had blood in their eyes and they scurried home to get their guns—pistols, shotguns, whatever they had. Others waited to be armed by the Sheriff.

In a short time the National Guard Armory was opened. The Sheriff arrived to take charge. Eighteen army Springfield rifles firing .30-06 cartridges of wall splintering force were passed out. These would augment the firepower already in hand. Men were dispatched to block all roads out of town. Others to guard possible escape paths to the river.

No one doubted where he would be. Where else was there to make a stand? His house was rumored to be a veritable arsenal of weapons—rifles, shotguns, pistols, even dynamite. His grocery, with its stone walls, was almost a fortress.

A man could make a stand there. A desperate man. Against a mob that size? One man? Alone?

Mr. Fallis and Carlos and Lucas had made it home without incident, but not without notice.

The sight of John Fallis hurrying through the streets on foot and in his shirtsleeves with a bloody boy at his side startled people. It caused them to stop. To stare. Some had heard the shots. No one interfered. No one dared.

Mr. Fallis had barely reached the house when a neighbor rushed up, breathless. "They're forming a posse, John. Men with shotguns. Lots of them."

Mrs. Fallis was in that house with the baby son. Shoppers were below in the grocery.

JF (that's Yancy's diminutive for Mr. Fallis, I might as well use it), JF gathered the family up as rapidly as he could and rushed them to a neighbor's house. He then dashed back to the grocery, shooed the shoppers out, closed it, locked it.

Yancey had already heard what happened uptown. He knew what to expect. Lucas didn't. But no matter. They wanted to stand with him.

He wouldn't let them. He sent them away.

And waited alone in the darkened house.

Uptown, the four bleeding men had been rushed to the hospital. Off-duty policemen were being called in. The Adjutant General was on his way in in the event the National Guard needed to be called out. The Governor was being informed.

Rumor and speculation burned across the city, swept through the neighborhoods. A cloud of apprehension hung in the air.

By ten o'clock the men of the posse were sworn in and organized and ready to began the long march from the center of town to the Fallis place.

People came out of their houses and congregated on the sidewalks to watch it pass.

They were quiet No one talked. There were no shouts or cheers or smart-ass remarks from the watchers.

From the police station down to the Old State House, then west along Broadway to the river, then north on Wilkinson to the Fallis place, a mile, maybe a little more, no one had seen a procession like it before. Men they knew, armed and menacing, walking abreast down the middle of the street

The only possible reaction was silence.

By eleven o'clock they were in place and had taken up positions surrounding the house and the grocery. The grocery sat on the corner of Wilkinson and Hill streets. The Fallis home was above it, with Fort Hill at its back. Gunmen took up positions along Wilkinson and up along Hill Street. Escape to the river was cut off by riflemen lined across Fort Hill. They had the target surrounded.

No light shown from the house. Nor from the grocery. Only the glow from the street light on the corner lit the scene.

They were a mixed bag, that posse.

Solid God-fearing, church-going, hard-working citizens who'd had enough of John Fallis's arrogance and lawlessness and wanted the town rid of him. And men with old scores to settle and saw this as their opportunity--men he'd beaten at business or at cards or at the polls. Men he'd intimidated or cuckolded. Men who had no particular grievance but thought it would be a fine thing to be known as one of the men who helped bring down the King of Craw. And a few who were three sheets in the wind and on the way to flying under full sail.

No one was sure how many of them. Fifty. A hundred. Enough surely.

They were prepared to do what was necessary. They even had dynamite to blast him out.

But give him a chance. Let him surrender.

A policeman named O'Nan was chosen to present the demand. O'Nan and JF were known enemies. O'Nan was one of those who regularly patrolled in the Bottom. They had clashed early. JF had backed him down in front of witnesses. On a Saturday night on a corner in Craw. A young solider so drunk he couldn't stand was draped around the lamppost outside the Blue Moon Bar. Not hassling anyone. Not mouthing off. Just trying to hang on

No one was paying him any attention. Drunks on lampposts on Saturday nights weren't unusual sights in Craw. O'Nan happened by. Stopped. Studied the boy. Saw something he didn't like—the boy's uniform, his looks, whatever. Tapped him on the shoulder with his nightstick. The young soldier could barely raise his head. Tried to focus. Couldn't. "Pay attention, boy. You're drunk, boy. You're a disgrace to your uniform, boy."

JF was coming out of The Peach Tree Inn across the street. Noticed.

O'Nan rapped the boy with his nightstick hard across the arm. "Pay attention, boy." The boy's head shot up. O'Nan jammed his nightstick under the boy's chin. "You're going uptown." The boy was bewildered. Had no idea what was going on.

JF crossed to them. "I'll take care of him," he said, seeming amused. "Just a poor country boy who's lost his way. No harm. I'll take him." Said it politely, started to move toward the boy.

"Like hell you will," O'Nan said. "He's drunk and disorderly and he's going to jail."

People were beginning to watch—the Saturday night crowd flowing up and down the sidewalk from bar to saloon to bar. John Fallis and a policemen arguing about a drunk. Gotta see this.

JF continued toward the boy, smiling. Said to O'Nan, "Don't make more of this than it is."

O'Nan was the law. He called the shots, not a two-bit gambler. Glaring, O'Nan reached to his belt. His handcuffs were there. Just as rapidly, JF threw open his jacket. His forty-fives were visible. He made no menacing move. Just stood there. Smiling.

O'Nan let his hand fall. He drew himself up. Considered. Decided. Tapped the boy on the cheek with his nightstick. Then pointed it at JF. Stared angrily. Turned and walked away.

JF took the boy's arm over his shoulder and helped him into the saloon.

That night was a bad night for O'Nan.

This night he had a posse at his back.

O'Nan stepped out the line of armed men ringed around the house and started across the street.

He led a squad of three—fellow Patrolman Quire and two civilian deputies caught up in the excitement of the thing who had volunteered and had been under arms for almost two hours.

At the foot of the steps leading to the house O'Nan stopped. Shouted.

"Fallis. You're surrounded. Give it up."

There was no response.

He waited a moment, then tried again.

"Surrender, Fallis. You're done."

Still no response.

O'Nan looked around to make sure the others were behind him. The house was dark There was no movement inside. Cautiously he mounted the steps, crossed the porch to the door.

There was still no movement. Emboldened, O'Nan strode to the door, unlimbered his shotgun. "Dammit, Fallis, open this door or I'll blow it open."

Almost immediately it swung open.

JF stepped out.

Loosed a shotgun blast at O'Nan.

Ducked back through the door.

Slammed it shut.

The blast blew O'Nan back and down, sprayed the others with buckshot.

Stunned, they stood paralyzed, O'Nan bleeding and moaning on the porch, they with wounds in their arms and shoulders.

Then, bleeding but upright, they rushed to O'Nan and, stumbling and falling, half dragged, half carried him back across the street to safety.

A wave of shock ran through the posse.

No one expected that.

The bastard shot O'Nan!

Right there on the porch. Point blank. The bastard shot O'Nan!

To hell with waiting.

Go get the sonofabitch!

Get him!

But the General had arrived. No, he said. Wait for daylight. Too much can go wrong with men shooting wild in the dark. Fallis can't get away. Get the wounded to the hospital and wait for daylight.

It was about eleven-thirty. Sunrise wouldn't be until almost six. Could they be held that long?

Shortly before midnight a man named Brewer showed up. He walked with a swagger. Lucas knew him. Gus Brewer. He had a body shop on Wilkinson, was part owner of a bar in Craw, thought of himself as force in the Bottom, a rival to JF. Lucas thinks this is wishful thinking. Yancey isn't so sure.

Brewer huddled with the Sheriff and the Police Chief for a long moment. "Why not?" the Sheriff said. They knew Brewer. Had had dealings with him.

Brewer nodded and started across the street, hands visible at his sides, empty, walking very, very slowly.

The crowd of onlookers that had assembled panicked. Most of the places in Craw had emptied out and many of the folk of the Bottom had rushed there, many hoping to see the King of Craw get his comeuppance, just as many pulling for him to get away. People start running and darting in every direction as if they expected shots to ring out and mayhem to occur.

Brewer gave it no attention. He continued his slow walk across the street. He stopped at the foot of the stairs leading up to the porch and gave a call. There was no response. The house was still dark and still silent. On any other night you'd think everyone was in bed. Brewer mounted the stairs, crossed the porch, stood in front of the door and gave a knock. A proper knock, a respectful, asking knock, not a demanding bang.

Still no response.

He began to speak then, saying something through the door. He was speaking softly. Whatever he said couldn't be heard in the street. He finished. Waited patiently. Still no response. He started to reach for the door handle, but stopped, remembering O'Nan. He stepped back. Said again what he had to say. And waited. Hands at his sides. Standing straight, composed. But alert.

The men watching fidgeted with suspense.

Minutes passed. The night got a little cooler.

Nothing.

Shaking his head, Brewer retraced his steps, talked briefly with the Sheriff, then disappeared through the posse line into the crowd. Vik was with him.

The moon was almost full that night and the sky was that velvety blue-black of early summer. The sort of night to conjure with.

Except there were men with guns all around and anger in the air.

One o'clock came.

There'd been no sign of movement in the grocery or in the house since the shotgun blast that dropped O'Nan.

Then two o'clock. The courthouse clock could be heard striking the hour.

Everything was quiet on the street, everything was still. Not even a bark from a dog.

Around three, a shot.

A rifle.

Jarringly loud.

No one was sure where it came from. But who the hell cared.

That's it boys. Go get the bastard.

It couldn't be stopped then.

Whether the General or the Sheriff or the Chief of Police approved or not, guns opened up all around, shattering the silence, jolting people awake up who were just beginning to get to sleep after the excitement of the midnight panic. Lights clicked on. Screen doors slammed. Night-clothed figures materialized ghost-like in the dim light on the porches.

The barrage of gunfire was like a rolling thunder, a wave of sound so loud it was heard all the way uptown. Rifles, shotguns, pistols—whatever they had they blazed away with. The firing was so continuous that individual shots couldn't be distinguished.

The rounds chewed up the wood, shattered the glass, ricocheted off the stone of the walls.

Eventually a shot, a lucky shot, or so many shots it was inevitable, struck a box of matches or exploded a can of kerosene.

The walls ignited.

Flames began to eat the building. In minutes the corner was a bonfire.

The shooting stopped then.

They hadn't intended to burn him out, but you take what's given you.

They waited.

Eagerly.

For John Fallis to come running out. Clothes on fire. Hair ablaze.

SIXTEEN
Mercurial And Dangerous

It was crazy.

The whole thing was crazy.

What could Mr. Fallis have been thinking? Was he thinking at all? A seventeen-year-old peeping in at a carnival show? What sort of crime could that be? Resisting arrest? Okay. A different matter, but considering the boy's age and his record of no arrests, no trouble of any type ... a fine maybe. Nothing more. A minor thing.

Why the hell go berserk?

John Fallis was home when Lucas came for him, at home with his wife Anne, his wife of twenty-one years, helping tend to their year-old son, the baby who was deathly ill.

JF was twenty when he and Anne married. She was eighteen. They'd had twelve children. Seven died before their first birthday.

Victor was six months old. Earl just two hours. Clarence, five months. Edward, seven weeks. Leona, five months. Marvin, seven weeks. Elmer, six hours and twenty minutes. JF had to be thinking not another, Lord, not another. Please.

So there was John Fallis that summer night, John Fallis, King of Craw, a man with power, a man who took care of people, that John Fallis, watching helplessly as his baby son struggled to breathe, taking that pain again, bending with that grief again, when Lucas burst in to tell him the police were clubbing down his eldest.

John Fallis couldn't do anything for his youngest, but he damn sure could for his eldest.

Lucas thinks that was the biggest part of it.

The other part, Lucas thinks, is that the police dared lay a hand on his boy at all. Anyone daring to do that would have been in considerable danger. That a policeman did it was beyond endurance.

John Fallis had detested police since he was very young—a ten-year-old coming home from a Salvation Army church service one night. Happy, singing down the street full of the spirit of the Lord, when out of the shadows stepped Big Belly Bob. Big Belly Bob the Bully, the cop on the beat. Everyone in the neighborhood knew him, despised his guts. The man was mean and arrogant and used his badge like it was a license to push people around. Especially kids.

Stabbing with his nightstick, he yelled at JF, "shut your show-off mouth, you little bastard, caterwauling like that." Grabbed him. Manhandled him uptown to the police station. Threatened to charge him with disturbing the peace. JF was battered and bruised and had a split lip and would have done more than kick at the cop's shins if he had his knife, but he hadn't gotten one yet and all he could do was twist and squirm. His mother had to come get him. From that day on his hostility to police was unbounded.

Six men have been shot. Two, possibly three, may die.

Buildings have been burned.

The town is in turmoil.

He's protecting his son and he doesn't like police.

That explains it? That justifies it?

Where am I?

SEVENTEEN
Signs

Lucas and Yancey were sitting on the low stone wall staring into the ruins when I got there. Neither seemed surprised to see me.

Yancey is a Melungeon.

Which explains, in part, his eyes. They are a dark deep brown, brown as dark as chocolate and so piercing you think he might be able to see what's hidden. And his size. Yancey is taller than most men, taller than my father or Mr. Fallis, but is built like Mr. Fallis, lean and strong.

He shaves his head and sports a small gold earring in the lobe of his left ear. You don't see earrings in the ears of men around here.

He wears a black derby hat. All the time. Indoors and out. The only time I ever saw him without it was in court the day of JF's trial.

A man in a black derby hat sitting beside a boy with curly blonde hair on a low stone wall on a sparkling summer morning waiting for the embers to cool in a burned out building across the street ... unreal, so unreal.

People don't know what to make of Yancey. He's not black. He's not white. His skin shades to olive. He has great presence. He walks like he's proud of himself and others had better respect it. It is generally understood that he is Mr. Fallis's deputy. He looks as if he could be lethal.

Yancey closes up at night. He tallies the take and locks the day's proceeds in the safe, then carries it up to the bank each morning and deposits it to the account of John R. Fallis. He walks. Carrying the bags. Everyone knows what's in them. No one has presumed to try to relieve him of the burden.

Yancey is the only Melungeon I had ever seen. Probably the only Melungeon anyone around here had seen. There were very few. There were no others in town.

When the first English settlers pushed away from the coastal areas and into the great unexplored wilderness that was colonial America, they expected the land to be empty of all but Indians. It wasn't. Little groups of people who weren't Indians were already there. They dressed in the English way. They had Christian names and they spoke English with an accent that was almost Elizabethan. But they weren't English. No one knew where they came from. They themselves didn't know. As more settlers pushed in, these strange people withdrew, pushed west and north out of the Carolinas and Virginia up into the folds of the Appalachians and sheltered in small villages in the remote mountain fastness.

In time they became a people of myth—ghosts in the forest. They were said to have powers. They could cast spells and change forms. Their men could see in the dark. They called themselves Melungeons.

I leaned my bike against the wall and walked toward them.

Yancey nodded as I approached, said to me, matter-of-factly, "JF is Sunday's child, did you know that? Born on a Sunday in April with a half-moon rising. The early settlers called the moon of that month the Planting Moon. The ground has thawed enough by then that a plow can be gotten into it and seeds sown."

The way he said it in that deep voice of his, with the charred remains of the grocery in the background and the smell of smoke all around, made me think I was in a dream.

"Remember the nursery rhyme?" he went on. *Monday's child is fair of face. Tuesday's child is full of grace. Wednesday's child is full of woe. Thursday's child has far to go. Friday's child is loving and giving. Saturday's child works hard for a living. But the child that is born on the Sabbath day is bonnie and blithe, and good and gay."*

"That sound like JF to you, that Sunday part?" Standing up and stretching, Yancey said softly under his breath, "Those fools."

He sat down again beside me, still looking up at the searchers on Fort Hill. "I'm Saturday's child. What it says about Saturday's child is true. Lord, is it true. What's your day, Owen.? Lucas, what's yours?"

Neither of us knew the day of the week on which we were born, but of course we knew the day and the month. Lucas, March twenty-nine. Me, May nineteen.

"Lucas, you're a Taurus. Born under the sign of the Bull. Owen, you're a Gemini... the sign of the Twins.

"People put a lot of store in the sign you were born under." He turned to me, serious. "Your sign determines the kind of person you'll be and what will happen to you as your sign rides around the Zodiac circle and the planets and stars play on each other. A slew of people believes this. You don't want to take it lightly. Take JF for instance. JF was born under the sign of the Ram. People born under the Ram are headstrong. They're impulsive. They do rash things. They've got lots of ambition. And they're proud. Oh, lord, they are proud. But generous to a fault. And soft hearted, you know. Just don't cross 'em. Bad news if you do. They can make a lot of mischief, but they're so likeable people just naturally draw to them. That sound like JF?"

Yancey said looking at Lucas, "You're Taurus. The Bull. Yeah, that fits you. Dependable. Faithful. Obstinate. Proud."

Turning slowly to me, looking thoughtful, "You're a Gemini. Gemini are smart. They can get along with almost anybody. They know how to use words and play on people's feelings to get what they want. They're curious. They're interested in almost everything. Excitement. Adventure. That's you. That's why you're down here, isn't it? You're burning to find out what really happens down here. That's you," he smiled, amused for a moment, "a moth drawn to the flame." Then he glanced back up to the hill and stood up, restless.

Lucas shifted anxiously on the wall. Police had put barricades around the ruins of the grocery. Traffic was down to one lane and a patrolman was filtering the flow of workers trying to get to their jobs at the Hemp Factory and the Distillery.

Already the curious were beginning to gather.

"Disgusting," Yancey growled. "Like buzzards circling a carcass." Then turning to us still sitting side by side, "Strange man, JF is. Hard to figure. You need all the signs there are ... stars, moon, chicken guts, owl hoots in the night. Even then you won't be able to. He don't fit any mold I know. The thing for right now is to stop worrying at that and start figuring out how can we help him?"

Shell casings littered the roadway. The smell of cordite and charred wood filled the air. Lucas and Yancey had been there all night. Lucas looked drained. Yancey looked like Yancey. Ready.

"They let it burn," Lucas said to me, disbelievingly hurt. "The fire trucks came, but they let it burn. They're supposed to put out fires, aren't they? Supposed to save things, aren't they?"

"Come home with me," I said. "Mom will make us breakfast."

He shook his head no, his gaze following Yancey's. "Where is he?"

Yancey stood up. Brushed the seat of his pants.

"He ain't up there where they're looking. Slipped past those fools on the hill and made it to the river. Got a johnboat and got across. He was gone before the fire started. He could be holed up over there on the other side. Or out in the county. Almost anywhere. No shortage of folk who'd hide him."

"If he made it out, why wouldn't he just keep going," I said.

Yancey looked at me as if the answer was obvious. "He won't leave until he knows about the baby."

Lucas nodded, agreeing.

"Go home, Owen. There's nothing for you to do here. Go home."

There was a note in Yancey's voice I hadn't heard before. Frustration. Tension. Not a note to argue with.

Lucas heard it too, tried to soften it.

"Tell your Mom I'm sorry you didn't get to see much of the carnival." A smile with that. A weak one, but he was trying.

As I I left I heard Yancey saying, "I wonder if the safe has cooled enough I can open it," and I thought what an extraordinarily ordinary matter to be on his mind on such an extraordinary day.

EIGHTEEN
Is He Coming?

"They seek him here, they seek him there, those Frenchies seek him everywhere. Is he in heaven? Is he in hell? That damned, elusive, Pimpernel."

I couldn't get that rhyme out of my mind.

No charred body in the ashes of the store. No fleeing figure darting through the dark.

His escape is complete.

No one has seen him.

His whereabouts are unknown.

Like the Scarlet Pimpernel, John Fallis has vanished.

It's Thursday.

By mid-morning the search on Fort Hill is abandoned. The roadblocks are dismantled.

Stores have opened on time and people have gone to work like they always do. But the mood is apprehensive. No one knows what to expect. No wants to think of John Fallis on the loose. After all that happened last night he's as likely to come back to town and shoot it up as he is to run for Mexico.

The Governor, at the urging of the city fathers, from his desk in the mansion on Capitol Hill, announces the posting of a reward for the capture of John Richard Fallis—a five-hundred-dollar reward to be paid from the state treasury. State money being put up for the capture of a local desperado, that's how serious the concern is.

Of the casualties, Patrolman O'Nan's and Patrolman Scott's lives are said to be hanging in the balance. Scott, the first to fall, is shot through the liver and the arm. Several times during the day his life is despaired of. O'Nan, who took the shotgun blast on JF's porch, is wounded in the chest, the calf, and the shoulder and is in great pain. The others have been treated and released.

Toward mid-afternoon the sightings start coming in.

JF is said to have been seen heading for Frankfort with two forty-fives dangling from his belt and a shotgun in his hand. He's said to be coming from the direction of Stamping Ground, a small community about twelve miles away. Then he's reported at a train station near Georgetown, further out, and has told the station manager he's on his way to Frankfort. A little later a doctor named Stewart says he saw him leaving Woodlake, which is closer, headed for Frankfort still carrying those two forty-fives.

All the reports are from roughly the same area, the country east of town where Fallis, because of his business dealings with the farmers there, has friends.

The reports are enough to shake the city.

The Mayor authorizes the addition of six special police. They're sworn in immediately. The Sheriff starts deputizing men again, sending them out to guard the approaches to town. Practically every physician is on alert and all off-duty nurses are being called in to help ... in case.

Throughout the afternoon and evening the newspaper and the police station are swamped with calls. Is he coming? Are we safe? There is talk of reassembling the posse. Even of calling out the National Guard.

The sun goes down a little after nine that night. Thursday night.

And while the town waits and marinates in unease, every scandalous thing that has been said or thought of John Fallis gets repeated and embellished upon.

Gambler, brawler, bootlegger.

Gangster. Ward boss. Bully.

Womanizer.

Devil.

He doesn't come.

Friday dawns clear. The sun is up by six-fifteen. Armed men still man the entrances to town.

That morning John Fallis, Jr., age fourteen, and a friend show up at the grocery on Wilkinson armed with shotguns and a rifle. Practically the entire contents of the house and the grocery have been destroyed by the fire. Why they are there isn't clear but the police, who are still on the scene, disarm them and take them to the county workhouse. They're questioned vigorously, but have no knowledge of JF's plans or whereabouts and are released in the late afternoon. The police confiscate their weapons.

By nightfall Craw is packed. It seems everyone who can crowd in has done it. The regulars and the uptown upper-crust, thrill seekers from all around, are drawn by the excitement and the suspense. They all want to be there for whatever happens, because something has to happen and it sure as hell is gonna be stupendous.

There is a constant flow of people on the streets, drinks in hand, laughing, jostling—like Bourbon Street at Mardi Gras.

At the Blue Moon and the Tip Toe Inn the bets are going down. He's coming back with two guns blazing to wipe out the rest of the police force!

No! He's running like the coward he is and will keep on running.

Very few are putting their money on him running.

A few fights break out. Nothing serious. The cops don't interfere. They usually don't, and anyway, this night they have other concerns to deal with.

The party doesn't wind down until almost daylight.

JF doesn't make an appearance.

On Saturday morning one of JF's sons drives a truck to a gasoline station on the edge of town, parks it, and leaves in another car. The truck is filled with clothes and food. The Sheriff follows the car, but loses it. Later that day the Sheriff announces that he's had word from an emissary of the fugitive. He says he knows the hiding place and will go alone, to apprehend and return him to justice.

No one sees the Sheriff go...or return. Whatever he does, when night comes JF is still on the loose.

My father is still away. We've talked by phone. He's seen the stories. There's been almost daily reportage in all the area newspapers. He knows we're all right.

"You saw the shooting?"

"Yes, sir."

"Are you okay?"

"Yes, sir. No, sir. I don't know. I think so."

"How's Lucas?"

"He's all worried about Mr. Fallis."

"Help him if you can."

I was afraid he'd tell me to stay away. He didn't.

"I'll be home Wednesday. We'll talk then. Take care of your mother." He pauses for just a moment.

"Yes, sir?"

"Don't do anything dumb."

NINETEEN
At The Riverman

Lucas.

I went down to the grocery Saturday morning hoping to find him.

No Lucas.

Only the burned out ruins.

There were still police barricades around the site and a policeman patrolling around the house where Mrs. Fallis was staying. A small crowd of gawkers clustered on the sidewalk, trading stories and floating theories on where he was. Or waiting for the King to return.

But no Lucas. No Yancey. Only the curious and the morbid.

I didn't know where Lucas lived, knew no one who knew him, had no way to leave a message. I hung around awhile, hoping he might show up.

My mother was anxious about Lucas.

"Do you suppose he's all right? He admires Mr. Fallis so. You don't think he's out searching, do you? Oh, lord, I hope not. He could get shot, all those men with guns looking everywhere."

"No, ma'am," I said. "He wouldn't do that."

Lucas was most likely with Yancey. Waiting. Even if Yancey knew where Mr. Fallis was, he wouldn't take a chance on trying to get a message to him. He'd wait and let Mr. Fallis get a message to him, tell him what the plan was, tell him how he could help. No. They'd wait.

By Sunday five days had passed since the Big Shoot-Out.

John Fallis's whereabouts were still unknown and his intentions the cause of considerable unease.

If Mr. Fallis had decided to run, he could be halfway to China by now. But there was no indication he had done that. The reports of the sightings and the Sheriff's claim of a contact by an emissary caused everyone to believe Mr. Fallis was still in the area. This made people very uneasy. Why was he still around? Why hadn't he run when he had the chance?

I thought he was waiting for something more than word of his baby son. I thought he was waiting for the news that ran in the newspaper that Sunday morning.

No one died.

Of the seven men he shot, no one died. The two most seriously wounded had been declared out of danger and were recovering. The others had been bandaged and sent home.

No one died!

It was the one lucky break of the whole sorry affair. He'd killed no one. That meant he wouldn't have to stand trial for murder. Which meant he could surrender if he chose. He could get the hunters off his tail. He could surrender and take his chances with a jury of his peers. He'd had good luck with juries before.

Might he do that? Would he do that?

"Be taking a helluva chance," Yancey said. "The cops might not let him surrender. Might shoot him on sight. They would in a flash if they got to him first."

Each day I'd made my little pilgrimage down to the grocery. Sat on the wall across the street. Watched the gawkers kick around in the ashes and the policemen standing guard on the corner.

And waited.

Lucas knew I'd be there. Sooner or later he'd come.

Now, that Sunday after church, that sunny Sunday afternoon as I sat on the wall waiting, Lucas materialized. On the far corner out of sight of the policeman. Motioned to me to follow. And walked off into the Bottom toward Craw.

Craw.

I'd still not been there. Had been told not to go.

"Don't you go there," Mom had said.

"Yes, ma'am," I'd dutifully replied.

Is "yes ma'am" a promise? I kept promises. Was my "yes ma'am" a promise? I hadn't said I wouldn't go. I'd only said "yes ma'am."

Lucas was a block ahead of me.

I decided that "yes ma'am" was not a promise and rushed to catch up.

We were on the upstairs floor of a two-story wooden building. The sign out front announced it the Riverman. It sat on a corner and was painted brown. Across the street was the Blue Moon; in the next block down, the Peach Tree Inn.

So far Craw had been a disappointment. Just little clusters of plain looking men on the sidewalks outside a string of bars and saloons, drinking and talking. No knife fights. No gun play. No magic or sparkle. The clusters would pulse for a while like driftwood caught in an eddy then break off and move on with the current to be caught up in the next little eddy. Maybe it all happens at night, I thought. Maybe the lights go on and the music starts and the excitement begins. At night.

Yancey set his coffee cup down on the edge of the table. Lucas was at the window. Muffled sounds from the street filtered up. Laughter. A car going by. A high-pitched voice calling out, "Get your ass over here, boy." A banjo plinking a tune I didn't know, a cheery tune, seemed hopeful.

Lucas left the window. "Well, you're in Craw."

"Not what I expected," I said.

"Your mother know where you are?"

"She thinks I'm over by the grocery waiting for you to show up."

"That's okay with her?"

"She's worried about you."

He closed his eyes and shook his head and looked away. "What does she think about all that's happened?"

I started to answer, but stopped. The tone in Lucas's voice was so plaintive that I realized for the first time how much he wanted her good opinion. What happened wasn't his doing but he was a part of it and he seemed to be thinking that what she thought of it would color how she thought of him.

What had happened appalled her. The shooting, the burning, the sense of chaos that hung over the town—that shocked and dismayed her. "Good Lord, Eddie, what sort of place have we moved to," I heard her say to my father on the phone. She knew Mr. Fallis was at the heart of the trouble and she knew Lucas admired him but she associated none of the mayhem with Lucas. She liked Lucas. She trusted him. She thought he was sweet and kind and considerate. She worried that some harm might come to him because of Mr. Fallis.

I thought it best not to tell Lucas that, so I shrugged and was fumbling for a reply when Yancey stepped in.

"Never mind," he said.

He'd been listening, watching us, interested in our interplay, but now impatient, standing on the edge of something.

"Never mind," he said again.

Yancey moved from the side of the table where he'd been sitting to pull up a chair beside Lucas. We were in a big rectangular room. Three rows of circular tables were strung down the length of it. A bar of polished walnut with a big mirror behind it stretched across the far end. Soft afternoon light slipped in past the green velvet drapes on the windows on the street side.

A fairly brisk business was being done downstairs. Drinking wasn't against the law. Making and selling the stuff was. By declaring booze illegal, everyone's thirst seemed to grow. It was up to the Feds to stop the flow of it, not the cops. Prohibition was a money machine for them. Let a little money change hands on a regular basis and the bars and saloons had no hassles or worries.

If things got a little rowdy—a shooting, a knifing—the operators took care of it. No one wanted the police involved, least of all the police. Street fights and barroom tussles were considered entertainment.

The only people unhappy with the arrangement were the church ladies and the Feds.

JF himself didn't run bars or saloons, and definitely not houses of ill repute. But he owned property which was sometimes leased to those who did, property like the building that housed the Riverman.

Which is how it came to be that Lucas and Yancey and I had its upstairs floor all to ourselves that afternoon.

Yancey rubbed his chin, adjusted the brim of his black derby hat, and studied me. I don't know that he liked me. I think he was mostly curious about me, an uptown kid hobnobbing with Lucas, hanging around. What was I after? Yancey thought everyone was after something. He figured he'd find out in time but for now, if Lucas and JF trusted me, he had no reason not to.

Which must be what he concluded, for he leaned forward on the table we sat around in that empty room, partially rose on his outstretched arms, and stared challengingly at me.

"JF is back. He has a plan. We need your help."

TWENTY
Don't Do Dumb Things

Once, fishing the Upper Big Thompson outside Estes Park. Late April. Just after ice had cleared the river. Fishing alone. In mid-stream. In water about thigh deep. I'm wading along and edge around a big boulder expecting to step onto a continuation of the regular streambed. But it isn't there. I've stepped into a hole that seems to have no bottom.

My waders begin to fill immediately, pulling me under. The cold of the water hits me like a zap of electricity. The hole I'm disappearing into, and which will drown me if I don't make it out before my waders fill, shouldn't have been there. I knew that stretch of river. The surprise of it paralyzed me as much as the shock of the icy water creeping up my chest.

That's how it hit me when Yancey announced "JF is back."

I turned in surprise to Lucas.

He was nodding vigorously, "He's okay. Not hurt," but with a worried, apologetic smile, "Will you help?"

Yancey broke in. "This ain't play, Owen. If anything goes wrong and you're caught, that's aiding and abetting. A crime. Get you sent to jail. Your momma wouldn't like that. You'd like it even less.

My father's words flashed in my mind. Don't do anything dumb he'd said. Help Lucas if you can but don't do anything dumb.

I liked Mr. Fallis. Not enough to risk jail for him, but enough to want to help if it wasn't too dumb a thing to do. More compelling was Lucas. Sitting there. Wanting my help. Needing my help.

Is this in that dumb category?

"Tell me what you want me to do," I said.

JF had arrived back in town last night, Saturday night, and got word to Yancey. I didn't ask how he'd managed to slip past the searchers or where he'd been or where he was now. All I wanted at that moment was to know what they needed me to do.

Yancey eased himself back down into his chair, glanced to the stairs, nodded to Lucas. Lucas walked to the stairwell, stepped down it to the bottom to make sure the ground floor door was locked, climbed back to the top, closed and locked the door to our room, and came back to the table.

He took a seat across from me, folded his hands, and waited. Though the outside windows were open and the ceiling fans were running, the room was so quiet I could hear my own breathing, and though afternoon light filled the room, everything around me seemed to be in shadows. Yancey and Lucas were all I could see. Lucas looked tense, Yancey, now that he'd come to it, was subdued and solemn.

"We have to get word to Bill Callahan. Tell him that JF is here, has a plan, and needs him to make it work. I can't do it. Neither can Lucas. The cops are watching us. You can. They don't know you. They're not watching you. I'll explain the plan to you. You'll memorize it then tell it to Bill."

"I don't know Mr. Callahan. Why would he believe me?"

"You'll give him this."

Yancey handed me a handwritten note. As he did, he reached to his ear and removed the small gold earring he always wore.

"Take this with you. He'll know the note is really from me. The note explains who you are and that JF and I trust you. It don't explain the plan. If you're caught, the cops would have it and then shortly they'd have JF. That's why you have to memorize it. Are you game for this? Can you do it?"

A courier. I'm to be a courier, slipping through enemy lines with a vital message, the secret committed to memory, my lips sealed, never mind the consequences. Adventure. Danger. Hot-diggity-damn! Yes, I can do it!

This was the plan.

I'd go to Bill Callahan (he's JF's cousin, Yancey knows where he is), give him the note, give him time to consider what it says, then tell him that JF wants him to make contact with the county judge before the day is out.

The Judge is the key. The Judge has enough authority to make things happen. He's friendly to JF (JF's Ward Three had gotten him elected three times) and JF trusts him.

Bill is to tell the Judge that JF is sorry for the damage that's been done and wants no more bloodshed. He is ready to turn himself in, if certain conditions are met. The conditions are these:

JF will surrender to the police—but not in Frankfort. He doesn't trust his safety in the hands of the local police. He'll surrender in Louisville.

The Louisville police will accept his surrender and escort him back to Frankfort where he will be delivered to the County Sheriff, not the city police.

He will be charged and then released on bail to await trial on whatever date the Judge sets.

He will not be jailed.

The Frankfort city police are to be ordered to stay clear of JF, to neither harass nor interfere with him.

The Governor is to be informed and is to guarantee safe passage to Louisville under the protection of, but not in the company of, the State Police.

All this is to happen tomorrow, Monday. The longer JF is at large, the larger the threat of more bloodshed.

And, there was a certain twinkle in his eye when he told me this, "Callahan is to get the reward. You have it all? Have it clear? Can repeat it all to Bill so he understands?"

"Mr. Fallis can't think he'll get all that," I said.

All Yancey said was, "He better."

It was almost two-thirty by the time I got to Mr. Callahan. He was at his home in the Thorn Hill section out beyond the prison drinking lemonade and pitching horseshoes in his backyard.

I would not have picked him as related to John Fallis.

He was older and shorter. Had a good smile and a strong handshake. He was friendly, but there wasn't that expectant look in his eyes or the sense of energy that JF radiated.

Mr. Callahan excused himself from the horseshoe game, walked me to a couple of chairs under a big shady oak, and gave me a glass of lemonade. He limped slightly. I learned later that he had once been in an explosion that injured him so badly doctors thought both his legs would have to be amputated. He wouldn't let them. He sent them away. He limped now. But he had both legs. That was a Fallis trait I recognized, that stubbornness.

"You're not from around here."

"No, sir. I'm from Colorado."

"Like it here?"

"It's different."

He chuckled. "I imagine. How did you and Lucas come to be friends?"

"He got my bike back for me."

"Is that right? You'll have to tell me that story sometime."

He turned his attention from me to the note in his hand. Read it once. Put it down. Stood up. Sat back down. Inspected the earring Yancey had sent. Looked around. Then back to me, frowning. Read it again. Sat back in his chair. Frowned again.

Finally said, "Tell me."

When I finished he sat silent for a long time. When he stood up, I stood up too.

"You think we can pull this off?"

"I hope so, sir."

A faint smile, "Me too, kid. Me too."

I went home from there.

I'd been told not to come back to the Riverman. Yancey and Lucas would be elsewhere.

As I walked along the prison walls and angled right toward the Old State House I thought Mr. Bill Callahan would have to work wonders to corral the Judge and the Sheriff and manage to meet with the Governor before the day was out that sunny Sunday afternoon. Even if he managed it, would they agree to JF's demands?

The image that came to my mind was a rogue lion roaring in the night while the natives shivered in their huts.

TWENTY-ONE
A Perfect Day For It

Monday.

Sunrise was at six-sixteen. I was up and out before that, finished my paper route and was home and cleaned up and at breakfast by seven-thirty. Dad was home, too. Came home late last night. With all the uncertainty in the air he cut short his trip to get back and be here.

We didn't talk last night. He got in too late for that. We will today.

Mom had been up since daylight. She'd made a big breakfast. Scrambled eggs, country ham, pancakes with real maple syrup from Maine and fresh churned butter, hand squeezed orange juice, milk, coffee. To celebrate Dad's return? Because cooking is one of the ways she works off tension?

Today's the day. The day the Powers That Be either accept JF's surrender on his terms, or....

She doesn't know that. Neither does dad.

I don't know what the "or" is. It can't be good.

Mom was standing at the stove, a long spatula in her hand. "Eat your breakfast. You're staring off into space. Are you all right?"

Was I?

She cocked her head and gave me that, you can't-fool-your-mother look. "You're fidgety this morning."

"No, Mom. I'm fine.

"Owen...," she frowned.

"No, really. I was just wondering where Lucas is. I thought I'd round him up and we'd go fishing."

That was almost true. The wondering about Lucas part. The fishing just came to me. A stroke of inspiration. A passport to get out and be gone all day and no explanations needed.

"Well, it should be a nice day for it." Then nodding to herself, "Yes, it would be good for both of you." She turned to me, smiling, "Be back by supper time. Don't be late. Make sure Lucas is okay," paused, "tell him to come to dinner soon."

It would have been better than a nice day for it. It would have been a perfect day.

The sky was red at sunrise. I thought rain might be coming ... "Red sky at morning, sailor take warning." As soon as the mist lifted from the river, though, the sun was up and bright, the sky translucent blue and cloudless. We'd had no rain for almost a week. Elkhorn would be running clear. My guess was that a black woolly-bugger worked around the holds in the stretch beyond the bridge at the Forks would be deadly for the smallmouth living there.

Except I didn't go.

Lucas and I had made no plans to meet. No one had said they'd bring me news. Still, dammit, I was the guy who'd carried the message through enemy lines. I was the courier. I deserved to know what was happening.

Did they give JF want he wanted? Was he surrendering? Or was there going to be more shooting? Somebody get killed this time?

Dammit, Lucas, come talk to me.

So I waited at the only place I knew to wait—on the wall across from the grocery looking over at the ruin and up at Fort Hill.

During the Civil War, there was an earthworks fort up there. From that fort the local militia turned back a raid by Confederate General John Hunt Morgan's men. After all this is over, I'm going to go see it. I should make a list. My father does that. He has a list of things he has to do and one of things he wants to do. I should do that. I should make lists.

Wilkinson Street was almost back to normal. Traffic was moving freely. People were passing on the sidewalk. A dog nosed around in the ashes of the grocery.

The cops had disappeared. The barrier around the burn-out was still up, but they were gone, not even keeping watch on the place where Mrs. Fallis was staying. Did that mean they'd given up? Or did that mean they'd captured him?

Dammit, someone come tell me.

So I sat on the wall and fumed and twisted and when the tension had to be relieved, got up and paced. Or fished that stretch of Elkhorn in my imagination (hung two, nice size). Or studied the mass of Fort Hill and tried to picture how JF managed to escape over it, if that's what he did. The police thought he'd make his run in the other direction, down the hill to the river then across it and head west. They put their sentries on the river slope. Yancey thought JF would head for the river, too, but he said he wouldn't bet on it. "JF's hard to figure," he said.

Fort Hill was much more than a hill. It was a steep, rugged spine of trees and thick understory that ran across the valley from the river to the pass that led out of town on the northeastern side. To navigate over Fort Hill and across it ... three miles, maybe more ... on foot in the dead of night, to do it silently, invisibly, while an army of men with guns in their hands searched for you, with only the light of the moon to move by, I had to admire it if he tried that.

A little after three o'clock from my seat on the wall I saw a large black Buick coming down the street from the direction of the Distillery. I noticed it because it was moving very slowly. The driver seemed to be looking for something, checking street numbers maybe.

There was a vacant house diagonally across from the grocery. The car slowed as it approached then pulled to the curb and sat there in front of it idling.

After a moment the rear door of the car opened and a man stepped out. He held the door open while he very deliberately scanned up and down the street. He was very thorough.

A moment passed. And another. When he was satisfied he stepped back and motioned.

I caught a flash of movement under the elevated porch of the vacant house. A man was in the shadows there. As he stepped into the light I saw he was dressed like a workman—a dark brown fedora, a wrinkled blue denim work shirt, black work pants, black suspenders, black high top work shoes. And carrying a shotgun.

That man slid rapidly through the open door into the waiting car. The other man closed it, walked around the back and got in the street-side door. The car moved away without hesitation and proceeded slowly past me up Wilkinson in the direction of the bridge and the road to Louisville.

In the front seat were two men I didn't know.

In back were Callahan and, riding shotgun for himself, Mr. John Richard Fallis.

TWENTY-TWO
What Man Wouldn't?

Of his own volition, John Richard Fallis turned himself in to the Jefferson County Sheriff at the Sheriff's office in Louisville at approximately six p.m. on Monday, June twenty-one—fifty miles away from the state's capitol city and six days after his actions there that drew national attention and traumatized the town.

He was sorry, he said. Sorry that anyone got hurt. Sorry for all the trouble. He had only done what any father would do. His son was being beaten bloody by the police. The boy was handcuffed and down on his knees and in danger of ... well. He only did what any father would do. He hoped people would understand.

On the way up to Louisville, he had wanted to stop and get a bath and shave. He feared he looked like a desperado. He wasn't a desperado. He didn't want people to think he was. But there wasn't time. As soon as he'd had a bath and a shave he'd be ready to get back to Frankfort, he said, and eager to get this thing settled.

He was contrite. He was sincere. He was manfully likeable. But not apologetic for his actions. For their result yes, but not for his actions. He was protecting his son. He did what any father would do.

The reporters waiting at the Jefferson County jail ate it up.

When I think back on it now, that comment at that time to those people was a stroke of genius. This was nineteen twenty-one. People got their news from newspapers then. There was no radio. No television.

I still wonder whether what he said was calculated or spontaneous. It made all the difference in the way a very large number of people came to think of John Fallis after that.

"Only Did What Any Father Would Do, Fallis Says" one headline read. *"Defending His Son From Police Beating,"* another declared.

That next morning this became the theme that drove much of the coverage of JF's surrender.

None of the stories downplayed what had happened—the shootings, the posse's attack, his escape. But that little conditioning line, "I only did what any father would do," introduced an almost justifiable reason for a series of acts that seemed barbaric—a man trying to protect his child from the violence of abusive police. People would understand that.

When JF came back to the Capital City, he arrived not as the mad dog some had cast him to be, but in the minds of many, a hero.

At the county jail when he arrived a crowd of friends and well wishers were waiting. They'd come from all over the county to shake his hand and to make sure he was safely received and respectfully treated. By the time the Sheriff got the place cleared almost two hours had passed.

The formal proceedings were concluded rapidly.

JF was placed under arrest on four charges of shooting with intent to kill without killing. He waived examining trial, was bound over to the September session of the Grand Jury, had bail set at five thousand dollars, which was immediately subscribed by four upstanding citizens, and released.

Released.

Set free.

At liberty to walk among us all.

Leland Morgan, his attorney, orchestrated it all. It was smooth and efficient—like a script was being followed. I didn't know Mr. Morgan at the time. I came to want to. I wanted to know how he did that.

JF and Mr. Morgan arrived at the Franklin County Jail about nine. A sparkling clear morning. Cool but expected to warm into the eighties by noon.

Mr. Morgan was driving. JF was beside him in the front seat. He had on a fashionable navy blue suit, a pristine white shirt, and a neatly knotted blood red tie. A new brown fedora was in his lap.

He was smiling.

There was just the two of them. No pistols. No shotguns. Only them.

Mr. Morgan had picked JF up at the Jefferson County Jail and made the long drive to Frankfort unescorted by police. They were just one other car on the road that morning, though trailing far behind and never losing sight of them, was a State Police car—the insurance JF had wanted and which the Governor had promised.

I was among those in the waiting crowd.

Lucas had called me the night before, his voice full of relief and eagerness. He explained what was going to happen, said I should be there—if I wanted. "Mr. Fallis wants to thank you. I do, too."

Yancey was there of course. He, too, was dressed formally. His black derby hat sat regally atop his shaved head. His black suit was spiffy. And, for I noticed this in particular, the little gold earring was back in place. Bill Callahan was also there and also suited. Many in the crowd were. It was as if this was a ceremonial event—hushed and respectful, a moment to mark as the liege lord makes his entrance and then a celebration to follow.

JF should have been an outcast. He'd shot six men, decimated the police force, traumatized most of the community. Even the Governor considered him such a menace that a $500 reward for his capture, dead or alive, had been posted. Yet he wasn't.

The reason, I believe, was that "I only did what any father would do" line.

The working man, the common man, the people who already looked up to John Fallis as protector and Samaritan, and others who only knew his name but had heard he stood up for the little man—they understood. The great unwashed understood.

Somebody beating up your child, someone from the establishment crowd who lorded it over you, people who felt they were better than you, a boss, a schoolhouse tyrant, a cop—running roughshod over your child, beating him bloody and breaking his bones, hell yes, you'd step in and stop it. What man wouldn't? What man would bear such an outrage? The cops had it coming, didn't they, always pushing people around, arrogant bastards showing off their power, bullies with their hands out for payoffs. Hell yes, they had it coming.

Even some of the upper class felt him justified. Over coffee or drinks at the club, in casual conversation after the Rotary meeting, when the matter came up, as it almost always did, they began to imagine what they might do if faced with a similar circumstance. And to wonder if to do less would not only be dishonorable, but cowardly.

A man protects his family.

A man does.

TWENTY-THREE
The Nicest Fellow I Know

The day had run its course. We were at Susan's Place, a restaurant at the far end of Wilkinson that overlooked the river on a bluff near the dam. There was Lucas and me, and Yancey and Callahan, and Mr. Fallis with Mr. Leland Morgan, his attorney.

Mr. Fallis had gotten his family settled in the house Yancey had found them. He had inspected the charred ruins of his home and grocery and was now winding things down with supper at Susan's. We had a corner table on the screened-in porch that looked out on the river. Susan's Place was a favorite of JF's. Susan was a favorite of JF's.

A soft twilight was settling in, the last of daylight silvering the river surface and nighthawks beginning to dart after insects over the dam.

Mr. Morgan rose to take it all in. As he did, we stopped our casual conversation and put our attention on him.

"Beautiful evening," he said. Then turning to JF, "Time for me to get along, John. I am glad you're back safe and sound." Not an attorney stroking a client, a friend being sincere. What he said next, though, caught us all. "But you need to understand that you're in a different game now. Before all this the police just didn't like you. Now they hate you in a very special way. You shot them up and made them look like fools. They are real enemies now, John. They will get you if they can.

"The police are only the obvious threat. The Mayor is embarrassed. The Chief of Police is embarrassed. The Governor and his people are embarrassed, so embarrassed they posted a reward for you dead or alive. You are an embarrassment to them all. They want to be rid of you.

"And there are men waiting in the wings to take you down. They'll think there is a good chance you are going to a jail for a long time now. They'll figure you are weakened. They're going to be coming at you as hard as they can. No holds barred. I mean that."

He held JF's gaze, frowning.

"The upcoming trial is one thing. This matter is more immediate. Watch yourself, John. Be careful. Put a hold on that temper of yours. Watch your back."

There was a long silence. Then JF said quietly, "Am I going to jail for a long time?"

Morgan looked puzzled, then began to smile. "After what I've just said, that's what concerns you? You are a constant wonder to me, John Richard Fallis, a constant wonder." He left laughing to himself.

"He wants me to be nice," JF announced. He looked around at us all as if astonished. "Why, I'm the nicest guy I know."

We all laughed with him and sat back, but Lee Morgan's warning registered in every mind and did not fade with the sunset.

I was there unexpectedly and delightedly. Mr. Fallis himself had invited me. He saw me standing on the edge of the crowd beside Lucas that morning at the jail and walked over and held out his hand.

"Come join us for supper. I want to thank you properly. Lucas will tell you where."

My mother had not asked where I'd been all day. I think she knew. Nor did she quiz me when I excused myself from supper by telling her Lucas had asked me to have supper with him. It wasn't a lie exactly, but I was uneasy with it. I don't know what she saw when she looked into my face. Whatever it was, she accepted my alibi without question and I loved her even more. All she said was, "Remember what your father says."

98

So I stepped out into the twilight cautioned. And pleased beyond saying to be included with Lucas and the others that night—Owen Edwards, the intrepid courier who'd slipped bravely through enemy lines to bring the vital message.

People kept coming over to the table wishing JF well. He was gracious and said how much he appreciated their interest and concern. Most of them he knew by name. If there were any in that crowd who wished him ill, there was no evidence of it. If there had been, Susan would have had the miscreant tossed in the river. Susan was pretty. She walked like she knew she deserved the attention men gave her. She had a confident air about her. She liked JF. He liked her. They liked each other. You could tell by the embrace and the way her lips brushed his check when she greeted him. The way his eyes followed her when she left our table.

Lucas and I sat across from Mr. Fallis, who sat facing the room where he could see everyone and everyone could see him. Yancey and Bill Callahan sat on either side of him. Yancey had his black derby hat on. He was the only man in the restaurant defying convention. All the others were hatless. He stood out.

Mr. Fallis thanked me early and simply. At the beginning he stood and walked around the table to shake my hand. "You ran a real risk for me," he said. "I am much obliged."

Everyone in on the porch must have noticed. I felt my face reddening with pride. Callahan put his finger to the side of his nose and made a little forward movement toward me with it, smiling. Even Yancey nodded.

To Lucas sitting beside me, he said, "You, also, Lucas. I'm glad you're with me," and shook his hand, too. Lucas beamed. The whole room seemed to glow.

Oddly though, there, then, in the headiness of that moment, I felt an anxious twinge—the feel I'd sometimes get high in the mountains hunting alone when an early winter storm starts building unexpectedly over the ridge and wondering if I can make it home before the snow starts falling.

Well, the King was back. No one died. The matter was in hand, so they turned to talk of how and what.

TWENTY-FOUR
A Little Stroll In The Moonlight

As well as I can remember, this is what JF told them. His words were directed to Yancey and Bill Callahan, but Lucas and I were at the table and he made no effort to exclude us from any of it.

The Night of the Posse (he didn't call it that, he called it simply "that night") he said he remembered it as if it were an hallucination. He said it was if he was standing off watching—caught up in the action, feeling the outrage, in tune with the fury, wanting the man he was watching, which he recognized as himself, to annihilate the men with the guns. Make them suffer. Make them pay. But he was watching it, not doing it.

This had happened before. Sometimes he got so mad at what people did to each other, or tried to do to him—demean him, cheat him, lie to him, threaten him—that he felt he'd explode. Sometimes he did. He knew it. They knew it. When he did, trying to remember what happened was like trying to recall images in a dream he'd just awoken from.

He was truly sorry if he'd hurt anyone. He didn't mean to hurt anyone. Sometimes it just couldn't be avoided. Still, he regretted the hurt.

That night, by the time O'Nan came bulling up on the porch and tried to force the door open, his fury had cooled. He wasn't standing off watching anymore. He was making decisions.

He wasn't sorry he'd shot O'Nan. He was sorry he'd been forced to. He realized that if he stayed where he was, he'd have to shoot others. He didn't want that. So after Brewer came and made his little show of bravado, he took his leave.

Yancey: "What did Brewer want?"

JF: "The posturing little bastard. He said that if I would surrender myself to him he'd see that the cops didn't shoot me on my way to jail and he'd make sure the reward money went to Anne for her and the kids."

Callahan: "And he'd be the hero who got John Fallis."

Yancey: "And he'd move in tomorrow on the uptown business."

Callahan: "And then try to take the rest of it while Johnny is in jail."

Yancey: "Have to do something about Mr. Augustus Brewer."

JF nodded. "Soon."

Yancey: "What?"

JF: "I'm thinking about it."

Yancey and Callahan exchanged glances, Yancey with eyes crinkled and a wicked grin forming, Callahan with brows furrowed and a look of worry.

Lucas and I sat spellbound, hardly breathing for fear they might remember we were present and send us away.

"After Brewer made his exit, I made mine," JF continued.

He had changed rapidly into work clothes and heavy shoes, grabbed an old fedora, a hunting jacket and a blanket-roll, picked up his shotgun, shoved his forty-five into his belt, made sure he had plenty of cash, and jumped down off the back porch onto the hill.

If sentries were posted to stop his escape over the hill, he encountered none. They were focused on stopping him from making a run to the river. If he made the river he could get to almost anywhere—north to Chicago, east to New York, west to San Francisco, south to New Orleans. Or head for Canada or Mexico. They'd never catch him.

He knew they'd think that way.

His destination wasn't the river, it was a place in the opposite direction, a shed on the farm of a friend near Stamping Ground. An easy drive under normal circumstances—five or six miles, a half-hour at most—if if you were driving.

He'd have to walk it. Up the cliff behind him and over the limestone ridges of Fort Hill, through the underbrush and trees, avoiding the gullies and the sink holes and coming down to cut the railroad behind the Shoe Factory on the east side of town where the railroad ran. From there he would follow the tracks up and out of the valley.

There were two high trestles to cross. Lose your balance on one of those and the fall could cripple or kill you. And miles of track to walk—wooden ties on crushed rock. By moonlight. Easy to twist an ankle doing that. Easy to misjudge a step and take a bad fall.

How long? He didn't know. He'd never tried it. Two hours maybe if he braved the trestles. If he chickened-out and had to climb the cliffs on either side of them? Too long.

Make it by daylight. Have to. Have to get there unseen. Slip in and get settled before anyone's around to notice.

He found the shed just at dawn, cleared a space on the floor, unwrapped his bedroll, laid his shotgun alongside, placed his forty-five near his head, and disappeared into sleep of utter exhaustion,

When he woke, it was midafternoon.

That was Thursday. He made his presence known to his friend. No explanation or excuses were necessary. He was welcome. They fed him and gave him what news they had. He learned that there was no organized search underway for him in the surrounding counties. That was good. The rest of it was bad.

He learned about the fire, learned that they'd burned down his house, burned down his store. He thought that must be a mistake. Surely they wouldn't burn down his home.

It was no mistake. They had to wait until almost dawn for the ashes to cool enough to search for his body. Only when they could find nothing, not even a belt buckle, would they admit that he'd escaped.

Burn him alive? Destroy and obliterate him? His anger was so great he almost started for town right then. But he realized the folly of that. He let his anger cool. He comforted himself with the promise that in time, in his own way, he would make them pay.

His friend was reluctant to tell him about the reward, but Mr. Fallis needed to know. Five hundred dollars. Dead or alive. That changed things dramatically. That meant anyone could be a threat to him.

He stayed at the shed that night, slept fitfully, dreamt of leaping flames and falling from railroad trestles.

Early the next morning, Friday morning, JF moved to a fishing cabin he knew on Elkhorn Creek near Peaks Mill. On the way he stopped at a little crossroads grocery and bought bologna and cheese, two apples, a loaf of bread, two cokes, and an onion.

The lady behind the counter didn't recognize him. She knew about John Fallis, though. She gave him all the details of the fight. How Mr. John Fallis had taken on the entire Frankfort city police force because they were beating his kid and shot them all to pieces. How the police were looking for him everywhere. There was a five-hundred dollar reward posted for him. Dead or alive! Imagine! Five-hundred dollars! No one knew where he was. They'd closed all the roads in and out of Frankfort. The policemen he'd shot were barely hanging on.

She was curious about a stranger on foot way out there in the county, but seemed satisfied when he told her he was on his way to the big fishing camp at the mouth of Elkhorn. There was a job for a carpenter there. He was a carpenter.

That night he stayed at the cabin by the creek. Made his bologna and cheese sandwich, slathered on mustard, added two big slices of onion, and opened the Coke he'd been cooling in the creek. For dessert he had an apple and a little cheese. He saved the other Coke for that little jab of caffeine in the morning.

It was very pleasant there by the creek with moonlight filtering through the sycamores and the whisper of water soft in the night.

He heard bobwhite calling to each other across the meadow and a whippoorwill off in the distance. It was peaceful. It was comforting. Lord, he needed a little peace and comfort.

He was soon asleep and slept the night through without dreaming.

The next morning, Saturday, he began to think about how to make his way back to town.

Yancey: "You had to find out about the baby, never mind the risk?"

JF: "Never mind the risk."

He was unkempt, unshaven, in rumpled clothes and a three-day beard. Not the John Fallis anyone who knew him would expect. He might be able to slip in unrecognized. Even if recognized, who would be fool enough to try to take him one-on-one? Worth the risk.

He caught a ride into town with a farmer headed for the livery stable at the foot of Wilkinson. He knew the farmer. The farmer knew him. They'd done business.

"They're looking for you, Mr. Fallis."

"I know."

"I think you did right, Mr. Fallis."

"Take me into town with you?"

"Take you any place you want to go."

He'd always been lucky. At most things. They thought his success at cards was due to skill. Skill was some of it. The bigger part was luck. The kind he made for himself. He was willing to take chances most men wouldn't.

"The Distillery. Not too far out of your way. Drop me there."

JF knew the Kentucky River Distillery property as well as he knew the way around his own grocery. He had worked there for almost twenty years. Began as a night watchman when he was a very young man, worked his way up to master distiller. He knew all the ways in and all the ways out, knew the layout of all the buildings, knew where to find a little privacy.

He gave the farmer a message for Yancey. "Tell him I'll be in the boiler house. Tell him to send a boy the cops won't follow who can carry my message back to him. Tell him to send a little food with the boy."

That night, Saturday night, he spent warm and cozy in the boiler room at the Distillery. He was back in town and had a plan.

As JF spun out this story, Yancey and Callahan were as absorbed as Lucas and me. They'd heard none of it, knew no more than we did about how he'd escaped or where he'd run to.

We paid no mind to the sounds or the bustle all around us. No one intruded. Susan came once to see if we wanted anything. "You look tired, Johnny," she said. He smiled up at her. "I'm okay." She started to say more, but didn't. She leaned down and kissed him lightly on the forehead and said to Lucas and me, "Don't let him keep you out too late, boys."

Yancey was there at daylight the next morning, which was Sunday, making sure he wasn't followed and bringing hot coffee and doughnuts.

People would be rising soon, families dressing and getting ready for church and deciding what to do with their only day off. JF thought he would like to go to church. He missed going. He missed the singing and hearing the words read aloud and the feeling of peace that came on him there. He missed the sense of refuge it gave him. He felt safe in church. He was a religious man. The uptown ladies might not think so, but he was ... in his own way.

JF knew Yancey would have no problem getting to him. Prohibition had shut down all operations at the Distillery except the production of medicinal alcohol and, though the Distillery property was fenced, there was only a skeleton crew and little emphasis on security.

Yancey strode through the Main Gate needing nothing more than a nod to the drowsy guard who waved to him with a sleepy chuckle. "Don't steal nothing, Yancey."

JF was standing outside when Yancey reached the boiler-house, looking down to the river where morning fog was tracing its course. Yancey was not a man for idle conversation.

Yancey: "You know about the fire?"

JF: "Everything's gone."

Yancey: "They were waiting for sun-up. About three in the morning the tension finally got to someone. A shot was fired, don't know by who, don't know at what, but all hell broke lose. Every gun started blazing and they kept it up until all their ammunition was gone. Rifles, pistols, shotguns. Thirty-ought-sixes from the National Guard Armory. They pulverized the place.

"One of the shots, hell, a lot of the shots, ignited something—a can of kerosene or a box of shells, some matches, we even had a box of dynamite in there, remember? All at once flames were shooting up. Damnedest thing you ever saw."

JF: "They wanted to kill me. Not capture me. Kill me."

Yancey: "Nothing could have lived through that barrage."

JF: "Who gave the order?"

Yancey: "It started spontaneously after that first shot."

JF: "You think the fire was accidental?"

Yancey: "Could be. Probably. Hell, I don't know. You think not?"

JF: "I think anyone with half a brain would know that throwing that much firepower into a building with flammable materials inside—kerosene, paint, matches, cloth—anyone with half a brain would know that the odds of igniting something are pretty high. I'm splitting hairs. If the idea was kill me, the fire was only icing. The barrage would have done it."

Yancey said nothing.

JF: "Anybody try to stop it."

Yancey: "Nobody could have. It was a mob. Carlos was shot, too. Not then. Earlier. He was coming out of the house as the posse was circling. Not serious. A rifle slug in the thigh. No bone hit. He's in the hospital. He'll be okay."

JF: "Why the hell..."

Yancey: "They thought he was you. They're charging him with resisting arrest and assaulting an officer."

"My god," JF said. "Charging Carlos? This can't be real."

He turned to look off toward the river again. He stood that way for a long time, not saying anything.

"Well," he said finally, "there's tomorrow," and motioned Yancey to a bench outside the door to spell out his terms for surrender. Yancey left after that.

JF waited until dark to make his way up Wilkinson to the house where his wife was staying. The baby looked so weak and frail, looked so small and vulnerable sleeping there in Anne's arms.

"He's holding on," she said. "Doctor Barr said he's a fighter. Keep him warm, keep him fed. Keep praying, Doctor Barr said."

The next morning, Monday, JF rose early from his cot in the boiler room and in the half light of dawn retraced his steps up Wilkinson to the empty house near his corner to wait for his ride to Louisville.

The baby died that night.

TWENTY-FIVE
Can Not Be Done

Mr. Fallis was determined to rebuild as rapidly as possible—raise his home and his grocery right back up on the foundations of the places the posse burned.

In eight weeks.

They would say it could not be done. A new home. A new grocery. Rising phoenix-like from the ashes. In eight weeks. Could Not Be Done.

He began laying the plans that night on the porch at Susan's Place. After he'd satisfied us all with the story of his escape and return and answered all our questions, he shifted the focus of our thinking from then to now.

That night, Mr. Fallis asked me if I'd like to be a part of it.

This would be construction work. Picks and shovels. Wheelbarrows. Mortar to be mixed and bricks to be carried, lumber unloaded, concrete to be poured. Start each day at first light and end at dark. Every day but Sunday. Hard work. Physical. Probably harder than anything I had ever done.

I'd be working with Lucas as part of a crew JF would assemble from around town and the county. Skilled men mostly—carpenters, bricklayers, electricians. The rest would be laborers doing the donkey work. That's what Lucas and I would be, common labor. We'd be the only boys in a crew of men. We'd be expected to pull our own weight. No excuses. No slack.

"You'd be sunburned and blistered and worn out, but by the time we finish, you'd be stronger and tougher than any kid but Lucas—and you'd learn if you can keep up with men."

I should see what my parents thought and if they approved, we would start Monday. I should not say yes unless I thought I was up to it. Yancey watched me with interest. I'm fairly sure he thought I wasn't.

One of the answers was easy. I wasn't as strong as a man, but I would be, and soon. I wasn't skilled at the work to be done, but show me how to do a thing once and I own it. And nobody, nobody, would work harder. I was up to it.

The other thing, my parents' approval—would they approve my working for John Fallis? Would people take that to mean they approved of him? After the shootings, after the arrest, and with the trial still to come and all the talk around town?

The church women would whisper, "What's that Jen Edwards thinking letting her boy go work with that gangster John Fallis?" Wouldn't they, most of them, wouldn't they? "Ed Edwards ought to know better than to let his son get in with a crowd like that Fallis crowd," the Rotarians would opine, wouldn't they, most of them, wouldn't they?

I broached the subject at supper. Waited until mom had put dessert on the table and dad was blowing on his coffee to cool it. He looked up sharply, frowned, set his cup down and turned to my mother. She folded her hands in her lap and looked across the table to me, studying me silently.

We sat that way, the two of them reading each other in the silence and me waiting. I had rehearsed a litany of reasons why it would be good for me and was ready to plead my case.

"Dad," I started.

"I know," he said, stopping me. "It would be good for you. You'll learn things and have fun and Lucas will be there. I know. You really want to do it."

My father sat at the head of the table. My place was on the left side, my mother's directly across from me on the right side. We had our evening meals in the dining room. My mother felt the evening meal should be the special meal of the day and the family should be together for it and come to it in respectable attire and with clean hands and face and hair neatly combed. We sat at the large cherry table her great-grandfather had planed and mortised himself. She kept it so highly polished it reflected light. When we had guests or there was a special occasion, she placed candles in silver holders in a row down the center. She was proud of it.

Not that the mood or the atmosphere at table was ever stiff or pretentious. Not that in anyway. It was relaxed and warm. I had the feeling now, though, that I was pushing up against a boundary we'd not approached before.

My father: "If you take this job, you'll lose your summer. You'd be laboring alongside men. At a man's job. Boys ought to run free and have fun in the summer."

He stopped again then and looked searchingly at my mother. They held each other's eyes for a moment. They seemed to have a way of talking with each other without speaking. He turned back to me.

"You know that John Fallis isn't the most popular man in town right now. I don't care about that, but you need to think about what your schoolmates will think ... what their parents will think when you come around ... working for the notorious John Fallis. I take him to be honest and straightforward and he seems to like you and I think he'd see to it that you'd be properly looked after. And you'll be working side by side with Lucas. Even so, what your peers think of you makes a difference. And we don't want you to grow up faster than you need to. We'll have to think about it, son."

I didn't get a chance to use my arguments.

My father was already at table in the kitchen when I got down to breakfast the next morning. Grey day. Looked like rain. Felt like rain.

Dad looked up. No expression on his face that I could read. Mom turned from the stove. Walked over to me and put her hand on my cheek.

"When you're at this job, you will remember that you are Owen Edwards. Not someone else. You are Owen Edwards from Estes Park, Colorado, You will remember who you are. Promise me that."

I knew immediately what she meant. There is a certain standard of conduct expected of me regardless of where I am or who I'm with or what I'm doing. I must not let the habits of others or the values they embrace erode mine. I know that. It puzzled me that she said it. "Yes, ma'am, of course. I know. I promise," I said.

Then I realized she was saying yes. "When you're at this job," she had said. That was a yes.

I looked to my father

He wasn't smiling. My mother wasn't either. This was something they were going to let me do. Not something they favored me doing.

"I told you last night that we don't want you to grow up too fast, but I also don't want you afraid to try new things. Take this job if you think you can handle it. But," and here he made sure he had my eye, "mind what your mother said."

Mr. Fallis didn't exaggerate.

I came home with blistered hands and a sunburned face and so tired I could hardly drag myself to supper. Mom had a special lotion to soothe the burn and a balm her folks had used on the hands of their men to keep them able to handle the wagons on the Oregon Trail. She smoothed them on me. I felt like a child again, tended to.

Lucas was tougher than I was. He didn't burn and he didn't blister, but Mom made me bring him home for supper the last day of the first week to check him over and make sure.

None of us spoke of the Big Shoot-Out or the Night of the Posse.

My folks already knew from me what I'd seen and how I felt. They didn't intrude on Lucas. Instead they kept the conversation light and focused on our jobs—for me the first full-time job I'd ever held.

There were awkward moments, but Mom's warmth and my father's genuine interest in what we were doing soon routed them.

To rebuild the grocery and raise a new house in just eight weeks would be unheard of. Many thought it couldn't be done.

Mr. Fallis assembled two crews, the best men that could be found anywhere near enough to get to the site on time each morning. The few he needed who weren't, he put up in boarding houses close by. He paid the highest wages in the area, so he got the pick of the best. To a man they were strong and tough, aggressively self-confident, and barely tolerant of a boy among them.

Each crew focused on its own project, the house or the grocery, and raced against each other. The first team finished would get a special bonus. Money motivates. JF was an early adopter of that principal.

He worked alongside us every day. He was there when we arrived in the morning. Worked with us until noon. Afternoons he had other business to attend to, but was back by quitting time to inspect the progress and set the goals for the next day's work.

He was as good as any of them. He was master carpenter, a stone-mason, a blacksmith. "Hell," Yancey said, "the man can do almost everything"

They all knew his reputation. No one challenged him. You could tell that one or two of the men from out of county were tempted. They never quite got up the nerve. Not all of them liked him, but they worked their tails off for him.

Would it be done in eight weeks?

Lucas was on the house crew. I was on the grocery. My team intended to win the bonus and I announced the same to Lucas as we sat down to supper. He laughed at my brio and said to my mother, "Miss Edwards, ma'am, this poor boy's dreaming. But I'll wake him up easy."

We had roast beef with onion gravy and mashed potatoes and peas and corn and yeast rolls and garden salad with Roquefort dressing and apple pie with vanilla ice cream for dessert—to help keep our strength up for the workweek coming.

When we dropped Lucas at the corner by the grocery (he still insisted on being let off there) my father said to him, "We're glad that you're Owen's friend." As we started to pull away he added, "You two watch out for each other."

My father and I didn't talk much on the way back. We didn't need to. We were comfortable in each other's company. We let the night take our thoughts.

JF moved his family in and staged the grand re-opening of John Fallis, Grocer on Monday the thirtieth day of August—eight weeks from the start.

He made an event of it—strung a banner proudly across Wilkinson, had the little jazz band from the Riverman playing on the corner. Gave out free soda and cookies and had balloons for the kids. Even staged a ribbon cutting.

The whole town took note. Some took umbrage. Some thought JF staged the affair to embarrass the city, to call back to mind the Night of the Posse— the savagery of that, the injustice of that. They thought it in the Mayor's office. And in the Governor's office. The police had no doubt of it. And the church ladies called the whole affair an arrogant affront.

I don't think embarrassment was his motive. I think he was honestly happy to have his corner back.

That people missed the place was obvious by the size the crowd and the relief of the mood. Some, like those who had relied on JF's largesse to help them through difficult times, had missed it desperately.

They all came back eagerly to celebrate.

TWENTY-SIX
Call Me Pharaoh

Yancey and Mr. Fallis.

They met in a reform school.

JF's mother had him committed.

He was running away, going to Frankfort he said in the letter he left for her, never to return. Not a smart move, that letter. She got the Louisville Police Chief, had him stop the train JF was on, take him off, bring him back to Louisville and deposit him in what was called the House of Refuge. That's where Jefferson County entertained its delinquents—the young hoodlums from the city's streets, the hardheads and the troublemakers who couldn't be controlled. There was an orphanage on the grounds, too.

The discipline was Dickinsonion strict.

It wasn't too bad a place, Yancey said. Bad enough, but not as bad as Jackson Camp in North Carolina or that abomination that was Jordonia in Tennessee. The House of Refuge was situated on pasture land at the southern edge of town. The buildings were red brick of two and three stories. Clean and neat. There were trees and grass.

The dormitories where the bad kids lived were high-fenced. All the inmates, good and bad, were locked in at night to make sure everyone understood where they were ... and why. A few on the staff were pedophiles. There were several bullies but no out-and-out sadists.

The kids, boys, girls, white and colored, ranged in age from seven to sixteen. They had classes in reading, writing, and arithmetic but the emphasis was on the uplifting virtues of honest work. Work is good for the character. Everyone knows that. So the kids, all the kids, orphans and delinquents, worked. They worked in the laundries and the shoe shop and the sewing room, in the gardens and the greenhouse, and on the farm, learning skills that could help them lead a useful life when they were let out into polite society

The school, of course, sold the kids' labor all around the county. This helped reduce the burden on the good taxpayers of Jefferson County and seemed only fair.

JF was thirteen or fourteen at the time. Yancey wasn't sure exactly. He himself was sixteen and boss of the boy's dormitory. Of that he was certain.

"They called me the Pharaoh," Yancey said, remembering.

None of them had any idea of what a pharaoh was except in their imaginings from the pictures they had seen in the illustrated Bible. Yancey was regal in their eyes, all powerful in their experience, and had a skin color none of them had seen before. He could sing incantations, conjure pictures out of smoke, weave spells that put them to sleep, or make monsters appear in their dreams at night. He could make magic.

Yancey never talked of where he came from or how he got to the House of Refuge...or how he knew about the other places.

JF was assigned a bed in the back corner of the third floor of the boys' dormitory near the window by the fire escape.

The moment that lights were out that first night and everyone seemed asleep he was out it and down to the ground.

Everything dark. Quiet all around. Just the fence to climb.

"Where you off to, Hoss?"

The Pharaoh stepped out of the shadows.

"Go away," JF hissed.

"Get back to bed," said the Pharaoh

"No way," JF said.

"If anybody goes over the fence, everyone gets the belt. You ain't worth it. Get your ass back in bed."

"Go to hell."

Yancey was older, bigger, stronger, street smart and, most commandingly, he was the Pharaoh.

"I admired his guts, this little guy standing off challenging me. To this day he thinks I used magic," Yancey said, smiling as he recalled it.

JF woke up in the bed near the window by the fire escape on the third floor of the boys' dormitory on the grounds of the House of Refuge on the southern edge of Louisville, in Jefferson County, Kentucky on the morning after his incarceration there at the demand of his mother.

His head was swollen. His eyes wouldn't focus. Yancey was standing there smiling down at him. "Nobody got the belt. Now don't you feel good about that."

They became friends that day and the friendship strengthened in the month that JF spent at the House of Refuge. Each found qualities in the other to admire.

When JF's mother came for him after church on a rainy Sunday in August, he and Yancey shook hands solemnly, said nothing, and walked away expecting never to see the other again, but feeling that they would.

Yancey believes JF's mother put him in the House of Refuge out of sheer exasperation. JF wouldn't mind. He was unruly, headstrong, impetuous— determined to do what he wanted to do regardless of the no's or the switchings or the nights without suppers or the days confined to the house.

It wasn't so much that he resented authority, although he came to in time and with full justification, it was that he ignored it.

He wasn't mean or unnaturally aggressive, or unusually acquisitive. He just wanted what he wanted.

None of the disciplinary tactics worked. Not even his father's wide leather belt across JF's bare behind. Not even the month at the House of Refuge.

As a last resort, his mother tried church. Immerse him in the fear of God, lock him up in the love of the Lord. Rise early Sunday morning for Sunday school and move straight from that into the full singing, shouting, preaching service at noon, then home for Sunday dinner, then right back to church for prayer meeting, then take your seat for the Sunday night service.

All day in the hands of the Lord and his faithful servants. Hallelujah amen!

On Tuesday night there was Bible Study and pot-luck-dinner. On Wednesday night church services again, then choir practice on Thursday night, All in the hope that all that reading and preaching and singing would get through to him. Discipline him. Get him to mind.

He loved it.

He loved going to the services. Loved listening to the readings and the preaching. Loved the singing. Sang so well himself that he became a soloist in the choir.

He believed.

Believed in God's love.

Believed in God's fury.

Didn't change him.

He still did what he wanted to do, though now he was sometimes sorry for what he'd done and would get on his knees and apologize and ask forgiveness, which he was sure he would receive, for God was loving and God was forgiving.

And in that confident expectation JF soldiered on.

Young John Richard Fallis.

God fearing.

Well intentioned.

Kind and generous.

A sinner doing the best he could in a world he never made.

His way.

Lord have mercy.

I tried to imagine Mr. Fallis as a boy and couldn't. I couldn't see the boy in the man. He was too elemental a character to think of him boy-like.

I know from what Yancey told us that JF was born in Jeffersonville, a town in Indiana just across the Ohio river from Louisville, which was a bustling industrial and rail and river transport center and the state's largest city. His father was a carpenter there, struggling.

His folks had kin in Frankfort and moved there sometime before JF's fourteenth year. Because work was too scarce in Louisville? Because they wanted to be closer to family? Yancey didn't know. He knew that by then JF had quit school and gone to work to help out. Which meant they were poor enough and that JF probably made it only as far as the sixth or seventh grade.

He worked as a night watchman at the Hemp Factory for a while and then, still in his mid-teens, talked his way into a job at the distillery. More money. More opportunity.

By age nineteen he was in the Army. The Spanish-American war was on and he volunteered.

Adventure. Glory.

But he serves only six months. He's injured in a fight aboard a train on which he is a guard, injured badly enough that he is medically discharged, badly enough that he's awarded a medical pension. He never talks about the injury, or even about the fight. That's a thing about JF to puzzle about, Yancey said. He never brags. About anything. That fight earned him a citation. Something to brag about if a man was a braggart, Yancey said.

Yancey had been skeptical when Mr. Fallis hired me. He thought I'd be too soft and pampered for real work—too "uptown." He came to start calling me that, needling me with that nickname as he worked on my ego. "Come on, Uptown, that little sack of sand ain't too much for your mighty arms. Get a move on, Uptown." All the other men he called by their last names. I was "Uptown." Soon I was Uptown to everyone.

It started derisively, but Yancey hadn't realized that the boys of Estes Park swung axes and wrestled boulders, pitched hay and dug ditches working summers on the ranches. Soft we were not. Our mothers would have been embarrassed if they thought we were pampered.

We learned to pull our own weight and not make excuses when we screwed up. We learned to be on time and not loaf or look for shade. We learned to do what we were told to do and do it the best we could. We already knew not to back down. There is no "uptown" in the forests of the Rockies.

Early that first week on the Fallis site, while we were taking a break, I heard a voice call out, "Bring me the water bucket, boy." I looked up. A big, beefy Irish guy called Dead Ready was pointing to me. "You, boy. I mean you," he said. "Get it, boy, I'm thirsty." Everyone on the site turned to watch.

I got up meekly, got the water bucket and dipper from the spot in the shade where it was sitting, walked across the space to Dead Ready. He was resting with his back against a post, legs sprawled out, a satisfied smirk on his face. I stood there for just minute thinking, well at least he's sitting down, then, with a nod to Mr. Charbonneau, threw the water in his face and swung the bucket against the side of his head so hard I knocked him out. Hadn't meant to knock him out but the statement seemed to impress.

No one was more surprised than Yancey.

When Lucas heard of it (he wasn't there, he was working the house site) he cocked his head and said, "It's not spontaneous is it? You're not reacting. You already know what you're going to do." He studied me for a minute longer. "People better be careful around you." I wasn't sure how he meant that, whether as a compliment or a caution.

After that "Uptown" was just a name and not an accusation and Yancey accepted me into his circle of the approved.

TWENTY-SEVEN
Happy, Happy Days

In the late afternoons after everyone had left, Yancey wandered the work site inspecting the day's progress, winding down. Lucas and I hung around and sometimes, depending on his mood, we'd get Yancey to tell us stories about himself and his time with Mr. Fallis.

Yancey seemed pleased at our interest and while he was a very private man and kept matters very much to himself, he felt us no threat and was relaxed in our company.

Every man has a need to tell about himself to someone. This is not a matter of ego, it seems to me. It is a need to connect. A need to be understood. A need to be acknowledged.

That year I wasn't sure where I placed Yancey on the spectrum of good guys and bad guys.

My father led the list of good guys. Mr. Charbonneau was on it and Mr. Leland Morgan, JF's lawyer (I didn't know him well then but what I'd seen of him I liked) and Mr. Harold Ames, my father's friend who ran the Sears store in town.

Yancey?

I wanted his approval. He was the sort of man whose respect you wanted, yet I wasn't sure he was genuine.

Almost eighteen years passed before Yancey and JF met again. Yancey was in the state penitentiary in Frankfort. Mr. Fallis was beginning his ride to the top of the Bottom and the kingship of Craw.

Yancey had been ushered out of the House of Refuge on the day of his seventeenth birthday. Reach seventeen you're out the door and on your own.

In a pair of blue jeans, a blue denim work shirt, a red sweat-jersey under a khaki windbreaker, and shod in brown high top brogans scuffed from wear, Yancey stepped into the outside world. A chill March wind was blowing in off the Ohio River. The sun was climbing toward noon in a cloudless sky. No one was waiting. No friends. No relatives. He had a dollar bill and a pocket knife. That was all.

Yancey wasn't apprehensive or intimidated as he walked out the road. Not a man yet, but not a kid. Big, or big enough at least, and as tough as he needed to be. He was delighted to be out, could hardly wait to get at whatever waited for him.

He made his way to the docks on the river downtown and signed on as a deckhand on a coal barge headed for New Orleans.

Happy days. Free again.

That he was a Melungeon didn't bother him. He'd stand out, sure, his skin color, but that would be an advantage. They wouldn't take him for black. They won't think he's Indian. A Moor maybe, or Egyptian. He'd use that to advantage. He'd hint of magic and mystic powers—could see in the dark, hear whispers from great distances, move unseen whenever he chose. They'd eat that stuff up in New Orleans. He'd play around there a while then hire on to a trading sloop and sail the Caribbean.

Happy days. Happy, happy days.

That's the way he told it to us, to me and Lucas, sitting on nail kegs in the shadows of the almost finished grocery, as he remembered out loud.

How much of Yancey's story is to be believed is hard to say. I'm inclined to believe most of it. You stand beside Yancey, see him work, feel his strength, watch his eyes—you can believe he did the things he said he did, knows the things he says he knows.

TWENTY-EIGHT
River Towns And Deviltry

Yancey made the run down the Ohio to the Mississippi to New Orleans. He held his own with the hard cases on the barge, got his pay, and abandoned the river. Yancey was from mountains. The open expanse of the ocean called. He found a sailing ship working the Caribbean trade and sailed off on a seventeen-year-old's high.

Jamaica. Cuba. St. Kitts. The Caymans. Rum and molasses on the long turn-around up to Newport and back again. Legal goods or contraband, made no difference.

His Melungeon looks with its whisper of the occult opened doors to Vodou, Santeria, Macumba—to strange worlds he never knew existed.

He grew stronger and bigger. Got introduced to a man's ways in the watering holes of Kingston and Havana. Learned the use of the knife and the big brass buckle on his seaman's belt. Learned about women.

Balmy days.

Soft nights.

Work he could handle.

Games he liked to play.

Almost paradise.

Yet he didn't let himself get careless.

He was very disciplined.

And smart.

That about Yancey intrigued me—how disciplined he was.

He roamed and rattled and had a helluva time. Bartended on Bourbon Street, gambled in Storyville. He was a bouncer at a bordello in the Quarter that specialized in octoroons. Smuggled arms to Marti in the mountains of Cuba while the revolution raged. A helluva time.

From New Orleans he moved up river to Memphis where he got in with bootleggers dealing in moonshine from Golden Pond and scotch from Toronto, then further north to Newport, Sin City they called it, on the Kentucky side of the Ohio just down from Cincinnati. River towns and deviltry attracted him.

That's where he killed the man.

By then he's almost twenty-five, managing the Five Aces Casino on Front Street.

Untypical.

Not the violence. He knew the uses of violence.

Untypical that he lost control of the situation.

The drunken Dago sonofabich went crazy mad when Yancey wouldn't okay more credit for the game upstairs. Drew to shoot him. Standing there at the bar. The room packed. Had no choice. Hesitate and die. Nailed him with his derringer square in the forehead.

Close quarters. Blood splattered all over. A little glob of brain on his lapel.

Damn.

He should have beaten the charge. But the little Dago's buddy and his girl swore Yancey pulled first. Turned out the little Dago was the nephew of the boss of the Second Ward.

First?

Faster?

It was self-defense, dammit. Self-defense.

Sure it was.

Five years in the state pen in Frankfort.

Next.

The guards started on his kidneys with their truncheons.

Had him suspended. Stretched up on his toes from the Learning Pole in the square outside the main cell-house. Stripped to the waist. Beating on his kidneys. Then moved up to his arms, not breaking anything, pulverizing the muscle, then down to his legs, working over his calves and thighs. Then up his back to get the lungs. When he started vomiting blood they unhooked him and dropped him down in the grit and the grime of the cold stone pavement.

"Now, ladies," the head guard said, standing astride the body beneath him, tapping his truncheon against his leg, "anybody else feel like saying no to something they're told to do. Well, step right up. The Learning Pole is waiting."

No sound came from the watching prisoners. They stood in long rows. Resignation on their faces. Fear. Submission.

The slice of sky that could be seen above the prison walls was fading from the blue of afternoon into the whiter wash of twilight. A guard threw water in Yancey's face. They left him lying there.

When he was picked up off the pavement and taken to the infirmary the next morning, six ribs were broken. Blood bruises covered most of his body. He had galloping pneumonia and was pissing blood. He hurt in places he didn't know he had and was so weak he couldn't even make a fist.

That was the second day.

There were eighteen hundred and twenty-four days left.

Yancey was too smart to let himself get killed in prison and too disciplined to let anger or humiliation put him on the Learning Pole again.

He set himself to decipher how to play the prison game—how to work the egos of the guards so they'd go easier on him, how to manipulate the dreads and superstitions of his fellows so that those who chose not to follow him would be afraid to cross him.

He began to become a presence.

They talked about him after lights out at night—that strange Melungeon guy the guards almost killed. He can put dreams in your head at night. Bad dreams. Make you squirm. Can make them come true. Or sweet dreams, dreams so sweet you taste the honey.

Most of the prisoners were congenitally superstitious. It was easy for him to plant these ideas in their minds.

He gained notoriety, began to become a power among them. If the spooky stuff wasn't persuasive, his fists were.

By the end of his third year in that hellhole he was a trustee and boss of Cell House A.

That hellhole, the Kentucky State Penitentiary in Frankfort, was the first penitentiary west of the Alleghenies. It dated from 1800. It stood like a medieval fortress on the eastern rim of town looking up at Fort Hill and out at Craw. It caged fourteen hundred miscreants in cells barely big enough for a bunk bed and a bucket for night soil. The cells were stone-walled cubicles. Frigid in winter. Suffocating in summer. Windowless. Dark as gloom at midday. Black as the pit at midnight.

The perimeter walls were chiseled blocks of Kentucky River limestone that rose twenty feet in the air and were thick enough to withstand a cannonade. Guardhouses nestled atop them. Two large Roman towers commanded the main entrance.

Abandon hope all ye who enter here.

The hapless and the forlorn packed the place.

It was the state's only maximum security prison -- the fortress where they penned the murderers and rapists and the thieves and the gangsters.

The unfortunates, too.

Not monsters, just men who broke under the pressure of wanting and not being able to have, who got caught up in a moment of rage or passion, who rebelled too violently at their lot of poverty and need. Someone's father. Someone's son. Someone's husband. Someone's brother. They were there, crammed in with the scum of the state.

Executions were by hanging.

Time served was at hard labor.

There was only one level of punishment.

Pitiless.

The whip, the belt, brass knuckles, the boot.

Starvation.

Solitary.

The Standing Man.

They shackled you to the top of your cell door and left you there. Stretched up on your toes, standing as long as the legs could take it, then hanging by the wrists until the head guard felt the lesson had been learned. No food. A little water. Three days minimum. No more than twenty. A man could go twenty days without food, maybe thirty. No one had ever made it to twenty.

The combination of the pain, which soon burned through the whole body, and the thirst and the hunger, that was grievous, but hanging there twisting in your own filth for all to see, that was the hardest, that broke the spirit and drained away pride.

A man could tolerate pain for a long, long time. But take his pride? Pride was all they had in there, even the most bestial of them.

Yancey was a prideful man. But a disciplined man. He never let pride disarm his discipline.

Yancey obeyed the rules. Gave no trouble. Saw to it the crews he was in charge of did their work.

That was all the Warden wanted anyway.

Meet the quotas. Keep the contractors happy.

That's all.

And a little bowing and scraping.

The state hired the prisoners out like slaves. Paid them nothing. Kept the proceeds for itself.

The Gordon Shirt Company, the Frankfort Chair Company, the Hoge-Montgomery Shoe Company, the Frankfort Broom Company, they had factories inside the walls, put their own machinery in, had their own foremen running things. Convicts did the labor. They made chairs and furniture and shoes, cut fabric and sewed it into clothes, assembled brooms, did laundry.

Outside the walls the prisoners worked as field hands on farms, busted rock to make gravel for roadbeds.

Hell, whatever you need the pen's got the workers. Get it cheap.

Twelve-hour days, six-day weeks, seven if there's a rush. Make your number or feel the whip.

When their time was up they were kicked out the door. Most were weak and sick. Almost all were brutalized and bitter. They trickled out into town like untreated sewage. They had no money, no job, and damn little prospect of finding one.

Your time is up. Get the hell outta here.

Yancey was on his eighteen-hundred-and-twentieth day. He had kept his pride in check and gotten on as well as a man could in that particular ring of hell.

He had six days to go and knew himself lucky that the TB hadn't tagged him until he was almost out.

He'd coughed up blood before. Didn't bother him. He'd thought it was the lingering effect of the beating that second day.

But when he began having coughing fits that dropped him to his knees, began losing weight and losing strength, he knew.

The prison doctor had no trouble with the diagnosis. Over forty percent of the prison population was infected. Packed in as tightly as they were in their cells and with the feeding hall located directly below the prison infirmary where infectious bacillus floated down through the cracks in the floor at every meal, they kept re-infecting themselves.

Not all would die of it. The overall odds were about fifty-fifty. But inside the infirmary, the odds were terminal. The prison doctor wanted to send him there.

Yancey wouldn't go.

He had his get-out-of- jail card.

He'd take his chances outside.

Not like getting out of the House of Refuge all those years ago, young and sassy and full of plans. Not young now. No plans. Nowhere to go and no reason to go there. Coughing blood and no prospects.

The twenty-third day of December.

That was the day he'd get out.

A Monday.

The eve of Christmas Eve in the Year of Our Lord nineteen hundred and twelve.

At high noon.

Open wide those prison doors and let this poor sick sinner out.

Merry Christmas.

Yancey rolled a nail keg over and sat down beside us. Lights were beginning to come on in the houses across the street.

"Be dark soon. You'll have to be getting along."

"No, Yancey," I protested. Lucas, too. "You can't stop now,"

He looked up at the sky searching for the first star of evening.

The three of us.

A big olive-skinned man in a black bowler hat and two boys sitting on nail kegs in front of an almost-finished building on the corner of Wilkinson and Hill Streets as daylight dimmed ... traveling through time.

Yancey: "It was cold and overcast that day, the day I got out. Felt like snow. I had no coat. No hat. All they'd given me was that cheap suit and the bus ticket back to Newport. I wasn't sure JF would remember me. Wasn't sure, even if he did remember me, that he would come. Wasn't even sure it was the same John Fallis I knew. If he hadn't pretended to blow himself up, I wouldn't even have known he was around anywhere.

Me: "Mr. Fallis was there?"

"Waiting," Yancey said.

Lucas: "Blow himself up?"

Yancey, laughing. "That's how I knew of him. From the stories in the newspaper. John Fallis, prominent local grocer, blown away by dynamite on the banks of the river, the headline said."

It was a bizarre story. It remains a bizarre story. I still don't know what to think of it. Had Mr. Fallis some plan he backed down from, some idea to run away and start a new life? Even today, knowing as much I know about him and understanding how little that is, I realize there will always be more questions than answers.

The story went like this:

JF is blasting out a portion of the hill behind his house on Wilkinson. He's keeping the dynamite in the house because it's more convenient than keeping it in his boathouse down on the river. His wife comes home and finds the children playing with sticks of it. "What in the world are you thinking of, John Fallis, to leave dynamite where the children can find it! Get it out of this house right now!" It's dark. Just before supper. He gathers the box up and starts down the riverbank. Somehow he trips and falls and drops the box of dynamite. It explodes on contact. The blast is so strong it's heard all the way uptown. People begin to run to the sound immediately. All they find is a gigantic hole in the ground. And JF's hat. No body. No body parts. A hole in the ground with smoke coming out of it and a headless hat. JF has blown himself up. Searchers comb the riverbank for remains. Others take to boats and start dragging the river. Two days they drag and search. Nothing. No signs of the remains of John Richard Fallis. Blew himself to hell and gone.

Funeral plans are begun. Life insurance policies searched for.

Two days later, four days from the blast, just as the family is sitting down for Sunday dinner, who appears but JF—unsullied, unhurt, chipper and spry.

An accident, he says. A misunderstanding, he explains. The explosion knocked him unconscious, he says. When he came to he was in Florida. Couldn't remember a thing, he says. Not how he got there. Not who he was. When he could remember, he came home. All's well, boys. Nobody's hurt, boys. Back to normal, boys, and pass the peas, please.

The tale is too outlandish to be believed. But no one challenges it. Not for the record, at least.

Yancey: "Is that my JF, I ask myself? Is that the boy I knew at the House of Refuge? Sounded like the sort of thing he'd pull. Devilish, that boy. Could this John Fallis be my John Fallis? A grocer? I'd never figure him for a grocer. What they hell was he trying to do? I could see my John Fallis trying something like that. But why? Just for the hell of it? If it is my JF, will he'll remember me? Will he hold out a hand?

"The guards knew of this John Fallis. Said he was a big man in Craw. I knew what Craw was. We had an inmate or two from there. They said he helped convicts sometimes. If he liked them. If he thought them solid. Especially cons with families living in the Bottom. Helped them find jobs. Helped them get settled. Hell, he might be my guy. Could be my guy. Worth finding out, I thought. Nothing else to grab onto.

"One of the guards I was friendly with said he'd get a message to this John Fallis for me. I wrote on a scrap of notepaper, 'Remember the Pharaoh? He needs a hand. December twenty-three. Main gate at the prison. At high noon. Free at last.' Gave it to the guard and hoped.

"Two days later, when I walked out through that gate, he was there. Waiting with a big black Buick idling behind him at the curb. He took my hand, pulled me toward him and looked me in the eye to make sure it was me.

"Pharaoh. I'll be damned," he said. "The spells didn't work this time?"

"No spell for this," I said.

JF laughed that big laugh of his. 'My god, it's good to see you. My god, I'm glad you found me."

As Yancey told us this, I felt like clapping.

John Fallis to the rescue.

TWENTY-NINE
The Games They Play

Yancey's little touch of tuberculosis turned out to be more serious than he thought. Five months slipped by before it was under control, almost a year before his body had fully walled off the bacillus.

Yancey spent those first five months in the Woodmen Of The World tuberculosis sanitarium outside Colorado Springs near Pike's Peak. At seven thousand feet of elevation, blessed with the cold, clean air of the mountains and almost year-round sunshine, it was one of the most advanced tuberculosis treatment centers in the U.S. and open only to members of the Woodmen.

The fortunate patients who managed to gain admittance lived in small, individual, octagonal huts that sat in rows along orderly walkways. The huts were left open to the seasons in all but the coldest weather so that the dry mountain air could circulate freely and keep the germs at bay. The occupants took the sun for hours each day and were fed tailored diets to help them regain their strength. Specially trained nurses attended them. Over seventy percent recovered.

JF got him in.

JF took him there. Went with him and saw to it that he had what he needed—a man he'd known only as a boy and then for only a month and hadn't seen in almost eighteen years. No obligation to him. No responsibility for him. Went with him. Took him there.

Colorado Springs is several hundred miles south of Estes Park, down below Denver. Although I'd heard the name, I'd never been there. I looked it up in the atlas in the library. It sits in high desert country at the foot of the Front Range.

Long way for JF to go, I thought. All the way from here to there. Three days by train. Louisville to Chicago. Chicago to Denver. Denver to Colorado Springs.

Strange this compulsion of JF's to care for and protect and defend. Lucas told me to quit puzzling about it. "It's just the way he is."

Yancey came back in the summer. Not fully recovered, but soon to be, and functioning. JF eased him back gently into work. On the boats at first. Fresh air and sunshine running the Kentucky River with lumber from the mills in town down to the Ohio. Then at the grocery which was the axis around which all JF's activities spun and where Yancey began to take on more responsibility, particularly for one activity which JF was just beginning to feel his way into and about which Yancey knew a great deal.

Yancey stopped his story at that point. Suddenly. As is someone had tapped him on the shoulder and brought his attention back to now, to him sitting on a nail keg on a construction site with night coming on and two boys hanging on his every word. He slowly raised his head and looked around, as if orienting himself, as if coming out a sleep or a dream. He focused on Lucas, then on me. Stood up. Shook himself. Then laughed. To himself? At himself?

"That Pharaoh," he said. "He had a time, that man did. I liked him. John Richard did, too. I doubt that he'd still be among us otherwise."

Lucas and I had risen, too, and were looking up at him.

"Curious, isn't it, the way the gods play their little games. JF and I couldn't have been more different. But something strikes a bond and it's stronger than steel."

His eyes were fixed first on Lucas. "You two," he said, turning to me with the same steady stare, "you two—a boy from uptown and a kid from Craw—I wonder."

On the final day of work, the day we completed it all, at the end of that day, at quitting time, Mr. Fallis called us all together there on the corner with the resurrected grocery rising behind us. To congratulate us. To thank us. Long bars loaded with big casks of iced beer and glass steins and had been set up on saw-horses on both sides of the grocery entrance.

Way the hell to go.

"Grab a beer, boys. We'll have a toast and pass out the pay," Yancey called.

I wasn't sure what to do. I stood off to the side while the men headed for the bars.

Yancey noticed. "You're part of the crew, ain't you."

"Yes, sir."

"Then grab a mug and fill it. When JF makes his toast, you drink it down. Show some respect for the men you worked with. Show some pride."

I'd never had a beer before. Had the strong feeling that I wasn't supposed to. No one had said so directly. Didn't need to. Let a drop of alcohol cross your lips and you're on the road to hell and damnation. That was the word. The temperance people who rammed Prohibition through made sure everyone knew it. Proper young men didn't drink. Boys? Good lord, the ground would open and swallow you on the spot!

Yancey smiled as I fidgeted.

Lucas was standing off to the side, curious too.

"They drink beer out in those mountains you come from," Lucas grinned.

"Sure they do."

"You?"

"Well...," I stammered. Hell, I didn't want to admit I hadn't done some manly things, didn't want to be laughed at for being a puss.

He stood there smiling and shaking his head at me.

"Didn't think so."

"Have you?" I said.

Still smiling, arms folded. "On occasion."

"And...,"

"Tastes real good on a hot day like to today. Makes you a little dizzy if you drink too much."

Lucas turned away from me to look out to the street. Two cops were standing on the sidewalk outside the construction site, watching as they'd been doing every day, but not daring to cross over. Pedestrians on Wilkinson looked in, too. A few paused to call out to the workmen they knew and wave and move on. The bars were in full view. Men laughing, gulping down beer and having a helluva time while the cops watched passively.

"No law against drinking the stuff." Lucas grinned, raised his eyebrows mockingly and bowed toward the cops.

To me he said, "Bets are being made on whether you'll join in. You'll get a new nickname if you don't. The crew will think you're a pantywaist after all. Mr. Fallis won't care but the others will. Yancey will."

"Will you?"

"Will I care? Well, your mother wouldn't like that you did it. I'd care about that. And I wouldn't like that the men would make fun of you. And we might find ourselves in a fight we wouldn't win. But what the hell, whatever you want to do is okay with me."

I drank the beer.

And Yancey grinned his approval and all the crew came and slapped me on the back, even Dead Ready.

And it tasted so good and I began to feel so good with all the laughing and talking that I had another. And then another. And maybe another, I'm not sure. It was still daylight. I think.

I remember Lucas calling my mother and explaining that we were having a little celebration to mark the end of the job and that it might run a little long and he'd take care of me and get me home safely, if it was okay with her that I stayed.

She must have said okay because the next thing I knew it was morning and I was in my bed coming awake with a headache so bad I didn't want to.

I was fourteen that summer.

When September came, I'd enter my freshman year in high school. A year would have passed since I came to this strange place.

So much had happened I often felt I'd dreamed it.

What I had seen and been a part of was too wild to be real. But whether dream or real, I could hardly constrain my eagerness for what might happen next. This left me with a nagging sense of guilt. Bad things had happened, violent things, and I had been immersed in them. I should have felt at least a twinge of guilt about that, but I didn't. So I found myself in the confusing situation of feeling guilty for not feeling guilty. Which made sense in a twisted Sunday-School-thinking sort of way. I tried not to let it bother me.

I stayed in contact with my friends in Estes Park but I didn't write them about any of these things—the Big Shoot-Out or the Night of the Posse or the return of the King and my role in it. I was afraid they'd think I made it up.

I did tell them about the town and how big and bustling it was and how it sat in a river valley with gently rolling hills and rich farm land all around. I explained that there were no mountains here, or bear or elk, and no trout in the rivers. But there were horses more beautiful than any they had ever seen and in the spring the grass was blue. They'd find that interesting.

I didn't know when I'd be back, I told them. Maybe never. But I wouldn't forget them or the place. Or the lesson Mr. Charbonneau taught us. I did tell them about Tubby and the revolt of the peons and how Mr. Charbonneau's lesson got me through it. And that they shouldn't forget the lesson either.

And I told them about Lucas and how we had become friends. And that I missed them and the mountains very much.

So much had changed.

Not just where I lived, but the me I lived in.

The ten-week course in the John Fallis School of Donkey Work accomplished what he said it would. I was stronger and tougher. I'd held my own in the company of hard men. I was fairly sure I could keep doing it.

I felt good about myself, but in a way sad, for in that summer of the Big Shoot-Out and the Big Build-Back, I began to shed my chrysalis of imaginings and fantasies.

I learned an awful lot that summer.

I learned that you must not let your understanding of a thing be clouded by wishful thinking or make-believe. Yancey had no patience for make believe or wishful thinking. A thing is what it is. See it. Accept it. Deal with it.

Most importantly, though, I began to realize that I could not be Lancelot or Hawkeye and that the Round Table existed only in my books. And reluctantly, for this I did not want to accept, I began to understand that the good guys might not always win and I might not always be able to tell who is who.

I let go of these fancies slowly and have not, even now, let go of them entirely.

THIRTY
Even Poor Boys And Crawbats

In the mid-afternoon of the sixteenth day of September, the Franklin County Grand Jury, in conclave assembled, indicted John Richard Fallis on four counts of shooting with intent to kill.

As expected.

The only suspense had been on when the jury would conclude its deliberations and make its announcement.

That was a Friday.

By suppertime word had spread all over the county and was being moved on the Associated Press national wire to newspapers across the country.

The moon was full that night, that September night, the night of the Harvest Moon—a shaman's moon, an auspicious moon.

After the grand jury returned its verdict, the Judge set JF's trial for the twelfth day of April—the Wednesday before Easter.

There would be a full moon that night as well. The Grass Moon. It, too, is propitious.

Yancey recalled that there was also a full moon the Night of the Posse -- the full moon of June, the Strawberry Moon. Its light helped JF escape.

Three portentous nights linked by the light of a favoring full moon.

Yancey took this as a sign, though of what he wasn't sure.

Lucas and I didn't learn of the indictments until we were on the bus to Shelbyville on our way to the first away game of the season. We overheard the driver and an assistant coach talking of it. School had been underway for almost two weeks. We were freshmen who were mostly scrimmage dummies for the lettermen, but had made the traveling squad and were proud of that.

"April. Not until April," Lucas said.

I slid in beside him. "Until the trial? That's good. Gives Mr. Leland Morgan plenty of time to get his defense ready."

"But seven months! Damn, why can't they get it over with."

I could see the distress building in his eyes.

"Mr. Fallis can't go to prison. He isn't Yancey." His voice had begun to rise and the guys in the seat in front of us were starting to twist around to see what we were talking about.

"He'd fight back. I know he would. They'd kill him in there, Owen, I know they would. The cops want to get him. They have influence in there. They have buddies there. If he goes to prison they'll kill him in there."

"Stop it," I said.

Lucas turned to the window and went silent, tormented I knew by the images rolling through his mind.

"Stop it," I said again. "You'll go batty if you start fantasizing about dungeons and tortures. He's not going to prison. Get your mind on the game."

As we rode through the autumn countryside and I thought about it, I knew that Lucas was right. If Mr. Fallis went to prison, he'd probably die there.

The animosity of the police was palpable. They came by the work site every day. Not crossing over, not stepping in, but standing on the sidewalk staring, tapping their nightsticks on their palms, radiating menace. They wanted at him so badly they could hardly contain themselves, wanted an excuse to get at him so badly they would have jumped at any feeble excuse to come, clubs swinging and guns blazing, to bring him down.

But the deal with the Governor was iron clad, so they had to take what comfort they could in the certain knowledge that if they couldn't get him here, they could, by damn, get him there—in prison.

No, not gonna happen, I reassured myself. Mr. Fallis's lawyer Leland Morgan is the best. He once got a man off who pulled his pistol and shot an unarmed state senator in the lobby of the Capitol Hotel with half the legislature looking on. There was malice aforethought and no obvious provocation. Another time he brought the whole jury to tears with his woeful tale of a woman who slit her sleeping husband's throat and was still standing with the knife in her hand and her nightgown drenched in blood when the police arrived. When Morgan finished his summation the crowd in the courtroom clapped. Even the judge had weepy eyes. "That man can make a jury believe anything," Yancey said.

Okay then, I thought. I pushed the worry aside and decided to trust in whatever magic Mr. Leland Morgan could make.

But Lucas, ah, but Lucas. He wouldn't be able to do that. He was too close to Mr. Fallis, had become even closer during these recent months. Lucas would angst until the verdict came.

Lucas was now—the closest word I can find to describe his duties is courier, or maybe, envoy—the bearer of confidential messages to and from important people under the seal of the King. Mr. Fallis had absolute trust in him, knew his loyalty was complete. Lucas was to be the pipeline for John Fallis to his ubiquitous empire.

So Lucas didn't have to rush to the grocery right after school anymore. He was part of the JF inner circle now, a junior member, yes, but nevertheless there and relied on.

I wasn't exactly clear on what Lucas did. I didn't find that out until later. He wasn't clear on it either, when, beaming with pride, he first told me about it. It was enough to know his afternoons were free and we could take a shot at all the things he'd been missing—like football. Football was the thing. The football players were the reigning elite. Though we were only freshmen we had aspirations.

Both of us had grown over the summer. Lucas stood a little over six feet tall and weighted about one-seventy-five. He was strong and fast. He had great hands. He had star potential. Just watching him on the practice field, everyone knew that.

I'd grown to almost five-eleven and Mr. Fallis's donkeywork brigade had hardened me up to one-sixty. I wasn't as fast as Lucas, but I was quick and could throw the ball well. They had me trying out for quarterback.

Our school ran the single wing. The quarterback in the single wing was primarily a blocking back. He did a little ball-carrying, did a little passing, but mostly led the way on the power sweeps. I liked that. I liked contact, liked hitting, didn't mind getting hit, liked clearing people away so the ball carrier could get gone. The quarterback also got to call the plays. That suited me, too.

We both got in the game that night. We were well ahead and Coach decided to see how a few of us held up under real game conditions. Lucas, well, Lucas blossomed that night. He made a spectacular one-hand catch over the heads of two defenders in the far corner of the end zone for a touchdown. Two series later he took a pass in the flat, ran over the linebacker, outran the safety and scored another. Two touchdowns in the closing minutes of the fourth quarter, the game's leading scorer, a rookie freshman—our home town crowd was on its feet shouting his name. People paying attention. To him. People roaring their approval. Of him. People cheering. For him.

That was the moment.

That was the moment he began to think that he might come up out of the shadow he lived in, might be able to throw off the Crawbat cloak, erase the poor boy stain. Might be able to rise above those hateful labels and step out among the unstigmatized haves.

I saw it in the way he walked, in the way he held his head.

I never saw him look so pleased.

When the bus delivered us back to town, the streets were quiet and the moon full and bright above Fort Hill. We shouldered our gear and started for home, talking some, mostly letting silence cushion our way. As we neared the courthouse the clock in the tower began chiming eleven.

Lucas stopped at the foot of the courthouse steps. I moved up beside him.

"This is where they hand out justice," he said.

"April," I said. "Easter week."

He nodded. "I wonder how they know what it is."

He stood there looking up at the courthouse doors. "Well," he said finally and started moving on, "it's been a good night. You played well."

"You played better."

"Maybe," he smiled. "Feels good. We're gonna have fun, right? Lots of fun."

"And then some," I said.

"Even poor boys and Crawbats," he said softly to himself as we turned the corner onto Main. "How 'bout that."

We did have fun that fall.

It was a glorious fall—the hills ablaze with color and the weather clear and crisp, frost sparkling in the fields as mornings dawned, a warming sun softening the afternoons and dialing back just enough to make a sweater comfortable as the days slipped away, then starlight and moonlight in indigo skies.

In the mountains of the Rockies winter announced its coming with less fanfare. There it was the crimson of aspen, the silver of birch. I missed my mountains, but not enough to want to go back. Too much was coming, too much here I still had to see.

So, yes, we did have fun that fall, though it was tempered by concern about Mr. Fallis.

He seemed not overly disturbed.

The newly rebuilt grocery was thriving. Deliveries of lumber from the city's saw mills down the river to the Ohio kept his boats fully loaded. "The business"—the business he was just beginning to begin and about which he knew almost nothing until Yancey, who knew a great deal about it, came back into his life, that business was booming.

So he was busy with all that. And there were other stimulating matters to occupy his mind—the overhanging menace of the police ...and the King of Craw wannabes. As Mr. Morgan warned, they sensed he might be wounded and weakened, sensed that the trial would put him away for a long, long time. They were circling like wolves ready to tear at the carcass.

Nevertheless, John Richard Fallis seemed to be in good enough spirits. Given the perils he faced, the only way I can explain this is that he had an uncommon ability to be wholly in the present. He concentrated on what had to be dealt with *now,* on what *could* be dealt with now. He wasn't knocked off stride by uncertainty. I was impressed by this. I thought this a very valuable ability. I hoped to develop it for myself.

And I hoped Mr. Morgan was as good a lawyer as Yancey said.

That Lucas and I had become the toast of the freshmen class helped distract us both from the thoughts of the consequences if Mr. Morgan wasn't.

Coasting still on the notoriety of the overthrow of Tubby and the King of the Hill gang during school last year, reinforced by our status as the only freshmen on the traveling squad, and envied for our closeness to the notorious King of Craw, in fact spooked a bit by it, the whole school was curious about us.

Everyone had heard stories about the Big Shoot-Out, none of them accurate but all of them dramatic. They knew of Lucas's connection to Mr. Fallis. They knew we'd both worked for him during the reconstruction of his burned-out buildings, they imagined we knew our way around the forbidden realm of the Bottom and were certain we knew the secret words and special handshakes that would open doors to the most exotic places in Craw.

That was enough. That was more than enough. In that strange way that teenagers pick heroes and are drawn to hooligans, we became the anointed. We were sought after and in demand, people wanted to be in our company, wanted our attention, desired our presence. We were "popular."

The attention and the praise pleased Lucas considerably. It bolstered his self-esteem and stroked his ego. He hadn't realized he had an ego. When he discovered that he did, he was embarrassed. He was at heart a modest boy— and he was shy. Which was noticed particularly by the girls. They were already attracted by the mystery and the hint of danger surrounding this worldly boy who lived among gamblers and ladies of the night. Now that he was found to be sensitive and vulnerable as well, well....

And he was being talked about as a rising football star. And had been chosen by Miss Lucy for the school choir. And he understood what Mr. Leathers was talking about in algebra class. And he had curly blonde hair and the nicest smile.

Irresistible.

Lucas realized this. He used it. Later.

But Lucas was not seduced by popularity.

He didn't trust people who looked down on other people because they were poor. He had contempt for people with power who took advantage of those that had none. He thought that the parents of most of our classmates were of this mold. He thought most of our classmates would grow into it, too.

He did not trust them.

But not trusting them didn't mean he wouldn't walk among them and take advantage of their admiration.

I was elected president of the freshman class. Lucas was named sergeant-at-arms. We were invited to join the Key Club and the Shelby Street Rangers. We had fun of a kind I don't think Lucas had experienced before. I hadn't.

I felt very good about it all—new kid on the block and boy from the wrong side of the tracks. Lordy, lordy, look at us. Don't it beat all how we shine.

THIRTY-ONE
Make Of It What You Can

April came too soon.

We wanted it to come, yet we didn't.

JF's trial was to begin on the twelfth day of April. We wanted it over. Yet we didn't. The outcome might be JF off to prison.

So we balanced on the sharp edge of apprehension and waited impatiently.

The weather didn't help. Though autumn was glorious and the winter mild, spring toyed with us. March was blustery and cold. April seemed reluctant to shed her winter coat and command the sun to shine as she should have done. The days counting up to the start of the trial vacillated between dreary and dismal.

The forecast for Easter Week was clouds and rain. Yancey was concerned about the moon. The full moon of April, the Grass Moon, was to rise on the eleventh day, a Tuesday. The trial was to begin on the twelfth day, a Wednesday. If clouds obscured the moon that night, or rain veiled it, that would be a very bad omen.

We walked to school through rain on Monday. And woke to rain on Tuesday ... soft rain, gentle and steady. We watched it make puddles in the schoolyard when we should have been paying attention in class. By noon the rain had slowed to a drizzle. By suppertime it had stopped completely and left only fine wisps of mist in the treetops. At bedtime just a thin scud of clouds hid the sky. At midnight I woke. Moonlight streamed through my window. I rose and went to look out and it was there, the Grass Moon, full and splendid, shining bright in a sky swept clean of clouds and speckled with stars.

The morning of the trial dawned clear. I met Lucas on the courthouse steps at seven-thirty. The doors would open at eight. The Judge would take his seat at nine.

We were cutting school that day. And would for the remainder of the trial. I thought there'd be an argument about this with my parents, but there wasn't. I didn't even have to explain why when I told them I wanted to be there. My dad simply exchanged looks with my mother. "Let your teachers know. Tell them we approve. Arrange to make up the work," he said.

No one thought it would be a long trial. JF shot them. Half the town saw him do it. The other half had heard enough about it that they thought they saw it, too. How long could it take?

A crowd had already gathered. We snaked our way through and showed the guard the passes Mr. Morgan had written for us. He frowned, but let us in and we slipped up the marble stairs to the courtroom on the second floor and slid into seats on the pew-style wooden benches where the public sat. In no time the room was filled and men were standing shoulder to shoulder around the perimeter. Those that couldn't get in filled the corridors and spilled down the stairs.

We took seats behind the railing that separated the courtroom from the well of the court. Across the aisle from us sat the aggrieved:

Patrolman William Helm—the man who'd started it all clubbing Carlos at the carnival grounds—shot through the right shoulder. Not serious. Painful.

Patrolman Vernon Quire—the man who'd come running with Patrolman Scott to give Helm a hand at the carnival and collar Carlos—shot in the shoulder but able to stagger to a doorway and fall. Not serious. Painful.

Patrolman Brady O'Nan—the man who made the demand for surrender on the porch at the Fallis home and was answered with a shotgun blast, the most seriously wounded of all—for a time it was thought he might die.

Patrolman Jesse Goldman—the man with O'Nan on the porch, wounded by the spread of buckshot from the blast at O'Nan—not serious. Painful.

And Sergeant Gerald Scott—the man who had turned with such fury and fired as Mr. Fallis rushed up to free Carlos there in the center of town—shot through the arm and liver. Condition serious.

Sergeant Scott glanced our way curiously as we slid in but gave us no mind. The others ignored us.

All were in their dress uniforms, crisp military-style navy blue coats and trousers, a flash of a ribbon, a glint of brass. Clean shaven. Hair neatly combed and parted. Fine figures of Kentucky manhood sitting steely-eyed and stern-visaged. They looked confident. They looked righteous. They looked like power.

Your humble servants, ladies and gentleman. Law and Order on display.

Lucas and I were particularly nervous and excited.

We had provided much of the information on which Mr. Morgan would base his defense. No one was closer to the events of that night than us. No one saw it from beginning to end like we did. We might give Mr. Morgan what he needed to cause the jury to set Mr. Fallis free.

We hoped.

And agonized, waiting to find out.

A month before the trial, Mr. Morgan picked our memories clean. In his office on the second floor of the building across the street from the courthouse. A raw March morning spitting snow, a Saturday so as not to interfere with school. We spent the whole day there.

Neither of us had been in a lawyer's office before and neither of us had been in a situation in which what we said could be of much importance. So we were tense and apprehensive. But Mr. Morgan calmed us and helped us see it all again, helped us remember what we saw, all of what we saw, not just the parts that stood out.

Strange the way his words worked on your mind. Strange how what he said could help you see things that you didn't realize you had actually seen.

I wondered about that afterwards, wondered if he could make you believe you'd seen a thing you hadn't, or hadn't seen a thing you thought you had. He couldn't do that, could he?

As he quizzed us, Lucas and I sat in two upholstered chairs in front of his desk and he in a banker's chair behind it. The desk seemed enormous. Polished and gleaming and large enough for a human sacrifice on its surface. The wall behind him was all books. The wall across from him all windows, large floor to ceiling windows that looked down on the street and out to the courthouse steps. The end of the room to his left is where we entered. A small conference table sat at the other end of the room. A neatly dressed older woman with a pad spread before her was there. She was smiling.

Mr. Morgan was smiling, too. "Mrs. Filstrom there," he said, nodding to the woman at the table, "will take notes on what we say to help me remember when I'm putting John's case together. We'll just talk. Just between us. All of it confidential." He smiled again and sat back.

"Let's begin at the beginning. You, Owen, you were there at the start. You saw the police beating Carlos at the carnival. When Lucas ran to find John, you stayed with them as they drug Carlos off to jail. You followed right behind them. You saw everything. You saw them clubbing him. You saw him stumbling and being jerked along all the way across the Old State House grounds to the police station uptown. You were following along behind them. Then John appeared. What happened then? Think now. See it clearly. Be certain. It is important to know who started this sorry mess."

"The police did," I said immediately. "They were hurting Carlos and Mr. Fallis came to stop it."

He shook his head, "No, my boy," he said. "Whoever fired the first shot started it. Can you remember? Do you know?"

I remembered my pulse beating in my ears. I remembered Carlos barely able to stand and blood dripping down his forehead. I remembered not knowing what I should do and being afraid I'd do the wrong thing ... or nothing at all. I remembered a voice behind me yelling' "Let him go." And Mr. Fallis rushing past me with a pistol in his hand.

"And?"

The memory of it came rushing back.

"The policeman behind Carlos, when he heard the shout he stopped, turned around, saw Mr. Fallis. He seemed to recognize him. He reached right away for his pistol and swung it toward Mr. Fallis. There was a shot. And then almost immediately another one. That policeman fell. Right away there were other shots and the other two policemen fell. People on the street started going wild, running, dropping to the pavement, yelling. Mr. Fallis and Lucas rushed up and grabbed Carlos and between them hustled him off down the street."

"Did John shoot first? What did you see?"

I saw fury in Mr. Fallis's face as he rushed by me. I saw loathing in the eyes of Sergeant Scott as he reached for his gun. I saw panic all around me.

"Did John shoot first?"

"I don't know."

"The policeman might have?"

"Yes, sir."

"Or John could have?"

"Yes, sir."

"You can't be sure which one did?"

It was so fast. There was so much tension.

"No, sir.

He turned to Lucas.

"You were right at John's side."

"I wasn't watching Mr. Fallis. I was watching the cops."

"And you saw Scott pull his pistol and point it toward John, but you didn't see what John was doing?"

Lucas nodded.

Mr. Morgan leaned back from the desk, looked us both over, frowned, turned back finally to me.

"Well, Owen, my boy," he said, "if you couldn't tell, no one could."

He then turned his attention back to Lucas. "Pick it up there. You and John arrive, see the police struggling up the street with Carlos. See he's hurt. You run after them. The shooting starts. The two of you rush up and grab Carlos and hustle him off down the street through the crowd cowering along the sidewalk. All the way home you take him, him bleeding and dazed., you and John on either side, half carrying him. All the way from the middle of town back down to John's place on Wilkinson.

"You barely get Carlos settled when word comes that an armed posse is on the way. John hurries the family off to a friend's place and begins to get ready to defend himself. Yancey has arrived by then. The two of you want to stay and help John against the posse. He won't let you. He sends you away. So you and Yancey find a place nearby to watch, to wait—to be of help if you can. It's dark now.

"You see the posse come. Fifty, a hundred of them. Marching through the night. Guns at the ready. They set up a battle line surrounding the house so that John can't escape. They wait. And become impatient. Patrolman Brady O'Nan takes a small squad to demand John surrender. Climbs the steps to the porch and tries to force open the door. John swings it open and blasts him. Brady's buddies, wounded by buckshot from the blast themselves, drag him back across the street and into the posse line.

"Furious and bloodthirsty, some of the men want to rush the house but the leaders tell them no, wait for daylight. That works for a couple of hours. But somebody gets impatient and fires a shot and that sets the whole gang of them off. They pour such a barrage of shells into the house and grocery that it triggers a fire that burns both buildings down. John's inside. Being eaten up by the flames? Suffocating in the smoke? You don't know. You want to try to run and save him, but you can't. You couldn't get through the line. Anyway, Yancey won't let you try.

"When morning comes and the embers have cooled enough so the posse can search through the ashes for his remains, there are none. No charred skeleton. No John Richard Fallis. He's gone. Out of that burning house, through that ring of vigilantes that has him surrounded. He's escaped. They can't believe it. They're stunned. Then almost apoplectically mad. That's right, isn't it? Did I miss any fact, anything crucial?"

He stopped, saw the answer in our eyes. He nodded to himself, rose slowly then and walked to the window. The whole block, from corner to corner, could be seen from there.

"Misty rain out there, boys. Looks cold. Well," he said when he turned back to us, "we've said it all, have we? Got the look and the feel and the facts of it? The shooting? All of it?"

He turned again to the window. Stood watching the afternoon fade. "Up to me then to make of it what I can."

THIRTY-TWO
It Begins

For reasons I did not understand, the prosecuting attorney decided to try Mr. Fallis on only one of the four indictments—that of the shooting of Sergeant Gerald Scott.

Thirty were called for the jury.

Six were truthful enough to admit they had already formed an opinion. They were excused from duty. The remaining twenty-four swore they had not, swore they would be open-minded and fair and could render a just and impartial decision.

I found this almost impossible to believe. No event in recent history had received more attention or been more talked about than the John Fallis shoot-out. But Mr. Morgan and Mr. Maxwell McCoy, the prosecuting attorney, went along with it and selected eleven of them. Why those eleven out of the remaining pool of twenty-four was an absolute mystery to me. I couldn't tell from listening to the prospective jurors answer questions, or from watching them as they did their sincere and thoughtful act, whether they leaned one way or another. Mr. Morgan could, I guess, and Mr. McCoy could—could see something in at least six of them (all it took was a majority) that they thought they could wheedle to see things their way. I'd have to ask Mr. Morgan about that. How do you tell whether someone is malleable?

The trial was to start at nine. The crowd had started forming hours before. The whole town was awake early it seemed. Breakfast business at the downtown restaurants was brisker than anyone remembered. Two pushcart vendors had set up shop on the curb out in front of the Courthouse and were dispensing coffee and doughnuts.

Lucas and I got there just before eight. I'd finished my paper route, had breakfast and changed into my Sunday clothes —my mother thought a touch of formality was called for considering the occasion. Lucas met me on the Courthouse steps. He'd dressed up, too, and looked anxious.

We made our way inside and slid into seats on the row behind the railing that separated the court itself from the spectators and scooted toward the middle to be behind the table where Mr. Morgan and Mr. Fallis would sit.

Lucas pointed out the gamblers he recognized and the saloon-keepers. Captain Ellis of the Salvation Army was there in his uniform and Pastor Dixon of the New Hope Baptist Church, the largest church in the Bottom, all black. The Mayor wasn't there but the Chief of Police was. And the County Sheriff and the General in charge of the Kentucky National Guard. I saw Mr. Nuchols, who runs the Newberry Five & Dime Store uptown, and Mr. Wright, who sings in the Methodist choir with Mom and me. Sitting close behind the cops in the row across from us was Gus Brewer, the man who'd been on the porch at JF's house the night of the Big Shoot Out, and standing back along the wall, Vik Braun.

There weren't many women, just a few, the most noticeable a clutch of six seated together near the door who had the stern look of ladies of consequence. Not too far from them sat Lottie Brown, a Madam of consequence herself among the Ladies of the Night and of more than nodding acquaintance with some of the more important and powerful men of the community.

Reporters filled a whole row on the side of the room across from the jury box. No one I recognized, but I was later told that a man from the New York Times was there, and the Baltimore Sun, and of course the Louisville and Lexington papers and our own State Journal and reporters from the wire service bureaus up at the Capitol.

And Billy Blue.

Billy hadn't a seat. He was a fixture in Craw, played street guitar to everyone's delight, but there were no seats for blacks that day. He was hanging back by the door trying to see in. He caught our eye. "Let Mr. Johnny know I'm here for him," he called.

I looked around to take it all in and marveled. All these people. Up early. Dressed in their go-to-meeting clothes. Making their way from wherever they rise to the center of town on a workday morning to see what happens when the King of Craw goes on trial. Losing the whole work day, maybe many days, to find out. What do they want that causes them to come and to wait like this?

To see the King go down?

To see the King go free?

The trial started promptly.

Black-robed and somber, the judge strode in as the clock in the tower above us sounded the hour. The hubbub stopped. The "Hear ye. Hear ye. Hear ye. This court is now is session" chant rang out. The Judge took his position on the bench, stood for a moment surveying the hushed courtroom, nodded to the already seated jury, took his own seat.

And it began.

Witness Sonny Lee Jamison for the prosecution: "The man is mean as hell. He'll beat the piss out of you for no reason at all."

Prosecuting Attorney Maxwell McCoy: "Be more specific."

Witness Jamison: "I'm standing on the corner minding my business when a Salvation Army gal comes by with her bucket and asks for a donation. I tell her to skedaddle. I don't give money to trumpet-blowing street-corner preachers, I tell her. Fallis is nearby. Comes over and says 'Be polite.' I say 'I am polite, I didn't smack her.' Before I can add the laugh, I thought it was funny, he smashes me in the face, knocks me to the ground. Kicks me in the ribs as I lay there. 'Put some money in the bucket,' he says. The man's got a terrible temper. There's no telling what he'll do."

Lucas, sitting beside me, nodded approvingly. I gave him a questioning look. The man was no threat to JF. He wasn't hurting the girl. JF was just a bystander. And yet, bang! He's dispensing mayhem.

"It's okay," Lucas said. "He was taking up for the girl. It's okay."

I guess I could see that. I guess I could rationalize that. Taking up for the girl, demanding a little courtesy on the street. Still, his sudden explosion disturbed me. Made me think back to the night of the Big Shoot-Out.

The testimony went on in this vein -- McCoy calling witnesses, each attesting to the wickedness of John Richard Fallis.

Mr. Morgan was strangely quiet during all this. He raised no objections. Seemed to pay more attention to the reactions of the jurors than to the witness on the stand. From time to time he'd lean in to Mr. Fallis, ask something, make a note, then return his concentration to the jury. What game is he playing, I wondered? How do you win if you don't seem to be in it?

Attorney McCoy to witness Alonzo Quinn:

"Tell us about the Senator."

Quinn looked to be about thirty. Medium build. Neatly dressed. A small black mustache and slicked-back hair. Smiling as he took the stand. Pleased with the attention.

"Well, sir, there is this newly elected senator, Soffit is the name, owns a couple of little coal mines near Hazard, first time in town, come for the legislature about to begin, down with his buddies to sample Craw, comes on Fallis at the Riverman, in the card room upstairs. At poker. Five of them seated around a table in the back. Marches in, his buddies at his side, one with a .38 showing in a shoulder holster underneath his coat. Stops. Looks around. The men at the table glance up briefly, return to their cards, pay him no mind. The man with the .38 whispers something in the Senator's ear. A big grin crosses his face. He squints at JF and says loud enough to be heard, "So that is the famous King of Craw. My god, boys, I am just plumb disappointed. He don't look like much more than a penny-ante gambler to me."

The room goes real still. Fallis glances up, fixes on the Senator. Says nothing. Looks around, notes the man with the .38, and the other. Disregards them. Lays his cards down slowly on the table. As he does the guys around the table begin looking for cover. And those close to the Senator start edging away. They don't want to get splattered. Fallis returns his attention to the Senator. Then abruptly shoves the table over, stands up, takes a fast stride forward, pounds down on the Senator's skull with the .45 from the back of his belt where he always carries it and drops him to the floor. Neither of the good ole boys move a muscle, Fallis standing there with a .45 in his hand. Fallis says to the crumpled heap at his feet, "Next time to you want to come to Craw ask my permission. And call me sir."

Attorney McCoy: "You were there? You saw this?"

Witness Quinn: "Plain as day. Blood on my shirt helping carry the poor man out."

Attorney McCoy: "Let me be clear. This was a Kentucky state senator he assaulted?"

Witness Quinn: "He did. Cracked his skull."

Attorney McCoy: "Did Mr. Fallis know his victim was a Kentucky state senator?"

Witness Quinn: "Would have made no nevermind."

Attorney McCoy: "Were the police called?"

Witness Quinn, laughing: "Hell, no. It's Craw, for chrissake."

The whole room laughed then, as well. Even Attorney McCoy couldn't help smiling.

The Judge banged his gavel. The room quieted.

"Continue, Mr. McCoy," he said. "Let's not waste time."

The next witness was a small-statured young man of serious mien and not quite convincing beard. He was neatly dressed in jacket and tie and well spoken. Sworn in as Jason Vail.

Attorney McCoy: "Mr. Vail, you are the son of Pastor and Mrs. Ambrose Vail of this city and a divinity student at Transylvania College in Lexington."

Vail: "Yes, sir."

McCoy: "You had as your guest Mr. Fitzhugh Pettigrew of Boston at the New Year's Eve Ball at the Hoge-Montgomery Clubhouse last year. Mr. Pettigrew is also a student at Transylvania College, president of the Letterman's Club, president of Kappa Alpha fraternity, of which you are also a member, and captain of the tennis team."

Vail: "He is."

McCoy: "You saw the cutting of young Mr. Pettigrew?"

Vail: "I did."

New Year's Eve. The Hoge-Montgomery Clubhouse. Chandeliered ballroom. Tuxedoed men and beautifully gowned women at candlelit tables. Music. Dancing.

JF there. Devilishly handsome in a tailored black jacket with satin lapels. There among the elite. As if he belonged.

I had no trouble picturing it. I had trouble understanding it. But then JF had business with all these people—the bankers, the politicians, the merchants. Of course he was there. The more proper folk of the city might think him a pariah, but the men who ran the city were pragmatic. They liked his money. They needed his influence. He was good company. That certain air of danger about him, that hint of roguery -- that attracted them, their women in particular.

The scene that formed in my mind as Mr. Vail gave his testimony was this:

JF is at the bar, talking and laughing when Mr. Pettigrew, a young man accustomed to being deferred to, just tight enough to be feeling good about himself and just egotistical enough to feel the need to show his disdain for the baddest man in the room, comes lurching up. He shoulders JF aside without so much as a pardon me, knocks his drink over as he does, and calls for immediate service from the barman.

Not even looking to see who it is, JF explodes. He backhands the man across the mouth, takes a half turn aside and with a knife already in his left hand swipes it down the intruder's cheek.

It happens so fast almost no one sees it except young Mr. Vail who is at Pettigrew's heels. But the shock of the moment, whether others see it or not, runs through the crowd. The music stops. Dancers freeze. Silence blankets the room. Heads turn anxiously to find the cause, settle finally on two figures at the bar—John Fallis in his immaculate tuxedo and poor Mr. Fitzhugh Pettigrew who'd let his vanity override his good sense.

Dead sober now and paralyzed with fear, Pettigrew puts his hand to his bleeding mouth, JF's backhand has loosened teeth, and then reaches to rub the pain in his cheek. When he draws back a bloody hand he cries, "Oh, my god, Oh, my god," slumps back against the bar and begins to whimper.

JF stares at him for a blazing moment, then returns the knife to his left jacket pocket, smiles to the paralyzed men standing aghast along the bar. "Sorry for the interruption. A matter of manners that needed attending to."

He motions to the bartender, calls out "Drinks on me," smiles again, and resumes his conversation while the stun wears off and the evening resumes.

Vail told it well. Enough outrage in his voice, enough anger -- but I could picture easily enough the smart-ass blueblood showing off to have no sympathy for him.

Attorney McCoy: "This was a vicious reaction to an innocent and accidental encounter?"

Vail: "In every sense of the words."

McCoy: "Where is Pettigrew now."

Vail: "In Boston. Our local plastic surgeons don't have the skills to repair his face."

As Vail stepped down and the next witness was called, I whispered to Lucas, "What's all this got to do with the shooting?"

But before the witness could take the stand, the Judge's gavel pounded and the court was adjourned for lunch. Reconvene at one-thirty.

People began to stand, make their way to the courtroom door.

Mr. Morgan and Mr. Fallis rose from their seats. Mr. Fallis turned, saw us and smiled, then let his eyes roam the rest of the room. A large crowd was still there, waiting, it seemed, for him to leave before they took their leave. An old man hunched over a cane let go long enough to flash a thumbs-up. Others nodded encouragingly as they caught his eye. They want him to know they're here, I thought, want him to know they're for him.

JF and Mr. Morgan left together through the same side door the Judge used. Lucas and I looked for Yancey in the crowd, spotted him easy with his height and I was surprised to see that he was hatless. Yancey had his derby in his hands. Later Lucas told me hats weren't allowed in the courtroom. It was the only time I ever saw Yancey without it. He and Callahan from the Riverman had a conversation going. He nodded briefly to us, but kept his attention on a small group of men gathered around the prosecution's table.

Lucas and I moved outside. The curbside pushcarts had hot dogs now. We joined the line, got ours, and found a place on the courthouse steps to wait for the trial to begin again. It was pleasant out there. A proper spring breeze played in the trees. The sky was clear, the sun was warm. April had eased in and we hadn't noticed. It would have been a grand afternoon had there not been so much apprehension in the air.

THIRTY-THREE
Bye- Bye, Bad Man

Attorney McCoy called fifteen witnesses that morning. I kept count. Each one attested to the wickedness of John Richard Fallis. He was a vain, volatile, violent man. Had a hair-trigger temper. Has no respect for law and order. Thinks the rules which everyone else is expected to abide by do not apply to him. He was a threat to peace and tranquility and a foe to decency.

This testimony abraded Lucas like sandpaper on a raw scrape. To him it was a pack of lies told by bitter, resentful people. They were envious of JF. They wanted to bring him down.

"Dammit, Owen," he fumed while we waited in the sun for court to reconvene, "why's Mr. Morgan letting them get away with those lies?"

"Maybe they're not all lies," I said gently.

"Don't you say that. If there's truth to any of it, he had his reasons. He had cause."

He so earnestly wanted me to see that John Fallis was the good and admirable man he knew him to be that he almost reached for my hand in supplication.

But I was bothered by the drift of the morning's testimony. The John Fallis those people spoke of wasn't the John Fallis I knew. Or thought I knew.

Who was he?

What was he?

Yancey understood him perhaps as well as anyone, but Yancey didn't know. No one knew. Not even Mr. Fallis. I doubt he ever even thought about it. But I did.

I wanted to know what happened that caused him to be so uncontrollable, so explosively brutal. His folks? Did they abuse him, punish him so severely he struck back hard at any threat, any slight?

Young as I was, John Richard Fallis had become for me one of those mysteries that grab your mind and won't let go.

Well before the appointed time for the trial to restart the courtroom was full and the hubbub muted. We all waited eagerly for the gavel to pound and the play to resume.

Yancey squeezed in beside me as the jury filed in. Given how packed the courtroom was, I looked up in surprise. The man who'd been on my left was scurrying up the aisle. "Shove over," Yancey said, settling himself, "Show's about to begin."

While we waited for the Judge, I tried to study the jury, tried to see what Mr. Morgan saw as he watched them. They looked ordinary to me. All neatly dressed like ready for church. No one preening, no one scowling. Nothing revealing that I could determine.

Two were farmers. I could tell by the band of white around their foreheads where their hats kept the sun from burning. One man looked older, dignified, had a gold watch chain across his vest. The others? Storekeepers, mill hands, tradesmen, mechanics? Couldn't tell. No one very young. Only the one older man. Two were from the city proper. The rest from the rural areas surrounding the town: two each from Peaks Mill, Wood Lake, Switzer, and Harvieland, and one from Bald Knob.

"Know any of them?" I whispered to Yancey. He looked down at me with a little smile. "Shh," he said.

Attorney McCoy called only one more witness. He had begun the morning with three of the four policemen. Their stories were consistent. Just doing their jobs. Keeping the peace. Protecting law-abiding folk from harm and disquiet when the defendant, John Richard Fallis, comes roaring up and starts shooting. They had the scars to prove it.

The fourth witness, the final witness, the man now taking the stand, was Sergeant Gerald Scott, Scotty to most. He was the hammer to drive the nail.

The Prosecuting Attorney had already painted JF as an unprincipled low-life capable of almost any degenerate act. He had the victims personally identifying JF as the man who shot them and eye-witnesses to back them up. What more was he after? Enough disgust on the part of the jury to put JF away for good?

"He'd like to, the bastard," Yancey said. "Scotty hates JF. They go back a long way. Now be quiet. I want to hear."

Sergeant Scott strode to the stand without glancing at JF. He had about him that air that made me think of Jigger Swinson back in Estes Park -- the overbearing air of the self-assured bully.

Scott raised his hand, swore his oath, took his seat.

A big, muscular man.

No sign of damage.

Though it had been thought he might not survive the bullet he took that night of the shoot-out, he looked hale and hearty now. Brown hair neatly combed and parted in the middle. Good color in his face. But his eyes -- there was a coldness in his eyes and a tightness about the mouth.

Prosecuting Attorney McCoy: "Sergeant Scott, that man there," pointing to JF at his seat, "is accused of shooting you with intent to kill while you were in the process of performing your sworn duties as a law enforcement officer of this city. Do you recognize the man?"

Scott: "I do. That man is John Richard Fallis."

McCoy: "You were doing your duty. You were in no way engaging with or threatening Mr. Fallis. You were simply doing your duty and he shot you. That's right, isn't it?"

Scott: "Yes, sir. He did that."

McCoy: "Tell the court what happened."

Sergeant Scott sat back in the witness chair, straightened his shoulders, seemed to become bigger, looked down at JF with scorn, slowly turned to the jury, staring, as if fixing each of their faces in his mind.

"There was trouble at the carnival. I was called for. I took Patrolman O'Nan with me. When we arrived we found Patrolman Wilhelm struggling with a young man. They were outside the fence that ringed the carnival grounds. The young man had Patrolman Wilhelm's nightstick and was stepping back to swing it at him. Patrolman O'Nan and I stepped in. We subdued the young man. On our way to the police station with him in custody, John Fallis came running up behind us. He overtook us at the corner of Main and Lewis streets, a block from the station. He informed us that the young man was his son and angrily demanded his release. Before we knew what was happening, Fallis had pulled his pistol and fired four shots. One hit me. One hit Patrolman Wilhelm, one wounded Patrolman Onan in the shoulder, and one went wild."

McCoy: "What happened then?"

Scott: "I didn't see much after that. I was on the sidewalk bleeding from the wound in my stomach. I think he grabbed his son and ran."

McCoy: "Those weren't warning shots or cautionary shots? They were meant to take you down?"

Scott: "Yes, sir."

McCoy: "Shots fired in anger with intent to kill?"

A hush settled over the courtroom. The rustling and bustling of people moving in their seats, shifting trying to get comfortable standing shoulder to shoulder around the walls, all stopped. This was the question. Not that JF had shot Scott. Everyone knew that. But did he mean to kill him? That was the nut of it.

Scott shifted his gaze from the attorney to JF, then to the jury. With an icy stare and in a venomous voice, "Yes, sir," and almost rising from his seat, "shots fired in anger with intent to kill." He strained forward toward the jury. "He would have killed me if he could have." He was practically standing by then.

McCoy seemed surprised by the intensity of Scott's statement and stood motionless and silent.

Scott eased slowly back into his seat. The room began to rustle again.

The Judge: "Mr. McCoy?"

McCoy: "Yes, of course, Your Honor," he said, regaining his pace. To Scott, "With intent to kill. But failed. How badly were you wounded"

Scott: "The bullet went in through my stomach, punched through my liver, tore up my arm as it come out. I was in critical condition for four days. They thought I would die."

McCoy: "You recovered. You are all right now?"

Scott pulled himself up ramrod straight. Said proudly, "I am that. I am fit and hale," and looking defiantly at JF said, "I'm too tough for you, Johnny boy. Too tough, by far."

As he was dismissed and was passing the defense table, Scott paused and leaned in to JF and said out loud, "Bye-bye, bad man," and laughed and took his seat.

McCoy waited until Sergeant Scott had settled himself before turning to the jury.

"John Fallis's attack on Sergeant Scott is just the latest, and most deadly, in a long string of violent attacks. In addition to what you've heard this morning, his record includes arrests for willful and malicious cutting and wounding, and wounding with intent to kill without killing. These are only the attacks that have come to the attention of the police. Who knows how many others there have been that have not been reported out fear and intimidation.

"So far he has not managed to kill anyone. But it is only a matter of time. John Richard Fallis is guilty as charged and he is a ticking time bomb. Your duty, to yourselves and to this community, is to put him away for as long as the law permits."

He raised his hands in that universal gesture with palms upturned and shoulders shrugging that asks what more can be said, what more is there to say. Then with a half turn and a respectful nod to the Judge, he announced, "Your Honor, the prosecution rests."

THIRTY-FOUR
And Then The Applause

When Lee Morgan rose beside John Fallis that day it was around two o'clock in the afternoon. We'd heard sixteen witnesses buttressing the prosecution case. Now we'd see what Morgan had in mind.

Lee Morgan wasn't physically imposing. Not like JF or Yancey. He was a small man. But he looked big. When you were right up next to him he wasn't much taller than a good-sized boy, but he had what the military people call command presence. When he entered a room the atmosphere changed. People noticed. There was no swagger or swing to his walk, yet he stood out. They paid attention.

He was a little portly. Graying at the temples. Had a friendly smile but a look in his eyes that said be careful. He wore round steel-rimmed glasses and dressed conservatively in somber suits. Very courteous. Very dignified.

There was something in his voice, some tone, some inflection, which made you think he had it exactly right. Nothing pretentious or inveigling. He could be eloquent, could paint a picture in words that could be seen as clearly as a reflection in a mirror. He seldom did. Sometimes, when he was making an important point, he talked so softly he could hardly be heard. You had to lean in, concentrate hard on what he was saying to get the meaning of it. Yancey said it was a trick. Made people really focus. Made them silence all those little voices that are always running around in their heads and really hear what he had to say. Made them pay attention. Better than shouting. I remembered that for later.

He started off oh, so softly. The courtroom quieted to hear. The jury leaned forward. Those in the back of the room standing along the walls stopped fidgeting. His diction was precise. His voice clear and resonant. He had a bit of an accent, that old southern accent that came up from Virginia with the landed gentry—courtly and melodic, the one everyone recognized and respected. They listened.

"Yes, John Fallis shot Scott and the others. He doesn't deny it," Mr. Morgan told them.

"He is sorry he had to.

"They were beating his son.

"He was afraid they would injure the boy seriously, perhaps fatally. He had no choice. He only did what any father would do. He had to stop it. He had to rescue his son. No man would permit such an outrage to continue." Here he paused to emphasize the word," no *man* would endure it."

Ah, I thought. The idea JF had voiced to the press shortly after turning himself in. That's the card he's going to play. Hot damn and hold the pickles.

Addressing not just the jury but the whole courtroom, Mr. Morgan told them he would let Mr. Fallis speak for himself, but first, and now his voice began to rise and his delivery to become more forceful, first he must set the record straight with respect to the unprincipled attack the prosecuting attorney had made on the character, actions, and reputation of John Richard Fallis.

Beside me Lucas stirred, sat forward eagerly.

"I could fill this room and take a month bringing people before you who will testify to the qualities of John Richard Fallis," he said walking slowly toward the jury box. "People who will swear to his generosity, to his loyalty, to his character. How he helps the weak and the poor, how he takes care of the sick and hungry, how he fights for their rights against the powerful and the privileged of this city. How he deals honestly with everyone. Never lies. Never cheats. How he is a successful and respected businessman. How he is an attentive father and husband. Yes, he sometimes lets anger or provocation lead him to actions he later regrets. Yes, he is a flawed and imperfect human—as are we all. Yet if you need a true friend, or require a real protector, there is no finer man in this town than John Richard Fallis. But I don't need to do that, Your Honor," he said, and turned to face the packed courtroom. "These fine people sitting here watching us trying to find where justice lies in this matter, they can attest to what I say."

He nodded to them, letting the idea take hold in their minds.

"John Fallis has already paid dearly for his actions. His home—burned to the ground by the mob that went after him that night.

"His family—displaced. An ailing infant son on the edge of death yanked from his warm bed and pulled out into the unhealthy night in order to escape the descending mob, dead three days later. His eldest son shot, then jailed when he himself was the injured party.

"His business—burned to the ground, his means of livelihood destroyed.

"Yes, he has already paid dearly."

Here he stopped, lingered to let the images sink in, slowly ran his eyes over the jury, then out over the throng and said, "I am not entirely sure who should be on trial here."

An absolute hush filled the courtroom. Not even the hint of a sound, anywhere, until, honest-to-god, they began clapping.

Attorney McCoy jumped to his feet, sputtering. The Judge banged his gavel down and roared, "That will be enough of that! Quiet, or I will clear the courtroom," and angrily to Mr. Morgan, "Save your speeches for the summation! Call your witnesses."

Morgan stood calmly waiting while McCoy fumed, the Judge scowled, and the room settled down.

Yancey leaned in to me, whispered, "Damn, Morgan's good."

Again the Judge banged his gavel. "There will be no more outbursts! You members of the jury, you are to disregard this. You are here to judge whether the defendant shot and wounded Sergeant Scott with the intent to kill. Nothing more. Not whether John Fallis is a good man or a bad man. Not whether he is a credit to the community or a threat. Only whether or not he shot and wounded with intent to kill. You understand that?"

He waited, looking sternly to each juror until they either nodded yes or said it. Finally satisfied, and the room quite again, he focused on Mr. Morgan. "You may proceed, counselor."

Mr. Morgan, trying to look contrite but not succeeding, moved away from the jury box and back to stand beside JF at the defense table.

"Your Honor, members of the jury," Morgan said, putting his hand on JF's shoulder, "our defense will be brief. Mr. Fallis shot Sergeant Scott. There is no doubt about that. He is sorry he had to. But he was justified in doing so. And he fired in self-defense."

The Judge scowled and nodded.

Mr. Morgan moved forward to take a position just in front of the witness stand.

"I have only four witnesses to call, and they only in response to the prosecutor's attack on Mr. Fallis's character. As for the rest of it, Mr. Fallis will speak for himself."

The first was Harold Aimes.

Harry Aimes was a family man and a foreman at the distillery, laid off now that Prohibition had closed them all. He was president of the Loyal Order of Elks and captain of the Stagg Distillery baseball team—a consistent winner of the inter-city league championship. He was well known and respected. All the people Morgan called were well known and respected.

There was Archibald Upjohn, who was in charge of the Methodist Mission in the Bottom and admired for his work with the kids of the Bottom; then Mrs. Henry Addison Clay, president of the Women's Charities of Franklin County, who marshaled the society ladies to open their purses and those of their husbands to help the poor and the needy; followed by Archibald Lee, president of the Capital City Merchants Association and one of the most respected businessmen in the country.

Harry Aimes's had known John Fallis since they were boys, worked with him, played baseball with him, went to church with him. Knew no finer man. Honest. Generous. Most of the working men in the Bottom were beholden to him, particularly now. He was helping them find work. Was carrying their tab at his grocery and not pushing for payment until they could. He makes a difference for a lot of folks. This shooting thing. That's bad. But John Fallis isn't. He is a good man.

Harry Aimes's testimony was the tone of the rest of it.

They all said that John Richard Fallis was a respected, respectable, and honorable man. He could be counted on and trusted. He was generous and kind. He was loyal. He played fair and kept his word. He was an asset to the community.

Take that, Prosecuting Attorney Maxwell McCoy!

Lucas was happy now. He beamed and nodded in agreement. Yancey stretched across me and tapped him on the knee. "Settle down," he said.

It was almost five o'clock by this time. We'd been at it almost eight hours yet the courtroom still seemed riveted.

Looking at the clock on the wall above the jury, the Judge said to Mr. Morgan, "You have another witness before we hear from Mr. Fallis. It has been a long day. Let's save Mr. Fallis for tomorrow. I'm sure you want everyone rested and fresh when they hear from your client. Call your witness, then we will adjourn."

Mr. Morgan nodded, said, "We call Mrs. Henry Addison Clay."

Mrs. Clay took the stand like royalty ascending. Hers was a family name old and honored. She herself was a Clark, of the George Rogers strain. There was no woman in town of higher social standing. Only one or two of equal influence. I found it surprising that a woman of such blue-blooded pedigree, one who was a pillar of the establishment, was standing up for the man called the King of Craw. She was in her late sixties, I suppose. She was a handsome woman. Tall and graceful. And rich. Rich enough that if there were some who did not care for her actions or opinions it caused her no distress. How she came to be a friend and admirer of John Fallis I did not know and never learned. It was enough that she was.

She sat straight, spoke clearly and confidently, without hesitation or diffidence. She spoke of his generosity and his, the word she used was courage, in standing up for the poor and the downtrodden against avaricious landlords and piratical merchants and money lenders who gouged them and insulted them and abused them at every turn. And against the city machine -- the politicians and the functionaries who took their tax monies but refused to put in the storm sewers that would carry off some of the overflow when the river floods, or patch the pot-holed streets, or put in the lighting that would make life safer and healthier in all the poorer sections.

She spoke movingly of his tenderness with the battered women who filled the shelters her charities supported, and the children who were hungry and without sufficient clothing.

She finished by saying, "I do not know what to think of this matter of the shootings. But I know this. If John Fallis is a bad man, we need more of them."

A moment of surprise seemed to take the courtroom. Lee Morgan looked taken aback by this. Even the Judge seemed startled. Recovering, Morgan signaled quickly to the Judge. The gavel descended. We were adjourned.

THIRTY-FIVE
JF Takes The Stand

When they began again the next morning, Lee Morgan rose, nodded to the Judge. Did same to the jury. Started to walk from behind the defense table where he had been sitting with Mr. Fallis as the Judge entered the courtroom, then stopped, turned back, leaned across to say something to JF. Mr. Fallis leaned forward. Morgan spoke softly, but just loudly enough, and I was sure it was intentional, to be heard by those in the jury box.

"You are certain you want to do this? It is not necessary. I can make the case without putting you through this."

JF didn't hesitate. He signaled forcefully with a nod of his head.

Morgan stepped back. Straightened up. Reached his hand across the table to shake JF's, turned to the Judge and announced, "The defense calls John Richard Fallis."

Mr. Fallis put his left hand on the Bible, raised his right and swore to tell the truth, the whole truth, and nothing but the truth, so help him God.

The room had gone deathly silent. There was no shuffling or movement. It was like the forest just before dawn—breathlessly still, expectantly waiting.

Mr. Fallis looked fresh. Eager. He didn't look villainous, felonious, or evil. He looked like a responsible businessman, a bit more fashionable than the establishment crowd, an air about him of confidence and authority, nothing like what you'd expect from the picture the prosecuting attorney's witnesses had painted of him. He was dressed in a suit of navy blue, a white dress shirt with a blood-red tie knotted into a perfectly proportioned Windsor, black wing-tip oxfords polished to a sheen, a white pocket square and, at his wrist, the left, the occasional glint of gold where the Omega band showed. A fine figure of a man. A credit to the community.

"Mr. Fallis," Morgan began, "before I let you start, we need to clear up one thing. That list of charges the prosecuting attorney recited before he turned the floor over to us, were you tried or found guilty in any of those?"

"No, sir," JF responded.

"Why not?"

"The charges were either withdrawn or dismissed—in two cases as having been fabricated by members of the police force."

"Nothing to them, then?"

"Yes. Nothing to them."

"One other thing. After that night, not then, but afterwards, did you feel that you were set up?"

"Set up?"

"Intentionally drawn into that maelstrom that night. There is bad blood between the police and you. That's no secret. You are a thorn in their sides. You interfere with their 'administration of justice' in the Bottom. They'd like to be rid of you. They know of your devotion to your family. They know of your quick temper. By making a spectacle of dragging your son across town bound and bloody, they knew word would get to you rapidly. They knew you'd come after him. They knew you would be outraged. They knew you would be combative. What better way to get rid of the thorn than to remove it during a three-guns-to-one shoot-out, with most of the town looking on? Do you feel it was a set-up?"

The Judge was banging his gavel down even before Attorney McCoy jumped to his feet.

"Mr. Morgan! Stop! Yes, Mr. McCoy, he is out of line. Treading on thin ice. Jury, disregard those comments. Mr. Morgan, put a rein on your suspicions."

The courtroom was abuzz, people turning to one another, whispering, shaking their heads in confusion. Did I hear him right? Did he say the police planned all this so they could take John Fallis down?

However strongly the Judge might admonish the jury to wipe that thought from their minds, it was too late, too late for either the jury or the crowd in the courtroom. The thought was planted.

I turned to Lucas. He had on his face the look of someone who has just received a startling revelation. Of course.

I turned to Yancey. He was smiling.

When order was finally restored, Mr. Morgan, unapologetic, strode from his spot in front of the witness stand to the corner of the jury box, giving time for everything to settle down and order to prevail. From there, having moved himself from the center of the stage to the side so that all attention was focused on JF, he said in a matter-of-fact voice, "Well, then, let's get to the heart of the matter. You shot Sergeant Scott?"

Without hesitation, JF answered. "Yes."

"And Patrolmen Wilhelm and McCoy and O'Nan?"

JF kept his gaze fixed firmly on Morgan, answered calmly, "Them, too."

"Why did you do that?"

"I had no choice."

Morgan had asked the first questions in rapid succession. He paused here, half turned, looked to the jury, waited, let his gaze wander to Sergeant Scott with McCoy at his side where they both sat with a look of bafflement in their eyes, waited another moment, turned back to JF, and speaking in an almost apologetic tone, as if asking that a very personal and painful experience be told, said, "Please explain."

Like everyone else, I held my breath.

Mr. Fallis shifted himself in the witness chair, raised his chin, drew in a long breath, almost a sigh, took his eyes from Morgan, turned to talk directly to the jury.

"I was home. My baby son was very ill. He wasn't a year old yet. We were very worried. I was helping my wife. We had just finished supper. It was eight o'clock or so. Had been a very pleasant summer day, not too hot, cooling now at dusk, the windows were open for the breeze, the kids were outside playing, we could hear them laughing.

"My wife had just gotten the baby settled when a young man of the neighborhood came running in, scared and excited, and told me that three policemen had Carlos, my oldest son. He said they had beaten him badly, torn his shirt off. He was so badly hurt and so bloody that he could scarcely be recognized, the boy said. He said they were dragging Carlos away across the Old State House grounds to the police station uptown.

"I acted on the impulse of a father. I started out the door at a run. To save my boy. I caught up with them about a block from the station. They had a hold on him and were dragging him and beating him. I demanded they release him so I could take him to a doctor, thinking he had been severely injured. When they refused, I attempted to take the boy. Then shooting started."

"You thought your son was severely injured and you wanted to get him to a doctor as fast as you could?"

"Yes."

"But the police wouldn't let you?"

"They laughed."

"What did you do?"

"I stepped in to take him."

"And the shooting started? Did you start the shooting?"

"I don't know. Scott had his gun out and was swinging it toward me. Whether he fired first or I did, I don't know."

"But he could have?"

"Yes."

"Were you trying to kill Scott?"

"No. I was defending myself and trying get my boy to a doctor."

"You are considered a good shot with a pistol? An expert?

"I can handle a pistol."

'You usually hit what you're aiming at?"

JF let that pass as obvious.

"I repeat then, were you shooting to kill?"

"I was not."

"Do you have anything to add to this?"

"I'm sorry these men were hurt. I'm sorry I was put in a position where I had no alternative. My son was in grave danger. I did what any father would do."

JF stopped then and turned to Mr. Morgan.

"More?"

"No," JF said. "That's all I have to say. It is the truth."

Mr. Morgan nodded and waited quietly while JF left the witness stand and took his seat again. Mr. Morgan followed. He stood behind JF, put his hand on JF's shoulder, and announced, it seemed with satisfaction, "Your Honor, the defense rests."

Attorney McCoy's head jerked back, startled.

The Judge straightened, leaned forward, frowning.

In the courtroom people started turning to each other, puzzled. Then the buzz started. The Judge banged it down.

"Mr. McCoy?"

McCoy rose, looked angrily at Lee Morgan, then said to the Judge, "I won't waste the court's time cross-examining this witness. He has admitted his guilt, which is as obvious as his lies. And this is the only closing statement this case requires." Here he turned to face the jury. "John Fallis is guilty as charged. Guilty! Guilty! Guilty!" And sat dramatically down.

Lee Morgan had been standing behind JF at the defense table through this. All eyes turned to him. He waited for the room to quiet.

When the hush was almost overbearing, he said, softly, "Your Honor, we don't need make a closing statement. John Fallis has spoken for himself. Everyone who heard him must know the truth of it."

And it was done.

It was nearing one o'clock then.

The Judge looked relieved. He immediately sent the jury to deliberate. If no decision had been reached by six, he said, he would adjourn court for the day.

Slowly, as if people were reluctant to leave, the courtroom emptied.

JF left with Mr. Morgan. Yancey disappeared.

Lucas and I made our way outside into the bright April afternoon to wait and worry.

By the time five-thirty came there had still been no word. The Judge called the jury back just before six.

"No decision?"

The jury foreman said, "Not yet."

So he sent them away to a boarding house for the night with the admonition to discuss the case with no one but each other. "We will reconvene at nine tomorrow morning," he said.

The courtroom, which had filled again rapidly when word went out that the jury was being called back, emptied slowly, packed as it was.

Again Lucas and I took a seat on the courthouse steps. Twilight now. Beginning to cool a bit. The crowd flowed out all around us. All of them talking, some arguing, a few looking dazed. There hadn't been a show like this in the Capital City since no one remembered when.

Lucas and I were wrung out from the emotions of the day. We had no plans, no idea how we'd handle the tension of waiting until tomorrow. Good Friday, that's what tomorrow would be. Good Friday. Easter weekend coming up.

"Come home with me," I said. "Mom will make us supper. I'll beat you at a game of chess."

He did. I didn't. But the time passed and we forgot for a while that eleven men were at a boarding house somewhere in town deciding the fate of Mr. John Richard Fallis.

The moon was full that night, the full moon of April, the Grass Moon. If you could see it clear, not obscured by clouds, big and full of light, a good omen. Yancey said so.

After Lucas left that night I walked to the bridge to see the moonlight on the river. My mother didn't believe in omens. She believed in prayer. I was willing to go with whichever worked. So I said a little prayer that night, looking downriver with the Grass Moon bright above me. It was the first time I could remember asking that someone other than family be looked after. As I think back on it, I'm not sure why I did that. I liked Mr. Fallis. I admired much of what he did. Still, there was something about him. The violence? The arrogance? Something,

THIRTY-SIX
So Sayeth The Jury

The verdict, delivered shortly after nine on the morning of the fourteenth day of April in the Franklin County Courthouse in the Capital City of the Commonwealth of Kentucky, by a jury of his peers, duly sworn and instructed, was six months in jail and a two hundred and fifty dollar fine.

Six months and two hundred and fifty dollars!

That's all?

Prosecuting Attorney McCoy rose in open-mouthed disbelief.

Sergeant Scott and his fellows jumped up in anger.

Defense Attorney Morgan immediately appealed the verdict, contending that the charges should be dismissed.

And John Richard Fallis, the focus of all this contention, walked out into the balmy morning a free man on bond.

You'd think there would be crowds marching in anger and shouting for justice, or folks celebrating in the streets, so heated had the matter of the Shoot-Out been. There wasn't. After the initial shock in the courtroom, the crowd filed out in a tide of I'll-be-damneds, and how-could-theys, and hurrah-for-Johnnys—but angry or happy, they were soon constrained and soon scattered.

On another day the reactions might have been more volatile, but it was Good Friday. Most things would close at noon. There were services to attend, the tortured way up Calvary to be remembered, men nailed to crosses to consider. Church bells would ring at three when the sky blackened and the heavens split asunder. The day would turn doleful. The mood become somber with sadness and guilt.

With that to face, the aftermath of the Fallis verdict was muted. The crowd dispersed, Lucas and I with them, but we walked away with that happily relieved feeling that comes when the cloud hanging over you disappears. If Mr. Lee Morgan had been there we would have lifted him on our shoulders and carried him jubilantly around. We shook hands, pounded each other on the shoulder and walked away, me toward home to get ready for church. Lucas toward Craw. Bodies on crosses and clouds parting not withstanding, I expected there'd be a victory celebration before the night was out, with Lucas at the table.

Even with the melancholy of Good Friday ahead of me, I felt really good that afternoon. JF wasn't going to prison. Even if the appeal failed, it would be only jail. Lucas could step out of the swamp of worry he'd been wading through and get back out in the sunlight. Spring was on us and summer would be here soon. And I'd discovered a new game I was burning to learn to play—if I could get Mr. Leland Morgan to teach me how.

As we wound down off the high of that Easter weekend and spring melded into summer, the trial, for me, began to fade into the background. Spring football practice would start soon. There were all those little delights at school to look forward to, like trying to pass Mr. Leather's algebra tests. And the mysteries of Craw still hadn't been explored. So my mind wandered eagerly and with relief back to matters that were commanding my attention before the Big Shoot-Out eclipsed everything.

Though the trial was behind us my father didn't think it had changed many minds about John Richard Fallis. But it had raised the question of who should have been on trial, which softened the attitude of some. It was easy to see, even by those who detested JF, how the police might have taken advantage of his son's curiosity to goad Fallis, who had a hair-trigger temper and was prone to violence, into a gunfight he wasn't likely to win.

Any other boy, one with a father who wasn't a boil on the hide of the police, might simply have been smacked and sent on his way. The incident at the carnival need have been nothing more than a hardly noticeable encounter on an otherwise fine summer evening—should have been nothing more than that. Did the police intentionally provoke Mr. Fallis? My father wondered. Whatever the case, JF's justification that he only did what any "man" would do to protect his family was an explanation many understood and accepted.

Still, you can't go around shooting up the police. There had to be retribution for that.

My father thought things would settle down now.

I didn't.

I was privy to some things he wasn't. I had a first-hand sense of the rancor between JF and the police. I'd seen it and felt it as they sulked menacingly around while we rebuilt the store. I had a second-hand sense, through Lucas and Yancey, that this new "business" proposition, the one Prohibition was opening the door to, might get very perilous.

I'd learned a lot about Mr. Fallis during the course of the trial. Heard the bad stuff. Heard the good stuff. Not sure of how much of either to believe. Some of it tracked with what I had experienced by being around him. Some of it didn't.

I heard him speak for himself about his actions. I believe he believed what he said -- now. What was in his mind at the time he acted I think was probably a little different from that. I think the anger button got hit. I think he went through the Shoot-Out not thinking at all. Just feeling.

Even so, I was inclined to Mrs. Henry Addison Clay's persuasion—if John Fallis is a bad man, we need more of them.

But with JF being who he is, the police being who they are, and all the temptations this new law prohibiting the making and selling of liquor was spawning, there wasn't a snowball's chance in hell that things would quiet down in the Kingdom of Craw.

The days began to become normal again. Lucas and I dropped back into our regular routines. We didn't talk about that night or what was to come if JF lost his appeal or any of that.

We met at the bridge and walked to school in the mornings ... like always. I made my trek down to the grocery for our study night sessions ... like always. We resumed our roles in the freshman class ... like always. But now I knew to pay attention to something I'd never had to think about before—that the world is fickle and it's best to be attentive. And I began to become aware that summer of how people have dimensions. And of how actions have consequences. And of how heroes are made.

THIRTY-SEVEN
To The Pennyrile

We coasted through spring.

The seniors won the traditional intra-squad game at the end of spring practice as they usually did, but Lucas and I performed well enough to believe that coach might elevate us to the varsity when the regular season began.

I paid attention to my class work, particularly to the algebra, and with Lucas's tutoring, managed to squeeze out a C on the final to join the ranks of sophomores when school resumed in the fall.

My reward was a summer in a distant forest.

Not my idea. My dad's. He felt I should get away from the Kingdom of Craw for a while. He liked Mr. Fallis more than he was willing to admit and respected him in an oddly provisional sort of way, but he wasn't comfortable with the experiences he thought I was being exposed to there.

This is not something he said. I knew it, though.

School ended the Friday of the first week in June. A week later I was packed, fed, hugged, kissed, told to remember to say my prayers, to be careful, to write, to ... too many things to remember ... and, sitting beside my dad in his black Model T, on my way to the Pennyrile.

Mom had a little going-away dinner the night before I left. Lucas came. She made my favorite—Swiss steak, mashed potatoes, fresh green beans sautéed in butter, garden salad with her famous red Roquefort dressing, home-made yeast rolls, and strawberry shortcake with loads of whipped cream for dessert.

Lucas was more comfortable around my parents now. We talked easily. He'd progressed from "yes, ma'am" and "yes, sir" to actual sentences that carried some information. But we didn't talk about Mr. Fallis. Or the trial. Or Craw or the Bottom or any of it. We talked about school and what we'd do for the summer.

I was headed to the State Forestry Division field office in Dawson Springs, way down in west Kentucky. The Commonwealth was just getting into the business of building state parks and a section of the Pennyrile Forest around Dawson Springs was a chosen site. The town was already famous as a health spa. People came in droves to "take the waters"—the rich mineral waters that were said to heal illnesses, banish pains, and make the halt and the lame dance again. A state park would be an added boon to the local economy. And it was being pushed by State Senator James Farrell Endicott, who had eyes on becoming Governor.

The park could become a jewel, my father said—a twenty-square-mile Eden of hardwoods and meadows with stands of oak and maple that were among the finest in the Southeast. I could help make it real -- hacking out trails, clearing understory, helping the surveyors, and mapping camp sites. It wouldn't be the hard physical work of last summer with Mr. Fallis, but close.

I'd work five days a week and not get home again until mid-August just in time for football. Ten weeks. I'd be gone ten weeks.

I'd never been away from home that long before. Never been that far away from home all by myself ... over two hundred miles ... in country totally alien to me.

Kentucky is a wide meandering state, five hundred miles or so from end to end.

Rivers mark three of its borders—the Ohio on the north, the Mississippi on the west, the Tug, a tributary of the Ohio, the eastern. The southern border is a fairly straight east-west line from the western tip of Virginia through the Cumberland Mountains across the top of Tennessee to the Mississippi.

The great plain of rich farmland and wooded hills that takes up most of the central and western parts of the state is the Pennyrile. The area took its name from the pennyroyal, the flowering plant that carpeted the land in spring and summer with its lavender blossoms and filled the air with the scent of mint. The settlers came to call the whole section the Penny Royal, after the flower. In time, in the lazy way people handle words, Penny Royal became Pennyrile.

I'd have a fine time, my father said. A real adventure. Be good for me. Good for a boy from the mountains of Colorado. Learn new things. Have new experiences.

Just a little over four hundred feet of elevation where I was going. Never been in country that low. What would the trees be like, the game, the air? Too thick to breathe? Would the pressure be so heavy I couldn't jump? Honest to god flatland. Would I like that?

"Yes, sir," I said.

Lucas's plans appealed to me more. He'd spend the summer working at the grocery. And he was going to play on Mr. Fallis's baseball team, the Hundred Proofs, the town's pride and joy, in the inter-city baseball league that everybody followed. They were the league champs last year and were expected to repeat this year. Mr. Fallis managed it. What could top that?

I was happy for him, and wished I could be a part of it, too.

Yancey gave me a present that night—Yancey whose opinion I was never sure of. Yancey whose measure of me seemed always ambiguous.

My dad drove us back down to the grocery and Lucas asked if I could come in for a minute.

Dad said take your time, so I followed Lucas inside to Mr. Fallis's office in the back.

Yancey was there waiting for us, leaning back against the desk. He nodded to me and handed something to Lucas, who took it, looked at it, and smiled, handed it to me.

I opened my hand to find a knife.

"Never go into strange places defenseless," Yancey said. He paused, stuck out his hand and said, "Now give me a nickel."

Confused, I began to fumble in my pocket.

"If someone gives you a knife, you give a coin in return to show your appreciation. Cuts the friendship if you don't"

179

Friendship? We were friends?

I didn't have a nickel. I had a dime.

He took it. "This will do fine."

I was so surprised I'm not sure if I managed to mumble thank you. I think I did. I hope I did.

I still have that knife—a five-inch Utica folder with a three-and-three-quarter-inch blade. It has brass bolsters and an impregnated hardwood handle. It is small enough for a pocket but the blade is sharp and of sufficient length.

When I got to Dawson Springs I found myself part of a crew made up mostly of locals. Only two of us were from out of county—me and Joe Travis. Joe was from Golden Pond. My dad's in with his park service friends got me the job. Joe's family was big friends of Senator Jimmy.

The others kidded us about our "connections," but practically no one on the state payroll got his job through ability or experience alone, them for certain, so we belonged to the same fraternity.

Joe and I were by far the youngest in the crew. We took ribbing about that, too. But as soon as they satisfied themselves that we'd pull our share of the load and wouldn't let ourselves be pushed around, they accepted us.

Our home was a bunkhouse about four miles out of town on forest service land. The bunkhouse slept eight in an upstairs dorm. Downstairs was an office, a big meeting room, a kitchen and mess hall. There was no electricity. A line hadn't been run out from town yet. And no running water. We got ours from a well. The privies were about fifty yards along a gravel path into the forest.

We worked hard.

Up at six. At it until dusk. Sometimes back to the mess hall for lunch, sometimes from our lunch pails in the field. Supper around the big trestle table in the bunkhouse kitchen. Then afterwards, cards or checkers or big talk and bragging by the light of the kerosene lamps.

That's when I taught Joe Travis to play chess.

The men played poker some, but mostly hearts. Hearts didn't have the cutthroat intensity that poker did and you weren't constantly being challenged to put your hard-earned wages up to prove your cards were better than the other guy's. It was far more satisfying to jump up and slam down the Queen of

Spades on the other guy's hand—so much more satisfying than to matter of factly beat his two pair with your three of a kind.

Joe and I weren't invited into the games. We were kids and we were newcomers. Hearts plays best with six at the table. The homeboys all knew each other. They'd worked together, or had in-laws in common, or been in school together. They didn't ignore us, they just made no effort to include us.

If Joe and I wanted company it had to be us. Which turned out fine. I'm not bashful and Joe was friendly. We're both curious. We hit if off immediately. So with nothing to do after supper, I taught him to play chess. His game was checkers and we played that for the first week, moving downstairs to the kitchen to get away from the racket of the hearts game, but after a week of pushing colored discs around I pulled out my chess board, set up the pawns and the knights and the bishops, placed the rooks on the corners and installed the kings and the queens in their spots. There was no more talk of checkers. My friendship with Joe Travis grew strong.

It turned out to be a grand summer, but that's not what is important to this story. What is important is that I made the Golden Pond connection that summer.

The workweek ended on Friday afternoon. By six o'clock the whole crew had scattered for home. That left me with no one to talk to and nothing to do until Monday when they returned.

Just me and empty buildings in a clearing in the forest.

I'd been alone in the woods many times. No voices to be heard. No one around for miles. That was fine. I liked that. But this. There was something spooky about this.

I felt like I'd been abandoned in a deserted village and left to fend for myself. I couldn't shake a nagging sense of unease and night was creeping up and there were no lights on anywhere.

When evening came I'd have to fire up the stove in the kitchen and make myself something, and afterwards find a way to distract myself until time for bed. Sit outside and look at the stars? Lay back in my bunk and read by lamplight till sleep took me? Sleep in that big open room surrounded by seven empty beds? Strange sounds in the night. Whispers at the windows.

I almost pulled down a bedroll and took it outside to sleep in the open, but realized I was letting my imagination run too freely. There were no assassins in the shadows, no monsters creeping up the staircase. Get a grip, sonny boy, this ain't the second grade.

Put out the lamp.

Turn over.

Go to sleep.

If I dreamed nothing woke me.

THIRTY-EIGHT
Dawson's Well

Those first weekends were lonesome. Lonesome was a new experience for me. I disliked the feeling very much.

To combat it, that first Sunday I walked the streets of Dawson Springs surrounding myself with people—well-dressed people with happy smiles, ambling along on their way home after church or to the fancy hotel in the center of town for a big Sunday dinner. I couldn't tell how many were locals and how many were hopefuls who had come to take the waters. They all looked pleased with themselves and with each other. It was like a picture in a slick magazine of a pleasant afternoon in a prosperous little town that knew it was lucky. I felt better.

Though the town was named Dawson Springs, the magic waters that made it famous didn't flow from a spring. Turns out a local businessman was digging a well on his property and hit an aquifer with water that had an odd taste to it and a curious smell. He started to fill it back in, but discovered the water had healing properties.

Word spread.

People came.

The town fathers thought Dawson Springs had better imagery as a name than Dawson's Well.

I tried the waters.

I was glad I wasn't trying to get healed of something.

The second weekend I nosed around, satisfying my curiosity. I found out that the Pittsburg Pirates came here for their spring training during the war years and that Shoeless Joe Jackson and Babe Ruth and Ty Cobb had all played here. Shoeless Joe and the Babe! Right here! I found the ballpark and climbed the stairs of the wooden bleachers at the field where they'd played and sat there conjuring them up until a voice rattled my imagining.

"What are you doing up there, boy, all by yourself looking at nothing?"

I looked down to see an elderly man standing by the railing.

"Looking for Joe, looking for the Babe? Tris Speaker played here, too, you know that, and Cobb, Ty Cobb. He was a sonofabitch but he could play."

The man looked around, waved his arm, "This place was packed on Sunday afternoons when the teams came. Ass to ass and two deep down the baselines. Hot dog stand there by the gate. Popcorn hucksters and cold beer vendors working the seats."

Looking up at me, smiling, "Those were the days. Never thought to see stars like that down here in the back woods, but they were here, Yes sir, they were here. And everybody for miles around came to see them. Sunday afternoons sitting here in the stands watching those legends play, my god that was fine. Sorry you missed it, son. Sorry those days are gone."

He shook his head. Took out a crisp white handkerchief and blew his nose. Shook his head again, then looked up. "Where you from, son? Why are you here?"

Mr. Bochert was the only person I every really talked with in Dawson Springs. I was rarely in town, and when I was it was usually with Joe Travis and some of the crew after work when we'd ease into one of the little cafes or the saloon by the dam where there was beer to be had. What talk there was had been between us mostly.

Mr. Bochert climbed up and sat down beside me. It was a warm afternoon, but not hot. Not a cloud anywhere to be seen, a little breeze now and then floating up off the river. A line of sycamores told me where it was. They'd built the stands down the third base line facing east, so the sun was at our backs.

He was a sturdy old man in a starched white shirt and a red bow tie. He had a seersucker suit coat over his arm, a wide-brimmed white straw fedora on his head, and helped himself up with a silver-headed cane. I had the impression he was a man of consequence, a prosperous farmer probably, just out of church. A widower? No wife in sight. Just finished his meal at the hotel dining room where the best folk would congregate if they weren't entertaining at home? Out for his afternoon constitutional? A pleasant stroll remembering good times?

"Al Bochert," he said, extending his hand, smiling.

We talked the whole afternoon. I never left my seat. Mr. Bochert is the one who told me about the well and about the town.

"Nice little town. Friendly. Safe. People get along fine here. Some of the best farmland in the Pennyrile. Make good livings farming. Go to church. Know each other or know of each other—except for all those people that damn well brings in."

He looked at me, almost challenging.

"Who would think a little evil-tasting, foul-smelling water would cause people to flock in like they do. Two hotels here now. Something like thirty rooming houses. Restaurants. Clothing stores. Souvenir shops."

He stopped, rubbed his chin, "It's not that they're rowdies. These spa people don't come to drink or carouse or gamble. They're just folk looking to feel better. Can't fault them for that. Drink the water. Bathe in it. Throw away your crutches and waltz the night away. More power to them. Just leave their money with us." He laughed then. "Sound like a curmudgeon, do I? I shouldn't fuss. That well is the best thing that's happened to this town since the railroad came."

He talked on in that vein for quite a while. Non-stop. Not waiting for a response. Telling me about the town, about his farms, about his wife of thirty years, passed on last spring, bless her heart, his two sons lying in the American Cemetery outside the village of Belleau in France. Jerry was twenty, Davey just eighteen. Killed in the battle in that damn forest. They'd be men now, ready to take over the farms. Start their own families. Damn that war. Damn it to hell. Well, his daughter had a good husband. The farms would be all right.

Finally, "What about you, boy? Tell me about you."

So I did. Who I was, where I was from, what I was doing. Sort of.

"You were there during all that foolishness last summer. That John Fallis thing. The battle with the police."

"You heard of it?"

"Oh hell, son, everybody's heard of it. A man takes on the entire police force of the state's Capital City and faces them down. Everybody's heard of it. Did you see it?"

I didn't want to talk about that. I let it slide by.

"Everybody went wild?"

"There was a lot of noise and shouting. A lot of confusion."

"I bet there was. Burned his house down. Awful. What do people think of this Mr. Fallis now? What do they call him? The King of Craw?"

"Some people think he's a hero. Some think he's a very bad man."

"If it had been my boy I'd have been tempted to do the same thing he did. Looks like he went out of his head for a while, though. You have to be careful around men like that. But I'd risk knowing him."

He laughed again, a big knee-slapping laugh. "Well, son, I have truly enjoyed our little talk. Glad you're here. Hope you enjoy our little town. Give Mr. Fallis, if you ever meet him, my very best regards. And don't you believe what they say about Shoeless Joe. He wasn't part of all that. He played to win. All the time. He was the real article."

He stood then, slipped on his seersucker jacket, picked up his cane and made his way slowly down the stands and out onto the field that Shoeless Joe Jackson had once honored with his presence.

It was coming on to dusk. Swallows were snapping up insects in the fading light. I had a four-mile hike back to my lonely home away from home. I walked it wondering why I hadn't told Mr. Borchet that I knew the King of Craw.

THIRTY-NINE
Major James

On the third week, Joe Travis took me home with him.

Whether he felt sorry for me there in the bunkhouse all alone, or whether he genuinely liked my company, I didn't ask. I happily went.

Mrs. Elizabeth Travis, Joe's mother, made me almost wish I lived there. She was standing on the porch waiting for us that first Saturday that Joe took me home with him, hand shading her eyes against the late afternoon sun as the car made the turn through the gate and into the yard.

She was a small woman with hair the color of red maple leafs in autumn and brown eyes full of welcome. She gave Joe a peck on the cheek and opened her arms to me. I was in love. You had no choice. There was so much warmth and goodwill about her that you loved her right away.

Miss Libby was a McFarlane, a descendent of Major James McFarlane, martyr of the Whiskey Rebellion when Pennsylvania farmers rose up in revolt against taxes being imposed by the new Federal government on the whiskey they made from their own corn. President George Washington had to lead out Federal troops to put it down. The Major was killed in the ensuing nastiness.

The Federals got their taxes. Many of the losers, outraged at the arrogance of any government, much less this new Federal government, presuming to levy a tax on something they considered as integral to their lifestyle and culture as the grains they made it from, and refusing to pay it, began a slow exodus across the Ohio River into the unsettled lands of what was then Virginia but would become Kentucky. Most were of Scots-Irish blood and temperament. They brought with them their skill at farming, their outrage at taxes and distrust of government—and their knowledge of how to make the finest whiskey that ever a man could make.

Miss Libby's people were part of that exodus. As were the Travises.

Joe was very proud of this.

They'd made up a bed for me in Joe's room upstairs. We stashed my gear and came back down to get acquainted. The Travis house was a large white two-story Victorian sitting back on neatly mowed acres on the south edge of Golden Pond. There were a couple of small buildings on the rear of the property—a shed of some type and what looked like a small barn, and a stand of trees and a pond off beyond. The town's main street ran along the front fence line. A roofed porch wrapped the house on all sides.

Joe's brothers—Rich, the eldest, and Kirk, the second in line—were in one of the swings talking, and baby sister Sally (they teased her, she was probably twelve) was standing next to her mother. Joe motioned me to the settee closest to them. Sally slid in beside Joe. Miss Libby pulled up a rocker across from us.

Miss Libby scolded Joe good-naturedly for leaving me out there in that lonely place when I should have been there with them enjoying myself, especially since I was a visitor and should be looked after. She smiled and patted my hand. "I will see to that," she said.

"Joe says you come all the way from Colorado. I have never in my whole entire life met anyone from Colorado. It must be very different there."

So I told them about the mountains.

They'd never seen real mountains, not like my mountains, none scratching the sky like my Rockies do.

They found it exciting to think about walking on mountain tops so high that people from the flatlands had trouble breathing. Where you could see all the way to tomorrow and then some. Where you had to be careful in the forest in the spring when a mother grizzly might rise up on you. Where there are fish that really are the color of rainbows.

And I told her about my mother and my father and that I would be a sophomore in high school when school started and admitted in response to her question that I was an only child, a situation she frowned at but was quick to say she was sure I wouldn't let spoil me because I seemed too nice a boy.

No one asked about Mr. Fallis or the Shoot-Out or any of that. After my brief exchange with Mr. Borchet I imagined they'd heard of it. And again I wondered, as I had wondered walking back to the bunkhouse that night after the talk with Mr. Borchet, why I was uneasy letting it be known that I was there, that I saw it, that I was part of it.

Maybe I was resisting opening that door in my mind again. I had locked all those whispers and shouts, all that apprehension and concern, away—didn't want to let them out again.

Or maybe I felt complicit and was embarrassed that I did.

But there was no need to hide from my memories or try to explain an event I could not explain. The mood was relaxed and easy. We laughed and kidded all the way to suppertime. Mr. Travis was home by then, Mr. Andrew Travis, Miss Libby's husband, Joe's dad, Andy they called him. He owned the Trigg County Feed, Farm Supply & John Deere Tractor Store in Cadiz, the county seat. He gave me an appraising look, held it for a bit, then a crinkly smile, stuck out his hand, took mine, shook it vigorously, and said, "Welcome, son. Don't you let these Indians scare you a bit. Libby Travis, what's for supper?"

What's for supper was golden, deep-fried chicken coated in a batter good enough eat by itself, corn on the cob, fresh green beans, mashed potatoes with brown gravy, sliced tomatoes straight from the garden, cucumbers in wine vinegar, buttermilk biscuits, ice tea, and apple pie ala mode.

Then and there I decided to sign on to the Travis clan if they'd have me.

The Travises were the most influential family in the county.

There were four brothers: J. D., the eldest, Andrew next, then Douglass, then Mark.

J. D. was Jabbo to his friends. Everyone else called him Mr. Travis. He was president of the Trigg County Grange and deacon of the Golden Pond Baptist Church.

Andrew had the Farm Supply & John Deere store. Every farmer in the county did business there.

Douglas was Sheriff of Trigg County, had been since the big flood of Ninety-Eight when the Tennessee and the Cumberland Rivers both rose up and almost drowned that whole end of the state. Doug Travis led the rescue efforts. Saved so many they started calling him Noah.

Mark owned Between The Rivers Livery & Automotive, had the Ford franchise. Not many were buying automobiles in that area at that time. Mark saw the future.

The aggregated clan, not counting in-laws, numbered thirty-one. Add in the in-laws and their friends and Doug Travis could get elected almost on the strength of the family vote alone.

Each of the brothers had farms. They grew corn, hay, tobacco and rye. Ran cattle. Operated a small dairy.

And they were the reason Golden Pond was famous far and wide.

I did not know this about them then.

I met the Travis elders that first weekend.

It was the Fourth of July weekend. The Fourth was on Tuesday. We weren't due back at work until Wednesday morning. Miss Libby had a family picnic that July Fourth afternoon. All of them were there. Trestle tables were spaced out around the lawn, babies on blankets spread under the shade trees, kids running and playing. There was a choose-up softball game underway, and horseshoes and mumbly-peg and croquet.

Each of the families brought their favorite dish and the tables were filled with the most lavish spread of food I'd ever seen. Some of it I'd never seen before. And under a very big elm by the pond sat a brass-bound oak cask with a dipper beside it and on a little table to the side, silver Jefferson cups and a pitcher of cold water. The men seemed drawn there. They'd tarry for a while talking, then amble back up to the horseshoes or the ball game in the pasture.

I was introduced by handshake to all the males and to all the girls and wives who, even the youngest of them, shyly nodded welcome or kissed me on the cheek.

When nightfall came they staged their own fireworks show.

Roman candles flared, firecrackers popped, sparklers etched trails in the night as the kids ran chasing each other. Joe and I sat on the porch watching, wanting to be kids again so we could play.

Mr. Jaydee walked out and sat down beside us. It was dark on the porch but enough light from inside that I could make him out clearly. A tall man, lean, older than my dad, the oldest of the brothers, maybe as old as Mr. Borchet. Joe stood up immediately, deferential and respectful. I did the same.

"Uncle Jaydee. Can I get you anything?"

"Sit down, boys. Enjoy the show."

We eased back down into our chairs, watching the rockets and the star clusters burst in the sky. We kept quiet, waiting for whatever Mr. Jaydee had to say. He sat quietly, too, relishing the noise and the colors. In a bit he said, "How are you finding our land between the rivers, Mr. Edwards? Andrew and Elizabeth and Joe here treating you well? Are you having a good time?"

"I'm loving it, sir."

That pleased him. "Move over to the railing there where I can see you better." He motioned toward the porch railing. The light from inside and the flare of the fireworks made us both more distinct. I sat there. He could see my face more clearly.

"This thing that happened in Frankfort last year, that battle with the police. Were you there then?"

"Yes, sir."

"This Mr. John Richard Fallis, the King of Craw. What do you know of him?"

Oh, damn. Fess up or lie. I wasn't going to lie to Mr. Jaydee Travis. Take a deep breath. Think. Answer slow.

"A boy I go to school with, a friend, works for him. I've met him. I worked on helping rebuild his house and grocery last summer after the posse burned them."

"He seems an unusual man. Doesn't seem to care much for authority. Interesting, a man who'd stand up for himself like that. Do you like him?"

Mr. Jaydee was asking out of real interest I sensed, not just out of curiosity. I'd been struggling with that. But I had to acknowledge it, because it was a fact, "It's hard not to like him."

That's what I told Mr. Jaydee, Travis, head of the Travis Clan of Golden Pond, Kentucky.

Mr. Travis leaned toward me. "A good judge of character, are you, Owen?"

I didn't try to answer. Just sat as composed as I could while he studied me. "How old are you, boy?" he finally asked.

"Almost sixteen, sir."

"Joe-boy, how old were you when you made the acquaintance of the Major?" The question surprised Joe.

"Sixteen, sir."

"Do you think Owen is old enough? He may not be this way again. Be a pity if he missed the opportunity, don't you think?"

Hesitant, as if unsure what answer would be the right one, "Well," a pause, "Yes sir, a shame," Joe said.

"Then why don't you take him down to the pond before you turn in."

Mr. Jaydee stood up then. Joe was already rising. I sprang up from my seat on the railing. A handshake, a smile I could barely make out in the shadows, "Goodnight, boys."

The night was well advanced. A soft mist was rising off the pond. The moon was down and the stars in command when Joe led me down. The cask was still on the table, and the dipper and the silver cups. Most everyone had left. The muted voices of a few lingering women drifted down from the house.

Joe didn't say anything. He placed two silver cups side by side on the table. Eased the dipper into the cask. Brought it carefully out. Poured the contents equally into the cups. Lifted one cup and handed it to me. Took the other himself. Held it up to the sky. Said, "the Major." Took the cup to his lips and drank it in slowly. Then raised his cup to me and nodded. I understood I was to do the same. "The Major, "I said, and drank.

I had never tasted starlight but surely starlight must taste like that. And there was caramel and clover and grass, raspberry in there somewhere, and oak. And something that touched a little chord that ran a warm chill of cheer all through me.

Damn! What was that? What is this?

Joe watched the expression on my face and smiled. "You've been introduced."

He stepped away, took my cup, placed it with his on the table, and walked me back up to the house.

And it came to me as we walked.

Major James.

I knew that name.

I'd heard it when Yancey talked with Mr. Fallis about Golden Pond whiskey.

Everything coming out of that remote slice of Western Kentucky they called "between the waters" was good. One particular brand was unbelievably good.

Major James.

Nothing topped it. Hard to get. Not much of it was made. All of it went to people the maker had been doing business with for years.

Finding out who the maker was was almost impossible. They were taciturn and suspicious of outsiders down there. Yancey had scored Golden Pond whiskey in his days at Newport, but never Major James. He couldn't make a connect to get Major James.

I bet I could. I bet I now knew people who could make the connect. I bet Mr. Jaydee knew who made Major James.

That nice warm glow I felt wasn't just from the whiskey. Part of it was from knowing I might be able to open the door to Golden Pond for JF if he wanted.

From the Fourth of July until time for me to go home I spent every weekend at Golden Pond with Joe Travis and his family. I remember it as one of the best summers of my life.

I was in an exotic land in the care of benevolent natives who were kind and cheerful and attentive to my comfort and amusement.

The house seemed to be constantly full of cousins and friends and they seemed to be enjoying the hell out of each other. They laughed, they argued, they fought, they teased. Compared to my house, where it was just my mother, my father, and me, it was pandemonium. All those people, all that energy, it felt like I was at a party that just kept going on.

Joe took me exploring all over. We hunted. We fished. We did Saturday night barn dances and played baseball in the big field in town on Sunday afternoons. I helped with the chores and Miss Libby, when she heard me singing one night with Joe, had me sing with the choir at the Golden Pond Baptist and seemed as proud as if I was blood-kin when people came up afterwards.

The land between the waters was unlike any place I'd ever been. It was a small and private kingdom hiding between two rivers and happy in its remoteness—a fifty mile or so finger of land poking north across the western tip of Kentucky from the Tennessee border to the Illinois line, twelve miles across at the widest point, rimmed on the east by the Cumberland River and on the west by the Tennessee. These were mighty rivers that drained a good portion of the upper South. Running parallel as they did in their final rush to the Ohio River and then on to the Mississippi, they created a landlocked peninsula of small farms and oak and hickory forests laced with creeks and ridges and inhabited by people who were sturdy and rugged and sufficient unto themselves.

Most families had been on the land since it was wilderness. They'd cleared it, planted it, harvested its bounty. It was their own private province and outsiders were welcome to keep out ... were encouraged to keep out. Among themselves, the between-the-waters people were a tight knit, protective, supportive community. A clan—not of shared ancestry but of shared values.

Isolation was a major part of its appeal. There was only one hard road in. It ran north-south down the spine of the peninsula. The borders on the east and west were water and could be breached only by boat or ferry. By ferry is how Joe and I made it back from Dawson Springs each weekend ... his old farm truck to the Canton Ferry across the Cumberland. Took over an hour, sometimes three depending on whether the river was up or the ferry operating.

Once inside, hard-packed dirt roads and rocky trails wandered across the countryside, their names known only to those who used them and unmarked as to destination. If you didn't know where you were, or how to get to where you were going from there, you didn't get there.

The creeks were used as much as the roads for transport—by john boat, flat bottom barge, canoe, even pirogues. The spine down the center on which the hard road ran was the highest land in the peninsula. Creeks on the east side ran down into the Cumberland, on the west side out to the Tennessee.

Golden Pond was the biggest town. No more than three hundred people. There was a grocery and a dry goods store, a hardware store and a tinker, the Baptist Church, the Post Office, and the Tennessee House & J.L. Hardin Saloon.

The other towns, Furnace, Turkey Creek, Laura, a few others, were little more than a general store, a church, a post office.

A few families in Golden Pond had generators to provide electricity for their own homes and businesses, but they were very few and night was mostly lighted by lamp light.

No one moved around much after dark—except Joe's brothers Rich and Mark would often leave right after supper and not be back until we were coming downstairs for breakfast. No one seemed to take notice of it or find it unusual. I didn't ask.

The morning I was to leave for home Miss Libby came in from the kitchen carrying a small white earthenware jug.

"This is for your father with our thanks for lending you to us for the summer." Joe, sitting across from me, was smiling, as were Rich and Mark who were at her side.

"This is something our family makes. The recipe is very old. It came with the McFarlanes from Ireland before the Revolution. It is very good."

She set the little jug in front of me, her pride in it showing in her eyes.

Inscribed beneath the finger ring, in bold patriot blue, were the words *Major James*.

Joe drove me to the ferry. We loaded my gear, shook hands. "You come back," he said. I dug in my pack, found it, pulled out my chess set. "You keep this," I said.

I'd developed a real fondness for Joe Travis. My friendship for him wasn't as it was with Lucas. The bond was different. It was more playful, less guarded. There was no cloak of foreboding on Joe's shoulders. No anger in his makeup.

Joe took the chess set, an are-you-sure look in eyes. Then nodded. No thank you need be said. The grin said it.

"The ducks and geese will be moving down the flyway in November. Be the best shooting you ever had. Bring your, dad," he shouted as I stepped up the ferry gangplank.

"Remember to castle," I yelled back.

FORTY
You Won't Believe This, Yancey

Lucas was waiting.

Lucas.

At first I didn't see him. There was a crowd around a car sitting off to the side. Then I saw, sitting at the wheel of the midnight blue Packard Phaeton, Mr. Fallis's car, the convertible, with its top down and its white sidewalls shining, Lucas—preening while people gawked.

"Owen," he yelled. He jumped out of the car and came running up to thump me on the back, grab my duffle, pound me on the shoulder, grin, pound me again and start us moving toward the car. "Damn, it's good to see you." The look on my face stopped him. "It's okay. No one's hurt. No one's sick. Your dad said I could come get you. A surprise. Just wanted to surprise you. Take you home in style."

Then my look of complete amazement caused him to laugh.

"Yeah, I'm your driver, pretty boy. Yancey taught me to drive. How the hell about that?" He was so proud of himself he almost levitated.

I laughed then, too, happy to see him and happy for him. Driving? There weren't many things more spectacular than that.

We threw my bag and sundries in the backseat while the crowd slid away to meet the folk they were waiting for or board the ferry themselves. Lucas backed us around and we climbed up the hill to the hard road, turning heads as the Phaeton roared, and headed home, both of us talking at the same time.

I was back at Canton Ferry hardly a week later. With me were Lucas, Yancey, and Mr. John Richard Fallis.

Waiting to cross.

My little white earthenware jug hadn't gone unnoticed.

Lucas asked what I was cradling so carefully as we rode. I unfolded the burlap cloth Miss Libby had wrapped it in to keep it safe. Showed him. Told him the story. Told him about Joe and the Travises, about my introduction to Major James.

"You know who makes it?"

"I told you. The Travises."

"You're friends with them?" Lucas shook his head, amazed. "Damn." He was pounding the wheel and laughing so hard I thought we'd wind up in a ditch.

"Watch the road."

"You've got to tell Mr. Fallis about this. Got to tell Yancey. Damn."

"Can I say hello to Mom and Dad first?"

Lucas was too excited to want to wait, but he wasn't about to interfere with my mother's plans and I certainly wasn't.

So he fidgeted through my welcome-home supper and sat trying to contain his impatience as I told them about my summer, answered Dad's questions about the work on the park and the land between the rivers and Mom's curiosity about my new friends the Travises and the magic waters of Dawson Springs.

Eventually, the evening began to wind down. Lucas asked if I could come with him. There was a dance at the Y. See friends we hadn't seen all summer.

"Of course," my mother said, "Your friends. Not too late, though. Church tomorrow morning."

Lucas hadn't made it up. There was a dance. And it seemed a very fine way to close out my first night at home all summer.

But we didn't go.

We went to the grocery.

Eleven o'clock.

A Saturday night.

Very little traffic on Wilkinson Street.

The grocery closed and dark.

Lucas let us in with his key. A path of light led back to Mr. Fallis's office in the rear. Yancey was there. At work by the light of a single lamp. He looked up as we entered, surprised, rising from the desk to confront whatever had intruded.

He had that black derby on. At work alone in a deserted building. In his shirtsleeves. At that hour. That derby. Damn. What was it? Some sort of talisman? Some magic charm that protected him, that brought him luck?

He was fully upright by then, glaring, but tension easing as he recognized us.

"Tell him," Lucas said immediately. "Yancey, you won't believe this."

"What the hell are you two doing here? Creeping in like that. I might have shot you." Slowly he lifted his left hand to show the forty-five. He let that sink in.

Yancey sat back down, motioned us to sit.

"Well," he said. "What won't I believe?"

"Owen has friends in Golden Pond. He knows the people who make Major James! They're friends! Tell him, Owen. Tell him."

Yancey turned to me, quizzical, frowning.

"It's true," I said. "I do."

Yancey's eyes widened, his frown deepened, puzzling, examining me with a look of disbelief, then slowly, the frown dissolving into a smile.

"Well, I'll be damned."

I made the call as Mr. Fallis asked me to.

Told Joe Travis that Mr. John Richard Fallis had asked me if I would ask if Mr. J. D. Travis would do him the honor of meeting with him to discuss a business proposal.

Joe's reply was, "Uncle Jaydee? I don't know. He's awfully picky about outsiders."

"Mr. Jaydee knows about Mr. Fallis. He was interested in him when we were talking on the porch that night. He might like to meet him."

"What's it about?"

"Major James, I think."

"Oh hell, Lucas." It seemed I'd asked him to give blood. "He only talks about the Major with friends."

"I'll come along with Mr. Fallis. Make sure he is introduced right. Doesn't get lost. Mr. Jaydee will like him, I bet."

No response.

"I don't want to put you in a spot you don't want to be in, but if you could see your way clear just to asking, I'd be obliged."

A long breath expelled, then, "Oh, what the hell. Okay. But don't be mad at me if he says no." And then a laughing grunt, "You're more trouble than you're worth."

A little under three hundred miles to Golden Pond.

Maximum speed for the Model T was forty-five. Faster in the Phaeton but Mr. Fallis wanted to attract no attention, so we took the Model T and the one-seater Ford roadster.

We could have all gone in the Model T, but if the talk with Mr. J. D. Travis went well, Yancey would stay to work out details and the three of us would come back in the bigger car.

South out of Frankfort to Lawrenceburg we went, just as daylight was breaking, turned west there and followed the road to Bardstown though Elizabethtown to Beaver Dam, nudged a bit further south to Dawson Springs, then to Cadiz and on to the ferry at Canton. Six hours and a bit. I rode with Lucas in the Model T. Mr. Fallis and Yancey were in the roadster.

We changed cars at Beaver Dam. Me to the roadster with Mr. Fallis. He wanted to know all I could tell him about the Travises—the kind of people they were, how they lived, what I thought of them.

I was nervous. I had never talked with Mr. Fallis just the two of us. He drove relaxed, but pushed the roadster as fast as it would go, taking the curves one-handed, shifting up and down for the hills with an easy motion, enjoying the swing and the sway, asking his questions, not interrupting my answers. Listening. He was a very good listener. He took in the countryside as we rolled across it and occasionally glanced to the side to make eye contact with me, but paid attention to the road. He paid attention to the road and he paid attention to me.

I began to relax. Not completely. I never felt fully relaxed in Mr. Fallis's presence. He spun off too much energy. But relaxed enough to get out what I thought might be helpful to him.

I knew I liked the Travises. I knew they were a powerful family. I knew they valued friendship and hard work and family. They were proud of their name and their place in the community and felt the land between the rivers was God's country and not to be mistreated. They did not put up with pretense.

I knew that Mr. J. D. Travis was the patriarch.

My only time with him had been that night on the porch when he decided I should be introduced to the Major. I knew from the way he was deferred to, the respect he was shown, I knew he was head of the family.

"He is a very formal man," I told Mr. Fallis. "That night of the Fourth, he came dressed in a black suit and starched white shirt, wearing a tie. The brothers were in short-sleeve shirts and khakis and jeans. He shed the suit coat before the fireworks started but never loosened the tie. Everyone except the women usually stood when he approached."

"Stern?"

"Not that. He was friendly. They all flocked around him. Stern's not the word. Dignified. That's it. He was very dignified."

JF considered that. Kept his eyes on the road. Said nothing.

"He's heard about you. He said you must be an unusual man to stand up for your family the way you did."

He glanced over at me then. Then back to the road. Only nodded his head. Kept driving.

FORTY-ONE
At Mr. J. D.'s

We made Golden Pond a little before noon.

The meeting was set for two o'clock at Mr. J. D. Travis's home on his farm north of town.

Joe Travis met us at the Tennessee House Hotel. We made introductions. Had lunch there. JF excused himself for the men's room. Returned with his hair carefully combed, a fresh white shirt and a burgundy silk tie, and a linen blazer of navy blue carried casually on his arm.

Dignified. The look.

Without comment he sat back down and finished his coffee. Joe looked around at us wide-eyed, but we continued our conversation as if nothing had changed. Being the smart boy he was, Joe let it pass and picked up where he'd left off, telling us how Golden Pond got its name. Long story. A pond nearby was filled with gold-colored fish when the first settlers arrived. Or a con man from the California gold fields had salted the pond with gold dust and spread nuggets around hoping to convince people the area was loaded and sell off a batch of worthless property he'd acquired, or, I liked this best, a platoon of retreating Confederates, escaping with the remains of the Confederacy's gold and being chased by a Yankee column, jettisoned it all in the pond before the Yankees caught them. The fortune sank and disappeared into the depths. It's still there, giving off a golden hue when the afternoon sun strikes the water just right.

"Aw, come on, Joe," I said.

"That's what they say," he laughed back.

We took the black Model T out to Mr. J. D. Travis's farm, Mr. Fallis and me following Joe in his old truck. Yancey and Owen stayed behind. They weren't invited. I wasn't either. I'd make the introduction and ride back to town with Joe, leaving the Ford there for Mr. Fallis when he finished.

Mr. Fallis didn't seem to want conversation on the ride out. He stayed quiet and I watched the country roll by, occupying myself with imagining the impression Yancey was making in Golden Pond with that black derby cocked on his bald Melungeon head and that gold earring in his ear.

Mr. Jaydee was standing on the porch waiting to greet us when we arrived. Must be a Travis thing, I thought, Miss Libby there waiting when Joe first brought me home, Mr. Jaydee standing there now. How do they know?

He could see us coming a long way. The stately old house sat on an expansive lawn in a grove of oaks. A long lane bordered by fields of corn led us to it. I could see white curtains fluttering in the upstairs windows as the afternoon breezes eased through. We crossed a small wooden bridge over a little creek, then up a small rise to the house. Mr. Jaydee was already walking down the steps from the porch as we pulled up.

Their meeting was like nothing I expected. Mr. Jaydee was warm, welcoming, and smiling. Not the stern, formal, reserved autocrat I thought would be his manner. Mr. Fallis was respectful and deferential in a way I'd not seen before. I couldn't tell whether his reaction to Mr. Jaydee was real or an act. Mr. Fallis had a remarkable capacity for empathy, an uncanny ability to read people. I wasn't sure.

Mr. Jaydee turned to Joe and me. "Thank you for delivering him." Then to Mr. Fallis, "You can find your way back if I let these two go?" Mr. Fallis smiled and nodded yes. "Then, Joe, I suggest you collect Owen and head on back to town. Mr. Fallis and I have some visiting to do."

"Yes, sir, Uncle Jaydee," Joe said and grabbed me by the arm and hurried me to his truck.

"Did you see that? Uncle Jaydee didn't even have on his suit coat. He was in his shirtsleeves with his suspenders showing. Never saw that before. Not with an outsider. Hell's bells and little green apples, what's going on?"

He backed the truck around and headed fast down the lane, shaking his head and muttering.

As we rode away I thought I knew what had happened. I think Mr. Travis already suspected he might like John Richard Fallis and when he met him, he did.

I think he'd done some investigating, talked with some people he knew back in Frankfort, and found John Richard Fallis to be an interesting and worthy man.

Or, and this was possible, he'd decided to present himself as a relaxed old farmer who was no real shakes at making deals. Lord, I thought, here's the King of Craw in a show of humility and the Patriarch of Golden Pond feigning guilelessness. Lordy, lordy, save us all.

Mr. Fallis returned a little after five that afternoon. I'd already thanked Joe and he'd said make sure you come back with your dad for the ducks this fall before he shook hands all around and departed.

Yancey found a table in the back of the saloon next to the Tennessee House. "I'll wait here," he said, and to Lucas, nodding toward me, said, "Take this poor useless boy somewhere and teach him to drive. No point in wasting the time sitting around doing nothing."

Lucas grinned at me. "Well, that ought to be fun," and motioned me to follow as he headed out.

There was a big level field outside of town, bumpy but flat, and nothing around that I could do damage to. By the time Mr. Fallis returned, I could steer well enough and shift through all the gears without making a godawful noise. All but reverse. I hadn't mastered reverse. But oh did I feel mighty.

I could drive!

Hallelujah, praise the lord. I knew how to drive! Sort of.

Mr. Fallis seemed as pleased as I felt when he found us. He took Yancey aside. Talked quietly. Gave him the keys to the roadster and left him standing there. He signaled to Lucas and me to follow him to the Model T.

We made it back to Frankfort just a little after midnight. He drove. Lucas rode up front with him and I climbed in back. We stopped for coffee and a sandwich at Leitchfield and put up the side curtains because it was beginning to rain. Lucas and I switched seats there and I rode the rest of the way up front with Mr. Fallis.

It was dark then and raining and Mr. Fallis was deep in his own thoughts. Lucas and I didn't want to intrude so we kept quiet and slipped into our own thoughts too, hushed by the hum of the tires on the rain-slick road and the swish of the wipers on the windshield.

I'm not exactly sure where we were when Mr. Fallis's voice broke into my dreaming. "Do your folks know where you are?"

Startled, I fumbled for an answer.

"I like your mother. I like your father."

We rode on silently, considering that.

"They wouldn't approve, would they?"

I could hear Lucas stir in the back seat. Sit up.

I answered with the truth. "No, sir, they wouldn't."

He drove on, not replying.

Eventually the question came.

"Why are you helping me? Yancey has a reason. Lucas has a reason. I've done nothing for you. Why do you help me?"

I didn't know the answer to that question. I struggled for something to say. Could find nothing to say.

Out of the darkness and the quiet behind us came Lucas's voice. "Because you're John Fallis."

FORTY-TWO
Delivery Boy

That summer weaned me.

Being away that long with only myself to rely on, living among strangers whose only interest in me was that I do the work assigned me, that weaned me.

There was a swagger in my stride when I came back (lord, I hope it wasn't a strut) and I was primed with self-confidence.

Lucas was way ahead of me in this.

He'd spent the summer playing baseball and delivering hooch.

At the time, JF was the biggest bootlegger in the county. He had his sights set on becoming the biggest in the Bluegrass. The only things standing in his way were the Feds, who wanted to jail him, and the wolves frothing at the edge of the kingdom. JF had to outfox the former and out-snarl the latter. He needed a band of dedicated partisans to accomplish this. Lucas had his hand up.

Lucas is a clean-cut, good-looking kid. Polite. Serious. No reason to be suspicious of him in any way. He's to be the delivery boy for the Fallis Grocery. But first he had to learn to drive. Yancey taught him—smooth with the clutch, firm with the steering, take the curves clean and be watchful for the unexpected.

Then he had to work at becoming so ubiquitous that no one noticed his meanderings. Make the home deliveries. Get the orders to the restaurants and hotel dining rooms. Keep the kitchens at the jail and the hospital stocked. Run all over town so that people get used to seeing the kid in the grocery truck making his stops and take no notice of it.

Then he had to learn the routes to get the booze to thirsty clients without being followed, without being stopped, without being noticed at all.

We eased back into into our school selves easily enough, but couldn't help feeling superior to our classmates. Even the seniors. We tried not to let that show. This was more difficult for me than for Lucas. He was incurably modest.

We made the varsity in football. Only three of us sophomores did. I repeated as class president and Lucas was elected to the student council. Lucas had less time for the social events now. His new "responsibilities" took precedence. We held on to our weekly "study" sessions, but began to spend less time with each other.

We had many similar interests, but also many that had no particular appeal to the other. So naturally we began to develop a circle of friends who had these other interests.

Or I did.

Lucas never mentioned any friends. I never met any. Other than the few we shared at school—teammates, boys we sang with or liked from clubs we were in, I'm not sure Lucas had any friends our age.

Nevertheless, he was popular. Especially with the girls.

By the end of the year JF was on his way to becoming the dominant supplier of contraband spirits to the better establishments of the Inner Bluegrass. Major James was the ticket. JF had exclusive access to it and everyone wanted it.

How he managed to be the only man in the Bluegrass that the Travises would do business with he never explained. Maybe it was with him and Mr. J. D. Travis as it was with Lucas and me—chemistry.

People called this business bootlegging and labeled the product moonshine.

The word bootlegging no more fit JF's skillfully executed process of collecting and delivering his much in demand elixir than the word crude fits an act of finesse.

And moonshine? An insult to the whiskey his oak casks contained.

The high-class saloons and the member clubs, they all lined up for it. And the country clubs and the hotels and the better restaurants.

And the American Legion and the VFW posts.

And the Loyal Order of Elks and the Independent Order of Odd Men. The Moose. The Woodmen. The Masons. Even the Governor's Mansion had its standing order for Major James.

All across the Inner Bluegrass, John Fallis and his Golden Pond whiskey was the ticket.

Which made him a highly successful diversified businessman—the grocery, his riverboats, now this.

Which wasn't new.

JF had been in the business of supplying spirits to the thirsty since shortly after Yancey came to work for him. This was before Prohibition, before the money spigot opened.

JF had his own still. He made the clear potent liquor the working class favored and could afford. He made it, sold it, and didn't bristle at the term bootlegger unless someone said it to his face—and then ... well, he was John Richard Fallis.

Moonshine's appeal was price and potency. It was cheaper than the output the legal distilleries sold and its kick much stronger. They offered hundred proof whiskey. JF's stuff was one hundred twenty proof minimum—sixty percent pure alcohol. Some batches went as high as one hundred fifty proof. That would take your breath and cross your eyes. Best tone it down with water or a glass of ginger ale or you'd fall down flat and lose your hair.

Moonshine made him plenty even then, before Prohibition.

With Prohibition, with the distilleries shut down and supply dried up—my god, that just made everybody thirstier and price be damned.

JF kept his local still going. It was easy money and his clientele was faithful. But his concentration now was Major James and Golden Pond.

When Lucas finally got around to telling me exactly what his job was at the grocery I was floored. It could get him arrested. I couldn't believe that Mr. Fallis would use him like that.

Prohibition was a Federal thing. The Feds had their own cops. They were tough. They could show up anytime anywhere. If they got you, it was jail or a big fine, or maybe both. And it was a Federal judge who handed down the sentence, not a local judge that JF might be able to influence.

I wasn't surprised Lucas would do it. I think he'd do almost anything Mr. Fallis asked, but to run a risk like that, to take a chance on being arrested by the Feds. Why would JF let him do that?

"Damn, Lucas," I said, "you realize what you're doing?"

A snort and a laugh. "Abso-damn-lutely. It's a game. A big game. Outsmart the lawmen. Get in and get out without getting caught. Win the prize."

"That's crazy. The risk..."

"The city cops don't care. Busting bootleggers isn't their problem. It's the Feds and they're spread thin. The risk? That's a pure rush. Lord, I love it. Love it."

The way he said it, with glee in his voice and a glint in his eyes, took away any counter I could mount.

"What about school?"

"I only make runs to deliver the Major. At night. No problem. Want to come?"

"You're kidding."

"Ride Shotgun."

"Now, I know you're kidding."

Lucas stood there with his hands on his hips looking eager and cocky. He was in the game and he was basking in the light of JF's approval.

I began to realize then that in a very fundamental way Lucas and I were on different paths. And I began to wonder to what uses JF was willing to put his followers.

FORTY-THREE
Write Your Check. Pack Your Bag

Four months later, John Richard Fallis is in jail.

The Kentucky State Court of Appeals upholds the Franklin Circuit Court verdict of six months and a two hundred fifty dollar fine for the shooting of Patrolman Gerald Scott. "The verdict was inadequate to the crime," Judge Turner, who writes the opinion, notes.

Attorney Morgan is outraged. "Damned sanctimonious twit. John is the victim here. His home burned down. His business destroyed. His infant son dead and his eldest son shot. Outrageous." Says as much to the press, omitting the "damned sanctimonious twit."

"That's it, though. No other steps to take. Write the check. Pack your bag."

There are things Leland Morgan can do, though. And he goes about doing them. He gets JF assigned to the county jail, not the city. Too easy for the city police to get at him in the city jail.

And he starts immediately working to get JF's sentence reduced.

Still, it's jail for JF.

Two weeks to get his affairs in order. Report on Monday, the fifth day of February. A full moon that night. The Hunger Moon. The heaviest snows fall in February. Hunting is difficult and game scarce. Not a good omen, Yancey says. JF doesn't care.

He reports to the county jail on Monday morning as ordered. Is treated like a guest, ushered to a corner cell on the first floor with a nice window, barred, but looking out to a hayfield and the perimeter barbed wire fence and, further on, a ridge line of cedars and pines.

He makes himself comfortable.

The cell door is left unlocked.

Yancey and Lucas and I visited him that afternoon.

I have a favored status now. I proved myself in the Big Shoot-Out. More important, I opened the door to Golden Pond. I'm golden. Yancey called me "friend," remember, and Lucas has my back and likes me, and JF appreciates that I seem to be on his side when there is no apparent reason that I should be and is curious about that and is appreciative of that. They know and trust me. I'm not in the inner circle, but I'm comfortably on the outer edge of the inner circle.

JF is sitting in a lounge chair and his cell door is wide open. It's a big cell, obviously meant for two but has been cleared out to give JF room. There's a bed, a desk with a lamp, a radio, another chair, a chest. He's dressed in slacks and a navy blue cashmere sweater.

Yancey: "This is jail?"

"Best Lee Morgan could arrange," JF smiles.

"Think you can manage in all this squalor?"

"Do the best I can," he laughs.

He waves us in. Lucas and I take seats on the bed. Yancey pulls up the other chair in front of JF.

Yancey: "Six months is a long time. Lots can happen."

JF: "It won't be that long."

Yancey: "Gus Brewer's gonna get ambitious with you gone."

JF: "His stuff is second rate. He won't be dumb enough to try muscle."

Yancey: "If he does?"

JF: "We've covered this. You've got the grocery and the business. Callahan has the Riverman and the boats. Make sure that word gets around. If anyone gets pushy, knock 'em down."

Yancey: "Don't get to liking it in here. If you're gone too long, the natives will get restless."

Afterwards, walking back, I asked Yancey, "Gus Brewer? He was the guy on the porch the night of the Big Shoot-Out, the one who walked up and said something through the door to JF?"

"Has the body shop," Lucas said, "and a bar in Craw called the same thing. Wants to be JF. Bad news."

"Might be. Hell, probably will be," Yancey said. "He's got a still. Makes decent enough hooch but's not moving much of it. He's an arrogant sonofabitch with a whale-size ego. Smart, though. Tough."

FORTY-FOUR
Out And In Again

Five weeks and one day later, John Richard Fallis was out.

There was an attempted jail break.

He stopped it.

Single-handed.

The Sheriff was immensely grateful. The President of the Chamber of Commerce issued a formal letter of appreciation "for this valiant act which kept a band of convicted criminals from swarming our streets." Even the Mayor, grudgingly, for he was no fan of John Richard Fallis, gave a statement to the press thanking Mr. Fallis for his act. This wasn't spontaneous. Leland Morgan put his friend at the State Journal up to asking the question.

I'm not entirely certain that Morgan and JF didn't orchestrate the whole affair.

With JF's contacts inside and a little cash, talking the inmates into staging a mock break-out shouldn't have been too hard to do.

There probably wasn't a man in that jail who didn't know who John Fallis was or didn't know his reputation. JF had friends in there who owed him. If there was the understanding that no one would get hurt and a few sentences reduced—not too difficult to organize at all.

And it went so smoothly.

Friday morning just after daylight. Town still asleep. Cell doors being opened to let the inmates out for breakfast. Jump the guards, take their keys, shove them in the cells and rush the main gate.

JF is standing there.

Legs spread.

Arms raised.

Stop!

By the time the jailer rushed up with the rest of the guards, JF had it all under control, had talked them out of it, had talked them down. Nobody hurt. Nobody gone. One man against the mob. Save the town from the criminal hoard. An act of heroism pure and simple.

Or a brilliant piece of theatre, planned, organized, and performed to perfection.

I had great admiration for the talents of Mr. John Richard Fallis and Mr. Leland Morgan, and I confess, even then, a tendency to cynicism. The Jail-Break Put-Down may have been exactly as it appeared. I have no information to the contrary—but I wouldn't be surprised.

Whether it was or wasn't, this was the deed that led to JF's early release. Letters and calls began to pour in to the court almost immediately citing JF's brave and responsible act and extolling his many virtues. They all urged the court, in light of his contribution to the community's protection, to show compassion and commute JF's sentence to time served--enough letters from enough persons of consequence on Lee Morgan's contact list that the Judge gave in.

JF walked out at high noon on a cold, rainy Monday the first week of March. Yancey was waiting. It reminded him of that day at the prison, Yancey told us later, that day when he got out and JF came to get him. Not the same, but it reminded him. I never suspected Yancey of being sentimental.

Nine months later, John Richard Fallis was back in jail.

The Feds descended.

A raid on his still in the neat little house with the split-rail fence sitting back on the river bank on the other side of Hemp Factory Hill.

CONCERNING THE MATTER OF THE KING OF CRAW

A big still, a two hundred thirty gallon still that would produce eighteen hundred pints of shine a run. At the usual price of two dollars a pint, that would get you thirty-six hundred bucks a run.

If you did three runs a week (a leisurely pace) that's ten thousand eight hundred dollars ... a week. Taking it easy.

JF was having coffee and talking with the two still men when the Federal agents arrived. Six of them. Two through the front, smashing the door. Two through the back, same way. And two lurking outside in case anyone ran. All with sawed-off shotguns. It was ten o'clock in the morning. A Thursday.

This was serious stuff.

And very bad luck.

If JF hadn't been there no charge would have been possible.

JF pleaded guilty. What else was there to do? Explained to the Judge he was just trying to make a little money to help pay his bills, but the Judge wasn't sympathetic.

The Federal agents were out of the Lexington office. No one had seen them before. They materialized unnoticed. City Patrolman Gerald Scott was with them. The Scott of the night of the Big Shoot-Out. Patrolman Scott took no part in the raid. He stood off to the side, arms folded, silent and smiling

The Feds busted up the still and poured the booze down the gutter, handcuffed JF and hustled him off. He was released on bail, arraigned, got the six months the sentencing guidelines called for.

Any chance JF could get a reduced sentence, walk out early? Not a snowball's in hell. Waltzing a client out of a Federal sentence wasn't being done just then. Lee Morgan did, though, manage to get the one-thousand-dollar fine relieved. More important, he got JF committed to the Franklin County Jail (he had just been there, had leverage there). JF could have been sent to the big Fayette County Jail outside Lexington. He would have been fresh meat there.

Six months to be served in his home town jail. Given the circumstance, thank you lord and don't go way.

Lucas and I were in school when the raid was made. We didn't learn of it until late in the day on our way home.

"Someone fingered him. Someone was watching him. Someone made the call to the Feds to tell them he was there," Lucas said.

"Gus Brewer's my bet," said Yancey,

"Scott was there."

Yancey shook his head, scowling.

"The city cops aren't usually in on these busts. The Feds don't trust them not to tip off the target if the price is right."

"What do we do," said Lucas, angry, steaming.

"We deal with it," said Yancey.

I kept quiet while they fumed. Turned up the collar on my jacket. It was getting cold there on the corner by the bridge where Yancey caught up with us. Be dark soon. Hard frost forecast. JF really in jail for six months? The throne vacant. The King out of action. Deal with that.

FORTY-FIVE
Abso-damn-lutley

Lucas and I headed for Golden Pond.

The Travises had to be told. They had to know there would be no problems, no interruptions, no complications in their arrangement with John Richard Fallis.

We carried a letter from JF to Mr. J. D. Travis to that effect—to be delivered into his hands. And we were to carry back any message Mr. Travis might wish to be delivered to Mr. Fallis.

We could drive down on Friday, have Saturday and Sunday there, and be back on Monday. Miss just two days of school.

My cover was the duck hunting invitation Joe Travis had given me when I left Golden Pond. Dad couldn't get away. I knew he couldn't before I put the trip together. So Lucas was my partner. I made no reference to JF or any of that in explaining the trip to my parents.

Both he and my mother continued to be very fond of Lucas, and in all honesty, my dad still had a liking for JF that he didn't understand but grudgingly accepted. But he was uneasy with my presence on the periphery of the Fallis world.

Anyway, I rationalized, bootlegging was an almost respectable crime. Only the prudes seemed to care. To most others it was a needed and acceptable service—not the violence that rapidly became associated with it after

Prohibition came in, but the practice itself. Some of the best people were involved. Bootlegging even carried a certain adventuresome panache.

Even so, my parents were very concerned that Lucas not in any way be involved with JF's bootlegging activities and hopeful that his association with me, and us, would help point him in a better direction.

We left before daylight, made Golden Pond just before dark. I drove part of the way. Joe Travis met us at the Tennessee House Hotel where I had planned to stay. He said his mother wouldn't hear of it. "She's expecting you for supper. Your beds are ready and made-up."

Miss Libby was waiting on the porch when we arrived. She must have seen our headlights turning into the lane. I never visited a Travis that someone wasn't standing on the porch to welcome me or holding open the door. It was as if they were truly eager to see you, really pleased to have your company. No need to knock or ring a bell. They were watching for you.

She wrapped me in a big hug and, to his consternation, took Lucas's hand and kissed him on the check. He blushed. Didn't know what to say, said "Thank you, ma'am." We all laughed, even him, and we were safely inside the cocoon of Libby Travis's benignity. Lucas was in danger of falling in love, too.

Joe Travis understood when I told him the real reason for my visit. "Uncle Jaydee is in Paducah. He won't be back until tomorrow night. I'll see if we can see him Sunday after church. We can hunt tomorrow. Ducks early. Quail in the afternoon. Your friend Lucas ever hunted ducks?"

He hadn't. He was a city boy. He'd hunted rabbits and squirrels on Fort Hill. Occasionally. More for food than sport. Was a good shot. Took the squirrels with a twenty-two, the cottontails with an old four-ten shotgun Yancey had. No ducks. No quail. The only other shotgun he'd handled was a sawed-off twelve gauge and he wasn't swinging on a mallard. Wing shooting. Fast moving targets, small and evasive. No, he hadn't done that.

"Will he be okay? Don't want to get my head blown off."

"We better work with him some."

My duck hunting had been confined to Colorado, which is on the outer fringe of the Pacific Flyway. I'd had good shooting but nothing to compare with what I expected here in the heart of the Mississippi Flyway, the richest and most productive in the country.

The flyways, these two and the Atlantic which runs down the Eastern Seaboard, are the roads in the sky that the waterfowl of the North American continent travel to get from their breeding grounds in the northern tier of American states and the lower third of Canada to their summer homes in Mexico and Central and South America.

Just ahead of winter they rise to the skies above these flyways and head south -- mallards and teal and canvasbacks and pintails, snow geese and majestic Canadas.

As they come down to feed or rest on their way, we hunt them.

In the beginning for food.

Now mainly for sport.

I'm not sure how I feel about this.

I forget about it entirely when a set of mallards cup their wings and start splashing in among the decoys and I swing on the target I hope to drop.

There is the excitement and it is so unabashedly atavistic.

The sapiens genes. They are in our blood.

We worked Lucas for an hour with clay pigeons in the meadow by the pond. Twenty-five birds. He didn't break a single one. Joe very carefully showed him how to bring the gun to his shoulder, find the bird and swing the barrel in tempo with its flight, judge the speed, and swing just ahead so that when you squeeze the trigger the shot arrives where the bird will be. A graceful, fluid motion. A matter of timing and reflex.

It was beyond Lucas. He was either shooting behind or shooting ahead. Too eager. No fluidity. No grace. Not an easy thing to do and it was unfair to expect him to get proficient in a single session. He took it in his stride. Not embarrassed. Not defensive. "I'll get it," he said.

We all three decided he should observe that morning. Not a chance he'd down a bird and a halfway fair chance he might get one of us in his excitement.

We limited out and were back at Miss Libby's just after twelve.

The shooting had been fantastic. We worked from a blind on a slough just off the river, mallards eyeing the decoys and peeling off to plummet down as Joe's calling lured them in. His call was so natural I couldn't distinguish it from the sound the real birds were making. Food here. It's safe. Come get it. Seductive. Convincing.

"Did you like it, Lucas," she asked as we shed our jackets and washed up outside. "Never saw anything like it, ma'am. Joe seemed to be talking directly with those ducks."

"Did he get you get some good shots?"

"I watched."

"Joseph Travis...," she said, turning, frowning.

"It's alright, ma'am," Lucas said hurriedly. "They were afraid I might hit them rather than the ducks."

"Joseph?"

"He'll get it right, Mom ... before he gets us. We'll be sure of that."

Lucas got no better.

We hunted the edge of plowed fields and down the fence rows expecting to find the birds in the grass and brambles.

We walked three abreast, about twenty yards apart, Joe on the left, me in the middle, Lucas on the right flank. The dogs ranged ahead and to the sides. If a bird flushed left, Joe took the shot. In front, it was mine. To the right, Lucas's. The rule was absolute. You took only your shots in your sector. You never swung in another man's direction or on another man's bird. Had nothing to do with sportsmanship or ego. Had to do with survival. Swing excitedly out of your sector on a fast moving bird and you're likely put a load of birdshot in your partner's brain. We thought it safest to place Lucas on the right.

We'd been flushing singles. Lucas had a shot or two. Missed, but was getting comfortable with the discipline.

Then we came upon on a covey. Our first. In the corner of the field. The dogs froze on point. We approached slowly. Carefully. We knew where the birds were. Knew they'd flush. Lucas had no experience with this. When a covey of quail flushes, it's like an explosion. It's loud. The birds rocket out in every direction. Although you know it's coming, the sound and the speed of it rocks you. Even the most accomplished wing shots have to compose themselves.

When this covey flushed, one bird came up directly in front of Lucas. He swung on it. It tacked left. He swung with it. Toward me. And still swinging, squeezed off the shot.

Pellets rained down on my head. The brim of my cap kept them out of my eyes, but one had enough force to lodge in my temple.

Stung me. Stunned me. I dropped to my knee, hand to my head but still with a grip on the gun.

Lucas stood frozen, then yelled and rushed to me.

That brought Joe running. He'd been concentrating on his own bird and hadn't noticed.

"I'm okay," I said. "I'm okay."

"Like hell you are. Stay down and let me see."

He took my gun, cleared the chamber and the magazine, laid it on the grass and took out a bandana to wipe the blood away so he could see the wound.

A scowl as he tilted my head. Silence as he inspected the wound. Lucas breathed heavily in the background.

"Oh, hell, you'll live," Joe laughed. "The BB didn't have a chance against your thick skull. It's in just deep enough that I can't pry it out with my finger. Might be able with my knife but that's sure to scar. How do you feel?"

I was starting to stand. Lucas rushed over to help me.

"I'm fine. Not hurt." I truly was fine. I wasn't trying to be macho.

"Want to keep going?"

"No," Lucas yelled. "Get him to a doctor."

Joe ignored him. "Owen?"

I knew then I must be all right. Joe Travis would not continue the hunt if he thought I needed attention. A test then, I thought. He's testing to see how tough I am. Travis tough? Or maybe how dumb.

"Abso-damn-lutely, I said."

He grinned.

We cleaned me up at the creek, dipping Joe's bandana in the clear, cold water to wash the blood from my forehead and cheek. There was a spot of it on my shirt collar. "Mom will get it out. Don't worry."

He cut a little patch from the bandana, pasted it over the small wound with a piece of tape he used to fix punctures in his wading boots, then turned to Lucas.

"That was first time you'd seen a covey flush, right? First time you'd seen so many birds flying is so many directions making so much noise you thought the sky was ripping, right?"

Lucas looked ready to fall on his sword if he'd had one and that sort of thing was done anymore. He waited.

"You got excited. You made a mistake."

Lucas nodded.

Joe extended his hand, encouraging.

"You won't make that one again."

Sheepishly, Lucas took it.

FORTY-SIX
With My Life

Mr. J. D. Travis saw us after church on Sunday.

We'd gone of course.

If you were at Mrs. Elizabeth Travis's, you went to church on Sunday.

Miss Libby had scolded Joe for keeping us out hunting rather than bringing me immediately back to her to be taken care of. "What will his mother think of us!" Eased the pellet out with a small pair of tweezers, mercurochromed me, put a proper little bandage over the spot, made me a hot toddy to ease the pain, of which there was none, but I took the toddy anyway. By morning, a small scab was forming, hardly noticeable. I was deemed presentable.

I'd come prepared, had a jacket and tie and had warned Lucas. When he came down that morning he was dressed in a blue blazer, English tan slacks, crisp white shirt, wine red tie and a perfect Windsor. His shoes were shined. JF must have advised him.

Miss Libby was pleased with us all.

Mr. J. D. Travis was waiting for us in his study in his home in that big grove of oaks back the long lane outside of town. I remembered the way.

He was cordial but formal.

Still in his Sunday church clothes. Jacket on. Tie knotted.

There was a fire in the grate. Wood. Not coal. Nice flame. Good smell. Oak, I thought. Warming the room and brightening it. It was a cold afternoon. Scudding clouds. Rain on the way.

I reintroduced myself but it wasn't necessary. Mr. Travis remembered me. Remembered that night on the porch and the fireworks and my introduction to Major James.

As I began to introduce Lucas, he interrupted, speaking directly to Lucas. "You are Owen's friend. The boy who works with Mr. Fallis. Mr. Fallis's apprentice. I am pleased to meet you. You must know him very well."

I explained why we were there—to deliver the letter by hand as JF had wanted and to carry back any message he might want us to give to Mr. Fallis.

He took the envelope. Inspected the address—in Mr. Fallis's cursive, his sixth-grader's cursive, not elegant, but bold. He studied it a moment, then laid it aside unopened.

"Mr. Fallis seems to have himself in a predicament," he said. "He seems to have a knack for attracting them."

He didn't say this unkindly or accusingly. There was a half smile on his face as if he was amused by the excitements in JF's life.

It was an observation, not a question. He didn't expect a response from us.

"You boys know Mr. Fallis well. Do you like him?"

"Yes, sir," we both said immediately.

"He's fair. Treats you well, treats you with respect?"

Heads nodding, looking to each other in agreement, "Yes, sir. Always."

He turned his eyes away from us to gaze out the window. Thinking. When he turned back, he asked, "Do you trust him?"

The response from Lucas was immediate.

"With my life."

Conviction in his voice. Devotion. No need to think about it.

Mr. Travis turned to me. "Owen?"

Did I trust John Richard Fallis?

To keep his word.

Yes.

To look out for his own.

Absolutely.

To be loyal.

Without question.

With my life?

Ah, well. Only Lucas would say that.

Could he trust JF? That's what he was asking.

I didn't answer right away. I let Mr. Travis see I was thinking about it.

Come hell or high water, JF would keep his word. It would be a matter of honor with him. A matter of ego.

"Yes, sir. You can trust Mr. Fallis."

FORTY-SEVEN
Bring 'Em On

Miss Libby sent us home with a dozen dressed quail ready for the pan and a note to my mother apologizing for the accident and reassuring her I was alright and if there was any scar it would be small and not mar my handsome face.

We reported back to JF in his cell in the Franklin County Jail, the same corner cell as before, as comfortably outfitted as before.

He had us repeat the entire conversation. Repeat Mr. Travis's questions. Repeat our answers. He looked as if he might tear up at Lucas's "with my life" response, nodded approval to me at my "you can trust Mr. Fallis" answer.

"Appreciate it, boys, I appreciate it." He truly did. It was apparent in his voice and eyes. What we'd done was little enough. A long drive. A small service performed. Done because he asked us to. That was important to JF. That he be cared about.

JF's time in jail was like a not uncomfortable leave of absence from the pressures of his world.

His cell was well-lighted and agreeable. The door was never locked. He came and went as he pleased. There were no impediments to visitors. He wore his regular clothes and drew no work assignments, though often he'd join a work crew just to get the exercise or the change of scenery.

The food could have been a better but women kept bringing him delicacies and he often dined with the jailer in his home, which was on the jail property.

JF's absence from the scene had not as yet emboldened Gus Brewer to make a play. Patrolman Scott made his daily drive-bys but spooked no one. And JF's letter to Mr. J. D. Travis apparently had the desired effect. There was no interruption in the supply of Major James. The businesses were running smoothly. Yancey came twice daily to report and to make plans. Lucas came with him at night.

The other inmates didn't resent JF. They could have. Might have. But his reputation and his manner disarmed them. Many were already friends. Men he'd helped—some money when they were broke, a doctor for a sick wife. They owed him.

He was attacked once.

A guy nobody knew who was brought in just before midnight by the city police. Next morning, breakfast line, rushes up and shoves aside the man in front of JF, whirls, has a knife in his hand, and, as the stumbling inmate's breakfast tray clatters on the concrete floor, yells at JF, "You sonofabitch," and starts at him.

The room is momentarily petrified. Those closest overcome their surprise and hurriedly back away as the guy with the knife closes in on JF.

Instead of falling back, JF instantly steps forward. The attacker starts a backhand slash. JF blocks it with his left arm. Swings his own tray hard into the attacker's face. Follows that with a swift hard kick to the balls. Breaks the guy's nose with the tray. Drops him down with the kick.

It's over.

JF looks pleased. Someone's just made an attempt on his life and he's grinning.

Bring 'em on.

Afterwards, when we puzzled on why a stranger would come at JF with killing intent, Yancey and Lucas thought the cops were behind it—Patrolman Scott most probably, with Gus Brewer in it somewhere. Had to be.

No one knew the man. None of the inmates had seen him before—a hulking Mick with the kind of scars on his left arm that knife fighters get. JF didn't know him.

The guy is arrested by the city cops but winds up in the county jail. Scott is the arresting officer. City cops take their arrests to the city jail, not the county.

And the knife. A fixed blade. A fighting knife. How did he get that in? No one searched him when he was admitted?

Had to be the cops. Had to be Scott.

JF didn't angst about it. He knew the police were his enemies. He knew there would be Armageddon one day.

At Christmas, Lee Morgan managed to get JF a two-day parole. On Christmas Eve JF held court at the grocery as he always did, shaking hands, taking kisses and hugs, passing out candy to the kids.

JF's policies hadn't changed while he was in jail. Would never change. Get what you need. Pay when you can. That he was in jail meant nothing to people crowding the grocery. They loved him. Damn Prohibition anyway. It had closed down the distilleries and put people out of work.

JF made his runs that afternoon.

To the sick and the lame, to the poor souls too broke to buy food and coal, to the few too proud to ask for a handout, he and Yancey made their deliveries. It was a very cold day, rain turning to sleet, desperate in the alleys of Craw, miserable in the shanties.

He didn't forget them.

JF got out of jail on Saturday the thirty-first day of May. Spring was on the edge of summer.

He was released at eight a.m.—peonies blooming, robins chirping, feathery cirrus floating in a sky that is indigo blue.

Yancey and Lucas were there. No blare of trumpets. No ceremony. Just out the door, a big, deep breath and a slow look around.

"Damn, it's a pretty day."

Laughing, he shook Yancey's hand, pounded Lucas on the shoulder.

"Take me home."

And off they went.

The happiness of the homecoming was short-lived.

FORTY-EIGHT
Just A Poor Orphan Boy

Women.

There was Annie, his wife.

And Anna Mae, his paramour.

And Susan, of Susan's Place on the river.

There was Ida Howard, handsome, classy Ida, the Queen of the Madams. And high society matrons and righteous church ladies. And casual encounters in the interludes.

JF's appeal to women, and his appetite for the most appealing of them, bordered on boundless.

Which Annie found not endearing.

They'd met when she was twelve. He was singing in the choir at a Salvation Army service and she was sitting beside her mother in the congregation when he spotted her. He kept his eyes on her the whole time. She was taken with his sassy looks. He with her shy smile when their glances met.

He followed them home that night, to the home of Mr. and Mrs. Jackson Crain in Woodford County miles away, and was back the next day, hanging around, hoping she'd come out.

She saw him from the window, was too well-raised to go outside to be in the presence of a boy she didn't know, but kept glancing to see if he was there.

He was. And then after a while, he wasn't. She rushed out to see where he'd gone and found him hiding behind a tree. He ran toward her. She ran away. Toward the house, frightened, to her room, slid in under her bed.

He was close on her heels and slid in right after her.

Her mother, catching all the commotion, startled, ran in, yanked him out by his feet and started whacking him.

"Who are you? What are you doing?"

"I wanted to kiss her and she wouldn't let me."

As angry as she was, Mrs. Crain almost laughed.

"You're crazy, boy."

"No ma'am," JF said. "I'm just a poor orphan boy and I'm hungry and lonesome."

He wasn't an orphan and he wasn't hungry but even then he was fast with a story and convincing when he told it. She believed it. Annie's big brother, who'd come flying to help, believed it, too.

Mrs. Craine melted, told him, poor boy, you're welcome here anytime, there's food here anytime you're hungry. You just come to us if you're lonesome.

Annie didn't believe it. She'd noted the devilish glint in his eyes while he was spinning his story. She liked that. He was interesting. He was exciting. He was funny.

He kept coming around.

They were married four years later. She was almost sixteen. JF was eighteen at the time and working at the Hemp Mill.

She was loyal. She worked beside him. She put up with his temper which was sometimes very bad but never toward her. She put up with his philandering. And his sins. And prayed for him.

She was a very devout woman. She wanted him to walk with God and he tried...hard. But he couldn't walk the walk the way she knew it had to be. There were too many distractions. She prayed for him anyway.

She loved him.

He loved her.

Less than a month after he came home from jail she kicked him out.

Anna Mae Blackwell was probably the reason.

Or Ida Howard.

Anna Mae was the most beautiful woman in town. Many thought so. Heads turned when she walked by. She was sweet-natured and soft-voiced and JF's affair with her was no secret. Nor was his with Ida Howard, though that was some time ago. He and Ida were just special friends now. Yancey said that with a smile that made me wonder what he meant by special.

Or maybe it was just that Annie finally tired of JF's carrying on. Lord knows she had reason, Yancey said. Not all his fault. Women were just naturally attracted to him and denying himself his pleasures wasn't in his nature.

JF moved out and into an apartment over a restaurant he owned on the corner of Washington and Clinton near the Old State House. Shortly after that Anna Mae moved in. She was divorced by then from J. D. Blackwell, who had been a friend of JF. That's how JF and Anna Mae met. Through J. D. Blackwell, JF's friend.

JF picked up the reins again. The Kingdom was in hand.

That summer I began working for Mr. Leland Morgan. I had decided I wanted to learn to play the game he played and he seemed to think I might have talent for it.

The plan was that I'd work in his office during the summers getting experience, get my undergraduate degree just up the road at the University of Kentucky in Lexington, his alma mater, then enter law school there.

Lucas had no interest in university. He had no interest in becoming a lawyer or an accountant or a business executive. He had no interest in any of the respectable occupations. Lucas thought most of the people in them were phonies. He wasn't about to become one.

"What do you want to be, then," I asked.

"Me," he said. "Just me."

I had no idea what that meant. I was already me. Wasn't Lucas already Lucas?

FORTY-NINE
Birds And Bees And Janie Watts

That fall Lucas and I became seniors, moved to the front row seats in the auditorium for assembly, lead the processions, basked in our glories.

We were co-captains of the football team. I ran what I thought was a brilliant campaign for president of the senior class but Tubby Boy beat me. He had evolved from the fat bully of our freshman year into the Svengali of the fashionable set. He and his minions worked at getting him votes. I let my ego mislead me. I thought my winning personality would do. "Pride goeth before destruction and a haughty spirit before a fall." Proverbs 16:18.

Point taken.

Lucas kept his school work up. He remained cynically popular (I say cynically because he had no real regard for the opinion of most of his peers but was happy to have their attention and, in the case of most of their girls, their interest.) He agreed to serve again on the Student Council, but wasn't around for much else.

His grades were much better than mine. He was more disciplined and more focused than me. He could have qualified for admission to any school around— UK, Transylvania, Centre, Georgetown—gotten a football scholarship, even an academic.

He wasn't interested.

"What a waste," my father said.

"What will he do? Surely not keep working down there," my mother said. "Surely he will get out of there. We'll help him, won't we, Ed?"

We invited him to supper one night expressly to make the suggestion. They tried to make it subtly with no hint of disapproval of Mr. Fallis, no scent of charity.

Lucas was polite and appreciative.

"We want you to do well, Lucas, to be happy and safe," my mother said.

"I know, ma'am. Thank you. Don't worry. I will be."

He said it with such certainty that I believed he believed it.

He wasn't a boy stocking shelves anymore, he was a player who was trusted and counted on. He was in a man's game, running risks. He was needed and respected. His self-esteem and his pride soared. I'd never seen him happier.

Until Janie Watts missed her period.

At our usual Mom-thinks-I'm-studying session in Mr. Fallis's office at the grocery, he told me.

Janie Watts.

Everyone knew Janie. She was the class of the class. She was pretty. She was sweet. She was nice to everyone. An honor student, the purest soprano you ever heard, a volunteer at the hospital and Homecoming Queen. Everyone liked Janie, all but the few girls who were jealous.

Janie Watts.

Missed her period.

Jesus H. Christ and save the apples!

We were all making our first clumsy tries at sex then. There was a lot of excited fumbling around and heavy breathing, but none of us knew much about it. There was no birds-and bees discussion in my house. There wasn't in any of the families that I knew of. What we knew was told us by the older boys. We knew we couldn't believe all of that. There was too much boasting and bragging involved.

We knew what missing a period meant, but we weren't in much danger. The girls we dated were the girls of our uptown world. Nice girls didn't go all the way.

Janie Watts?

Aw, Lucas. Not Janie.

A baby?

They're seventeen, eighteen? We haven't even graduated high school yet.

Ah, damn!

Lucas sat at JF's desk all hunched over that night. April outside. Light mist on the river. Orion distinct in the sky. He seemed stunned.

What could I tell him? What did I know?

Finally, I managed, "What can you do?"

Yancey had walked in. He already knew about it.

"He can marry her," he said, "step up to his responsibilities and pay for his mistake. Make an honest woman out of her."

He walked over, shaking his head, disgust in his voice, "Dammit, Lucas, you know better. You know better."

Lucas looked up, "It just happened. I wasn't expecting it. I wasn't ready." Yancey ignored him.

"Or we can find a doc who can make it go away." Lucas sat with his head down and didn't look up.

"Or she can leave town for a while and have it and put it up for adoption and cock up some story."

Still standing there, still scowling, still with disgust, "Or he can disappear and hope her folks don't send someone looking."

"I wouldn't do that," Lucas shot up straight, "I wouldn't run out on her."

"Well, I'd think about it," said Yancey. "Her dad's a prominent man. There'll be hell to pay one way or another."

Yancey standing, scowling. Lucas in the chair, tense, defensive. Me to the side, thinking I'm on the edge of something between Yancey and Lucas they'd both regret.

"What does Janie say?"

That broke their attention. Lucas swung to me, anger gone from his face. Misery there instead.

"She won't talk to me."

"How did you...I never even saw you two together anywhere."

He flicked that off with a toss his head. "Talk to her, will you? She likes you. I'll do anything she wants. I feel so damn guilty. Please, Owen."

Later—not then, then I was too taken up with his distress but later, I wondered. Lucas hadn't said he was sorry. He said he felt guilty. To be sorry about a thing is to to feel regret for having done it. To feel guilt is to feel blame. He took the blame. But he wasn't sorry. Janie Watts was important to him. A girl he cared about?

Lucas wasn't given to attachments.

Of course Janie wouldn't talk. You think she was going to admit to anyone that she and Lucas Deane, the boy from the Bottom, had had "intercourse"— that Janie Watts, chaste and serene, had, I couldn't bring myself to use the F word in reference to her even in my mind, had "done it" with Lucas? Ridiculous!

"There's something I'd like to talk with you about," I said, "about Lucas."

She smiled at me with ice in her eyes. "Oh, I don't care to talk about Lucas, thank you," she said and swirled and walked away to join the the cluster of girls waiting at the steps. She turned back, gave me that icy smile again, "Hurry. You'll be late," and swung through the school's front doors as the assembly bell rang.

It was a hellish week, Lucas agonizing over his plight, the suspense of not knowing what would happen draining even me.

The crisis climaxed on Thursday. I saw Lucas and Janie walking together across the school yard talking. Nothing that anyone would take notice of particularly, except Janie hardly looked at Lucas and he hardly took his eyes from her. They separated at the corner. Janie hurrying away, Lucas standing looking after her.

That night we learned that Janie hadn't missed her period.

She was late

And scared.

But not pregnant.

When she found out, she was so relieved she cried, then danced around clapping her hands and laughing, then cried again and dropped to her knees to thank the good Lord for his mercy, and jumped right back up laughing again and feeling she might faint out of sheer happiness.

She didn't tell Lucas right away. She was furious with him. He should have shown more control. He should have been more responsible. She was sorry for what she put him through, but think of what he had put her through. Her mother would shrivel up with shame. Her father would kill her. She wasn't sure she ever wanted to see Lucas again. Maybe not ever.

"Bitch," Yancey said. Yancey had a very keen sense of character.

I still had this image of Janie the princess, in my mind, and wasn't quite ready to go that far, but I was leaning.

Lucas said, "No. No. She's right. I should have. My fault. She had every right."

Janie Watts had a hook in him.

FIFTY
Courtesy JF

By the time graduation came we'd gotten past the scare.

Janie was talking with Lucas. She had even agreed to be his date for the dance on graduation night. Which was a surprise to almost everyone because they had seemed to take no special notice of each other through all our time at FHS.

Yancey dialed back his irritation with Lucas, which had nothing to do with Lucas seducing the daughter of one of the town's most prominent businessmen. It had to do with Lucas's stupidity in doing it unprotected. He knew better. He'd been taught better.

JF knew nothing about any of this.

Yancey didn't tell him and told Lucas to be damn sure he didn't either. JF would have had the same reaction as Yancey. He would have stood by Lucas, but he would have questions about Lucas's suitability for the sorts of responsibilities he was beginning to get. Of more concern to Lucas, JF would have been disappointed in him.

I was glad it was over. But puzzled. Lucas was remarkably disciplined. He had steely self-control. Who did the seducing, I wondered.

It was a summer of temperate days and tranquil nights that summer, the summer of our senior year.

Lucas and Janie began dating openly.

I was absorbed by my work in Mr. Lee Morgan's law office.

JF, after his six-month visit to the county jail and Annie's decision to boot him out, was settling in with Anna Mae and getting his affairs moving forward again, peacefully it seemed.

Pleasant summer.

Golden.

That summer I was initiated into the primal mystery.

By a prodigy.

A whore.

Jarring word, isn't it?

Cruel.

Mouthed by people who think themselves better than those they use and mean to demean.

I don't like the word.

I favor something more generous ... like Working Girl or Lady of the Night.

I lean to Lady of the Night. What do you do for a living, Lizzie? Oh, I'm a Lady of the Night. That's more respectful, isn't it?

Or better yet, Courtesan. I doubt few in Craw would recognize the word, but the ladies might appreciate it. Most of them take a defiant pride in their profession.

Some of JF's closest friends were, how shall I call them ... Ladies of the Night? Courtesans?

Ida Howard was. He had no better or more loyal friend than Ida.

I'm sure it wasn't a spur-of-the moment thing. I'm sure he discussed it with Lucas. I'm sure he smiled to himself as he planned it.

It began as a special dinner at Susan's Place on the river—JF, Yancey, Lucas, and me. A belated graduation present. We had the corner table outside on the porch where he could see anyone who entered and everyone could see him. The river was running clear. The night was soft. No clouds in sight.

Susan greeted us warmly, nodded with a mischievous smile at JF, and led us to our table. She seemed especially pleased to see us. She kissed Lucas on the cheek. She knew him. And me, though she knew me not that well

"A special night," she said to me. "Oh, you'll have fun. I just know it." She kissed JF playfully on the cheek. "The things you do."

I don't fully recall what we ate that night. That memory got crowded out by those I accumulated later. Whatever we ate would have been the best Susan had. JF only had the best. And I would have enjoyed it immensely. I know we had wine. I wasn't used to wine. And a small jigger of Major James, neat, following desert.

We talked and laughed until Susan came to the table and reminded JF it was time for his game. He paused then, raised his wrist to look at this watch. Nodded, looked at Lucas, looked back at his watch, unstrapped it and handed it across to Lucas. Confused, questioning, Lucas took it.

"Look on the back," JF said. Still confused, Lucas turned the watch over. A gold Rolex Explorer. He leaned closer to read the words inscribed there. *"To Lucas Deane. In appreciation of his loyalty and help. John Richard Fallis."*

When Lucas looked up there were tears in his eyes. He started to speak, but JF held up his hand. "You are very welcome." To me he said, "I have a little graduation present for you, too, Mr. Edwards. Lucas will take you to it." Then he rose smiling and left with Yancey following.

Mrs. Ida Howard's house on Clinton Street.

On the corner.

Big, friendly-looking house. Two stories. A swing on the downstairs porch. White wicker rockers on the upstairs porch overlooking the street. Lace curtains at the windows and roses on the trellis by the steps.

Her name was Rachael.

She wore a green ball gown and had sparkles in her hair.

The thing I remember most about her is her skin, the way her skin was sweet to the touch. She was pretty. Not old enough to be called a woman yet, but older than any girl I knew. I was very nervous. For a while.

Lucas knocked on the door just before daylight.

She washed me.

I dressed.

He drove me home through the silent streets.

Neither of us made conversation. Lucas smiled to himself and would glance at me now and then and smile. I was deep in my own thoughts.

He dropped me at the curb by my house.

"You okay," he said.

"Better than that," I said and let myself in without waking anyone and slipped into my own bed and slept until noon.

If there were bags of guilt to pick up, fires of hell to be faced, bring 'em on. Little Owen Edwards ain't no virgin no more.

FIFTY-ONE
Surprises All Around

Lucas was happy as the summer rolled on.

He was cheerful and light-hearted and outgoing.

JF noticed the difference. Yancey, too.

Janie was the reason.

The big surprise to me was that her family permitted her to be with him.

He had no pedigree. He was a protégé of the notorious King of Craw. He was anathema to almost everything they and their crowd valued.

The bigger surprise was that Lucas tolerated them—the overlords, the people who thought they were better than everyone else and trod their arrogant way over the rest, the top of the list of the people Lucas couldn't stomach.

Surprises all around.

Lucas must have found something in Janie that softened his anger.

Janie's parents must have found comfort in the thought that this foolishness would be over soon.

Like me, Janie would be off to college in a few months. The excitement of new surroundings and new people would clear her head of this Lucas Deane, would get her focused on a more suitable squire.

Could happen. Good chance it would happen. Janie didn't strike me as a girl who'd have a long term interest in a boy with no ruling class prospects.

For now, though, Lucas was happy.

And I was.

And Janie was.

And for the time being, there was no foment in the Kingdom of Craw.

Lucas and I had a long talk the night before I was to leave for university. We realized our paths were parting. We realized we had different interests and were pursuing different goals. We realized we would see little of each other and rarely be involved in things together anymore. We vowed we wouldn't let this change our friendship. We shook hands on that. We believed it.

I went up Highway 60 to the university.

Lucas went down Wilkinson Street to Craw.

FIFTY-TWO
Hit Or Miss

So we did. We saw each other infrequently and were rarely involved in things together, but we kept our friendship strong.

I'd come home on weekends occasionally. Sleep in my own bed. Sunday morning church and a big Sunday dinner. Mom treated these visits like an occasion. She missed me.

At school I had a room in a house near the campus where a nice lady rented to students. I made new friends and developed new interests, but I always saw Lucas when I was home. Sometimes at the grocery, sometimes at our place. Mom always invited him to Sunday dinner with us when I was home, and always, at Thanksgiving, invited him and his mother to be with us on that special day. And he always declined—politely and apologetically, but firmly.

Yancey explained why when he got tired of my fussing.

"She's dead. His mother is dead. When Lucas was six, when she was sick. She didn't get well. She died. That's when they came and got JF and he went and got Lucas. Took him to Ida Howard. Ida and her girls raised Lucas. JF kept watch and provided. Ida raised him in her house on Clinton Street. She took good care of him."

He shook his head in exasperation at me. "That's why he keeps turning you down. He doesn't want you to feel sorry for him. Lucas doesn't want anybody to feel sorry for him about anything. Don't tell him I told you. And quit forcing him to say no."

I didn't tell my mother about this. She would not have been able to hide her sorrow.

So that Thanksgiving Day came and passed. Lucas spent it however he managed to pass such days. I feasted on turkey and apple pie and realized how lucky I was to be Owen Edwards, son of Jennifer and Edward Edwards of Estes Park, Colorado.

The year flowed into spring, and summer, then fall again.

I was a college sophomore.

Eighteen.

Five years out of my mountains.

In danger of becoming ensnared by this lush, coquettish land—seduced by the look of it, the scent of it, the feeling of welcome it gave me. Not a Kentuckian yet, but dangerously close.

I spent that year caught in up school and the diversions that came with it, trying to avoid the temptations I knew I should be be stronger than and working hard enough to keep my grades acceptable. Not too hard. There were parties and games and passionate arguments over matters of great consequence to divert me. And girls. Oh, lord, Kentucky girls. They were as lovely and as luscious as the country they sprang from.

The Kingdom of Craw and its suzerain were nowhere in my thoughts ... until I saw in the Lexington paper that JF had been attacked.

It was a small story on an inside page that I might easily have missed. I was having coffee in the cafeteria between classes, glancing through a copy of the Lexington Herald someone had left. The headline stopped me. *King Of Craw Fights Off Attackers.*

According to the story, two gunmen had stepped out of a shadowed alley as he passed. He was on his way to a meeting of the Loyal Order of Odd Fellows uptown, was a block or so away from his destination.

They came at him from behind, hit him with a blackjack and knocked him to his knees. He was momentarily stunned but recovered rapidly. He rose reaching for the pistol in his overcoat pocket. By the time he was fully upright he had it out and the gunmen were running ... one down the alley, one to the cover of the trees across the street. He got off two shots. In the dim light and hazy mist of the drizzling night might have hit one. He saw him stumble.

JF reported the attack to the city police and continued on to his meeting. His fellow Odd Fellows cleaned the wound on his head, put a patch on it, and proceeded with the business of the meeting.

The reporter thought the attack was a robbery attempt.

I didn't.

There was no history of anyone ever trying to rob John Richard Fallis.

What then? The meeting time and place had been publicized. JF was a member and an officer of the club. The likelihood that he would be at that place at that time was very high.

I went home that weekend.

And found a different Lucas.

Not quite a year had passed, but there was an edge to him that wasn't there before—as if he'd been tempered, as steel is tempered in flame and made stronger. He had the same easy charm and the same engaging smile. But he was harder. Stronger. He brooked no insult, would not be cheated, would not be pushed around. He bent a knee to no man—except John Richard Fallis.

I found him at The Riverman. It was his seat of operation. Lucas was now a full-fledged member of the JF inner circle. He had been given responsibility for maintaining the relationship with Golden Pond, for making sure the flow of Major James wasn't interrupted or interfered with. The Golden Pond connection was the most important asset in JF's business, so Lucas was a key player now. He'd become friends with Joe Travis when we were down there together and was a much better ambassador to the Travises than Yancey. More important in the longer run, he had assumed a special role as a sort of aide-de-camp to JF. He undertook tasks which JF wanted to keep masked. He often knew things Yancey and Callahan didn't. I imagine a great deal of strain came with the assignment.

JF's operation had grown while I wasn't paying attention. He had come back from his sojourn in jail with a vengeance. He rebuilt the destroyed still, enlarged it to two-hundred-fifty gallons of capacity and located it on the backside of Fort Hill in an old farmhouse on the side of a slope with unobstructed views in all directions. No one would be slipping up on it. A fake chimney was the holding tank. Drive up and fill your Coke bottle from the ash trap in the backside of the house if you were of a mind. Or slide a pint into your pocket on the porch and walk away happy.

A second still, of the same size, was snuggled into a fishing camp near the mouth of Elkhorn Creek where it joined the Kentucky River.

There were distribution points at crossroad stores and wayside repair shops throughout the county. No one with a thirst need go dry. JF's corps of bootleggers saw to that. Counting the premium accounts locked up with Major James, very little business was left over for everyone else.

There had been trouble. Nothing too bad. A few broken heads. Gus Brewer sent Vik Braun and a few boys to hijack a delivery to the little saloon at the Peaks Mill crossroads store that JF supplied. It wasn't successful. Yancey had lookouts everywhere. Saw them coming. Sent them packing with bird-shot in their behinds. No real damage. None intended. Birdshot stings but is no real danger to life or limb unless they get too close. Just enough hurt to remind people to stay the hell away from JF's turf. Try to keep it civilized. None of the craziness like what was going on in Cincy and Chicago. They expected these sorts of skirmishes, but they hadn't expected this.

"So it was a hit" I said.

"A try," Lucas said.

"Gus Brewer getting back?"

"Maybe."

"If it wasn't Brewer, who?"

"Could have been the cops. They were surprised when JF came walking in after the attack in the alley. They didn't expect him to be standing."

Lucas looked away. Then back at me with a wicked smile.

"Oh, no," I said. "You're not going after the police. He can't take on the police. Not again. That's not what you're thinking."

"Well, he sure as hell isn't going to run. And he's not going to back off anything. You know him well enough to know that."

"So?"

"Yancey and I'll have his back. He'll handle anyone who comes at him."

"That's a plan?"

Lucas had absolute confidence in Yancey. And in himself. And he knew no one was as good as John Richard Fallis.

"Abso-damn-lutedly!"

The mood had changed in the Kingdom of Craw. There had always been a sense of danger there, but danger cloaked in excitement and adventure. There was menace in the air now.

I left my talk with Lucas and headed uptown to Mr. Leland Morgan's office. It was late afternoon, a Saturday. The stores had their Christmas decorations up and early shoppers were bustling busily around.

He'd be there. He always worked until five on Saturdays except UK football home game days. He'd be at his desk, files open all around, scribbling on a yellow pad. The office would be quiet. There'd be no secretary out front. He let her off at noon on Saturdays. I'd have to let myself in and announce my presence myself.

He heard me opening the outside office door and was looking up quizzically when I stepped in.

"Well, I'll be damned," he said rising to greet me. "Owen Edwards. Come in, boy. Come in. How are you?"

FIFTY-THREE
A Singular Case

Leland Morgan had been legal counsel to John Richard Fallis since the Semonis cutting when JF was a young man.

No one knew him better.

Some had known him longer—Annie, his wife, Yancey, his shadow—but they knew only the face JF showed them.

The face he showed Lee Morgan was less disguised. JF was open with Lee Morgan in a way he was not with others. He trusted Morgan with his thoughts, sometimes even with his feelings. He knew that what he told Morgan would be known only to Morgan. He felt Morgan accepted him for what he was. Did not judge him. He felt safe with Morgan.

Lee Morgan felt John Richard Fallis was a singular case and deserved his special care and attention.

Morgan had always been for underdogs and JF had touched a chord in him. As he came to know JF, he began to feel that JF was the quintessential underdog—a Quixote tilting at the windmills of privilege and power. They would chew him up and spit him out, but until that time came JF deserved his special care and attention.

"Yes, I know about the attack," he said.

"Was it the police?"

"Does it make a difference?"

He stood up, walked to the window looking out to the courthouse. He had a habit of doing that while he considered what he wanted to say. He turned back, brows furrowed, eyes sad.

"You need to understand how much ill-will there is out there for John. At least as much, perhaps more, than the affection a good part of the town holds for him.

"Most people don't understand that Craw and the Bottom are quite important to our fine and principled uptown businessmen. They make a lot of money there. They're the slumlords who own the shacks and hovels that pass for shelter in the back alleys of Craw, the landlords who rent out much of housing in the Bottom.

"John is in an almost constant fight with City Hall to get regulations that will force the landlords to patch the holes in the roofs and replace the broken doors and do something about the leaking outhouses before the whole place comes down with dysentery or worse. City Hall doesn't like him. The landlords don't like him.

"Most of the bars and saloons in Craw aren't owned by the men who run them. Their owners are uptown. They don't like it that John controls the booze supply. They want to change that.

"And there is the church crowd.

"And the police.

"They all want to be rid of John.

"And who knows what outsiders are nosing around. Bootlegging has turned into such unbelievably big money that gangs from New York and Chicago and Cincinnati are competing for markets around the country. The Bluegrass is prime territory. John has much of it locked up. Is someone coming after him?"

He shrugged. Shook his head sadly.

"The police? John keeps that alive as much as they do. He taunts them. He dares them. He's the King of Craw and he acts like it. Craw and the Bottom are his territory. The police rarely go in. John has absolutely no respect for the police and he shows it. The people take their cue from him. If they've got a problem, they come to John. Someone steal from them, beat them, cheat them, they come to John. Not the police. They know the police won't do anything. John does. He'll break an arm, snap a few fingers. Uses a baseball bat on wife-beaters and child-molesters. Makes the loan sharks play fair. Slaps around the two-bit punks harassing the old and the lame. He can be brutal. They respect John, but they fear him, too. They know he is likely to cause pain if you are out of line or make him mad.

"That animosity with the police will keep festering. There are a few who would be willing shake hands and let it go. Not the ring-leaders, not Scott and Helm and O'Nan. He's trashed their egos too badly and done them bodily harm. They are mortal enemies.

"Might the police have engineered the attack the other night? They might have. Or Gus Brewer. Or the slumlords. Or the city functionaries. Or a solider for Mr. Capone coming down out of Chicago. Or some combination of them all.

"The point is that the game John is playing has gotten murderously serious.

"Consider that, Owen. Consider all the powerful forces he has against him. The only way he can win is to get out of it. He won't do that. And that's the tragedy of it. Flawed though he is, John is one of those rare men who stand up to power and authority and makes a real difference for ordinary people. He's going to get killed for it. It didn't happen this time. It may not happen the next. But it will happen. You be careful you are not in the way when it does."

I let myself out. Night had come while we were talking. I took myself carefully down the darkened stairwell and out onto the street. There were lights and people there, but a cold wind was blowing and rain just beginning. It was a bleak night. I wished he hadn't told me.

FIFTY-FOUR
A Surprise For Lucas

Nothing happened.

I expected daily a headline in the newspaper announcing the demise of the King of Craw or a call at night to tell me to come, but nothing happened. After the first few months of apprehension, the marker in my mind began to fade.

I did not lose the worry entirely. It just got layered over by matters of more immediate concern—would Jodie Gaines be my date for the Derby Ball, did my paper on anarchism get the A it deserved—matters on which the fate of the universe hung.

By summer I had managed to submerge my concerns and was ready for days of learning at the feet of Mr. Lee Morgan and Sundays on the river in the company of pretty girls and gin-laced lemonade, with Lucas sometimes and sometimes not.

Janie was home.

He was spending as much time with her as he could.

I was wrong about Janie.

I thought she'd tire of Lucas fairly rapidly. That once she got to school and began to be caught up in the sorority whirlwind of parties, and dances, and dates with boys of her own class and sensitivities, she would kiss Lucas a tender goodbye and move on happily to the life she was intended for.

But I was wrong.

Janie was ambitious.

She seemed to have found in Lucas a spark of promise that she thought she might be able to fan into something of consequence—a man as fine as her father, Mr. Paul Elmer Watts, president of the Farmers & Citizens National Bank, perhaps. Or even greater. Perhaps, with the right care and stimulus from her, even Governor.

Lucas had the looks and the charm. He was as smart as any boy she knew. He was relentless. When he wanted something, no obstacle deterred him. And his story. A perfect story. A poor boy pulling himself up out of the meanest section of the Capitol City through hard work and merit (not to mention the love of a good woman) to aspire to the Governor's chair. He could be great. She would make him great. She fancied living in the Mansion.

Janie was open enough with me about her hopes for Lucas. She wanted my help. She felt he'd need encouragement from someone he trusted, someone besides herself telling him how grand he was.

Lucas? Governor?

The sip I'd just taken caught in my throat and I dropped back coughing onto the blanket we'd spread for the picnic.

When I recovered, I looked out to find him. He was about halfway across the river, swimming alongside my date, strong strokes moving him smoothly through the water.

I sat back up into Janie's eager and earnest gaze.

"Janie … Governor?"

"Oh not right away. Don't be silly. First he's going to be the youngest vice-president at our bank. Then he'll become the youngest governor in the history of the state. If he wants. I want him to be happy. In time. Only if he wants."

"He's going to be a vice president at the bank," I said in disbelief.

"Daddy doesn't know that yet. But he will. I'll see to it."

On the far side of the river Lucas and my date were climbing out, shaking off droplets of water and laughing delightedly. She'd made it. My date. She wanted to swim the river but wasn't sure she was strong enough. Lucas said "You can do it," and swam beside her to make sure. Standing there in the afternoon sun, lithe and muscular, relaxed and happy, he looked like a young Adonis. I might be able to imagine him as a politician. That would be a stretch, but I might. But working in a bank? I could never imagine that.

"Does Lucas know about this?"

"Oh, no" Janie said. "No. No. I'll have to lead him to it carefully." A playful smile. "I know how to do that."

Lucas didn't become a vice-president of the bank that summer, though Janie introduced him to her father, and no attempts were made on JF's life.

As each month passed, the specter grew dimmer until finally it became one of those little terrors that slip into dreams but are forgotten when you wake.

Late in the year, Mr. Fallis filed for divorce from his wife Annie.

In the complaint JF said there had been no co-habitation for years. Mr. Morgan gave me the details. He handled the filing for JF.

JF transferred all the property he owned into Annie's name, acknowledging "the natural love and affection which the first party bears to the second party, which is his wife."

He was living with Anna Mae at the time. She lived with him until he died. They had a son.

"Explain this to me," I asked of Mr. Morgan.

"There's no explanation for John," he said. "I am not certain even he knows why he does what he does."

And tried Yancey.

"He loves her. He loves them both."

And Lucas, who said as if the answer was as obvious and uncomplicated as the rising of the sun, "Because he's John Fallis."

Because he's John Fallis.

The second time he'd told me.

FIFTY-FIVE
Straws

John Fallis prospered.

His legitimate businesses rolled smoothly along and his success in the enlarging commerce of Bluegrass bootlegging was being noticed. This is not to say that there wasn't blood. He was beginning to nose into the Lexington market. The organizations already there didn't appreciate that. And the men who lusted for a bigger share of the local market kept trying to force their way in. There were hi-jack attempts and occasional unpleasantries over clients, but JF kept his name out of the papers and attended to his affairs. Kingdoms aren't sustained by pacifists.

Lucas carried much of this responsibility. Golden Pond whiskey was his charge. They brought it by boat up the Ohio to the Kentucky to the transfer point at the mouth of Elkhorn Creek, or by truck on back roads through the Upper Pennyrile to the Bluegrass to a warehouse in the railroad yards behind the prison—Major James in bottles snugged in hay-packed crates, Golden Pond Regular in oak barrels banded together so they wouldn't move. Over three hundred miles, wolves lurking all along the way.

Lucas got tougher and harder and reveled in the game.

Poor Janie and the bank had not the hint of a chance.

Things were stable in a tense sort of way and there seemed no unusual pressure for JF's head. I stayed in touch and didn't worry.

The trigger, I think, was the Come-And-Get-It Train and the Haines Alley Fire.

The winter of twenty-nine was the hardest winter the region had seen— weeks of temperatures in the low twenties dipping below zero at night, sunless days of snow and sleet.

There was suffering throughout the county, but nothing like the suffering in the Bottom and Craw. January was bitter. February brutal.

So many were out of work. So many had only marginal jobs that barely paid the rent. So many were old and feeble and had only the generosity of the churches.

They couldn't buy coal. They couldn't get warm. They hadn't the money.

The city was no help. It had no allowance for the poor and the needy.

If the cold continued much longer, the suffering would turn fatal.

Word went out from the grocery.

Take your wagon, take your wheelbarrow, take whatever you have that will carry coal and be in front of the Old State House by three o'clock. The afternoon L&N freight will come through with two hopper cars full of coal in tow. It will stop there and dump it all. Two car loads. On the street in front of the Old State House. Go get it. Take it home. Get warm. John Fallis.

People came not just from the Bottom, but from all over town. A mountain of coal in the middle of Broadway with snow falling down and people laughing and shouting and filling wagons and carts and big burlaps bags with coal, coal to keep the cold away. If they hadn't loved him before, they loved him now.

City Hall didn't. The police didn't. He was showing off again.

The last straw was the Haines Alley Fire.

In one of the hovels slapped together from old lumber and driftwood, a fire broke out from someone cooking over an open grate. A light breeze fanned the flame and spread it next door, then further, then all the way up the alley to Fort Hill before the fire trucks came. The places were like tender. They went up like fireworks. Ten people died. Six of them children.

Should not have happened. The building code shouldn't have permitted fire trap hovels like those to be built. Or rented. JF, with a young preacher from the Methodist Mission and the pastor of the Abyssinian Baptist Church, were beating relentlessly on the Mayor and the City Council to get new regulations that would stop such outrages. Sermons were being preached in the local churches. The ladies' clubs were mobilizing.

Uptown businessmen who owned the properties weren't happy. Make him stop was the message to the Mayor.

Were these enough?

Were these finally enough? A grandstand play to the poor with a little coal. A do-gooder's coalition threatening the bottom-line? Had they finally been pushed to the point they said no more. Were these the final insults?

Get rid of him. Get the the hell rid of him.

Or were the bootlegging bastards the ones?

FIFTY-SIX
A Sunday In August

The eighteenth day of August, nineteen twenty-nine.

Two o'clock in the morning.

Most of the town asleep.

A full moon glowing red through hazy mist. Heat-lightening whitening the sky.

A Sunday.

JF was born on a Sunday. "A child that is born on the Sabbath day is bonnie and blithe and good and gay."

He is dead.

Lying on the green felt of a craps table in the backroom of a saloon called the Wide Awake on the corner of Clinton Street and Gas House Alley on the edge of Craw.

Shot five times—four in the body, one in the head.

My father came and got me.

By the time I found Lucas it was past noon.

JF had finished for the day. He was home, getting ready for bed when they came to get him. Yancey and a few men he knew from the Riverman.

Yancey tells him that a new guy in town is running the table at the Wide Awake and bragging. A brassy guy. Thinks he's something. He's moving here. Thinks it's time to crown a new King of Craw.

JF isn't interested.

He sent you a challenge, Yancey says. Play me. Prove who's best.

There's fifteen, maybe twenty guys around the craps table. They all hear it. He makes sure they do. Go get Fallis, he says.

JF is inclined to ignore it. He's tired. Has had a long day. Doesn't need to prove himself to some no-name hustler. Tell him to go away, he says. Come back another day.

He said you'd make excuses. Everybody heard him, Yancey says. He said you'd be afraid of him. Best to put him away now and be rid of him.

JF is still inclined to ignore it. But there is his pride. No one, certainly no two-bit out-of-town gambler, can call John Fallis afraid. Damn him anyway.

So JF dresses. Walks with Yancey and the others up the street to The Wide Awake. It is a little before one in the morning. JF notices the moon. Points up to it. "Lucky?"

Yancey shakes his head. "The Red Moon. The heat haze of August causes it."

JF doesn't have his guns. He has dressed hurriedly. He's tired. But he has Yancey. Yancey has his back.

The game is craps.

The challenger is Rigsby, Everett Rigsby. Youngish, handsome, arrogantly confident. JF dislikes him on sight.

The craps table is in the middle of the room. Men move in around it. JF rolls and wins the dice to start. Holds them up to show Rigsby and begins to roll. He makes his point. And yet again. And still again. Onlookers are now beginning to be bettors and crowd in to get their money down.

Ten minutes pass and JF still has the dice -- and a pile of money. Rigsby doesn't look worried. Smiles confidently. Waits.

At about twenty minutes in, JF still rolling and still making his point, Rigsby suddenly grabs JF's arm. "You're cheating," he yells. "You're throwing loaded dice!"

JF stares at him in surprise. Shakes off Rigsby's hand, says, "Why you sonofa...."

And Rigsby has a pistol in his hand and before JF can move starts firing. He puts four slugs into JF's body and a fifth into his head as he lies already lifeless on the floor.

The room is stunned, deafened by the shots, in shock at the action.

Rigsby calmly puts his weapon back in his pocket, walks out the door and up to the corner where he surrenders to Police Sergeant Scott who seems to be waiting for him—Scotty, of all the police on the force, JF's worst enemy.

"I have just killed John Fallis and I want to surrender," Rigsby announces and hands over his pistol and they stroll off to the city jail.

At the Wide Awake, the crowd mills about uncertainly. Yancey lifts JF's body from the floor up to the gaming table. Lays him there.

Police arrive almost immediately. The crowd scatters and the room is empty except for the two cops by the door and Yancey. There is silence and the smell of spilled beer and blood.

While they wait for the coroner, JF's boys come. Dazed. Enraged.

Carlos, the eldest, takes up a post at the foot of the table near his father's feet, John at the head shaking with sobs. Outside the door Benjamin, the youngest, hysterical and vowing vengeance.

Protect him. Keep the ghouls and the snoops away. Don't let them see his mutilated body. Protect his pride.

A woman arrives. Not his wife Annie. Anna Mae. She has a child in her arms. The boy at the door curses her, but she pushes in. She clings to the body until a policeman takes her away.

Word spreads rapidly through Craw. The bars and the saloons empty. The cards are put down and the roulette wheel stops. The bordellos jettison their johns and the ladies dress and go. By the time the coroner's crew arrives the corner is crowded. The crew lifts JF's body and conveys it to the hearse through a corridor of watchers standing silent and still. When the hearse leaves, the woman with the child in her arms walks off into the shadows, alone and weeping.

Annie doesn't come.

That's what happened.
That's what Lucas had learned.

I found him at the Riverman. He hadn't heard of JF's death until morning. He'd been with Janie. By then almost everyone in town who was awake had heard of it.

Lucas went immediately to find Yancey. But Yancey was nowhere to be found. Lucas went to the Riverman. Callahan was there. Found out from Callahan that he had been with Yancey when Yancey went to get JF and had walked with them to the Wide Awake. Saw the shooting. Watched Yancey lift JF from the floor up to the gaming table. Thought he saw tears in Yancey's eyes. Had stayed until the hearse carried JF away. Didn't know what had happened to Yancey. Didn't know where Yancey was.

And after looking everywhere he could think of, Lucas didn't either. Yancey had disappeared.

"He did it, Owen. He set Mr. Fallis up. He betrayed him." Lucas, distraught and drained, strained toward me. "Yancey betrayed him and now he's on the run."

"What are you saying?"

"It was a hit. Rigsby is a pro. Yancey set Mr. Fallis up. He got him to where Rigsby was waiting. Yancey knew. He made it happen. Mr. Fallis didn't have his pistol, but Yancey had one. Yancey's supposed to have Mr. Fallis's back. Why didn't he pull it out and shoot this Rigsby down right there, right on the spot? Yancey knew what was going to happen. He got him there. He's the Judas."

"Surely not, Lucas. Why would he?"

Lucas was near tears in anger and frustration.

"I don't know. I don't care. I'll kill him. When I find him I'll kill him."

I could think of no reason why Yancey would do what Lucas thought he had done. But I could think of no possible reason why Yancey would disappear when his presence would be so needed.

What I thought wasn't important. What Lucas thought was. When he found Yancey, I had absolutely no doubt Lucas would do what he said he would do.

It was Sunday afternoon. I went home. And stayed the night. And tried to find Lucas to talk with on Monday morning. But couldn't.

I don't know what I would have said if I'd found him.

You're wrong.

But he might have been right.

Don't try it. Yancey's too dangerous.

That wouldn't stop Lucas.

Whatever I might say would make no difference.

Lucas was John Fallis's creation.

Mr. Fallis's funeral was held on Tuesday in the Frankfort Cemetery on the hill overlooking the river.

The funeral cortege wound all the way through town—up Wilkinson Street to Main, then up East Main Hill to the cemetery. It was long and somber. Men and women in black. Everything stopped as it passed. Cars and carriages, everything moving on the streets pulled off to the side and stopped. Pedestrians stopped and took off their hats and stood respectfully still. At the gravesite, the mourners crowded the cemetery's road and overflowed the grounds. There was much crying. Much sorrow.

I looked for Lucas and found him standing on a small rise behind the row of chairs for the family by the casket. He was beside Mrs. Ida Howard who touched a handkerchief to her eye but stood proud and regal in a genteel black dress. Lucas was in black, too. Black suit. Black tie. He looked forlorn. Abandoned. My father and my mother were with me. She, too, dabbed at her eyes.

It seemed that most of the working class of the town was there. Men from the shops and the factories and the sawmills. Women who took in the wash and cared for the uptown ladies' houses. Waiters. Bartenders. Clerks. A smattering of Ladies of the Night dressed demurely in black. Ditch diggers. Farmers. Most had walked all that long way through town and up the hill, many in a group behind the hearse. All of them in black. Black was the color of the day.

And businessmen were there and preachers and ladies of the church and state workers. And the Mayor and councilmen and the Chief of Police in his dress uniform. Some, no doubt, to make sure they were rid of him, but the others, all that great crowd of people, to see him safely to ground.

I stopped trying to identify the types and simply realized how widely John Richard Fallis had touched this town.

And was moved that so many had come to pay their respects to the King of Craw.

FIFTY-SEVEN
Afterwards

My office is on the second floor of the bank building on Main Street. That's where I'm writing this. I can look down and see the corner where the Big Shoot-Out took place.

I am president of the bank now.

Janie Watts didn't get her governor. She got me. I may run for governor, though. Janie has a way of getting her way. Of which I am proof.

Mr. Leland Morgan took me aboard when I graduated law school. In time I was to be made a partner—Morgan & Edwards, Attorneys at Law. Janie had a different vision for my future. Her father had to give in. I managed to hold out a year or two, then joined the bank, rose, purely on merit you understand, to my present lofty position and am happy enough.

Lucas is dead.

He found Yancey.

He didn't survive the encounter.

I had his body brought home and we buried him in the cemetery on the hill not far from JF's grave.

Lucas had so much promise.

It was such a waste.

My mother cried and cried.

I did. Once. As we were leaving his grave. I cried.

Dammit Lucas!

I don't know what happened with Yancey. I don't know why he did what he did. I don't know who paid him, or what he got. Money? Had to be money. Enough money that he didn't have to be anyone's number two any more. Enough money to be free.

I don't know where he's gone. It was in New Orleans that Lucas found him. Maybe he's off somewhere in the Caribbean. Drinking rum. Reverting back to his days as a conjurer of spirits and maker of magic. Maybe Lucas did manage to kill him. I don't know. I had no urge to go after him. I wasn't under the same spell Lucas was.

I don't know who bought JF's killing.

I have given that a great deal of thought.

The shooting was no gambler's argument. The police were expecting it— one waiting on the corner to get the shooter safely to jail, others arriving almost immediately when the police rarely made patrols in Craw and when no call had gone out.

Rigsby was known in certain circles. He had been called on before.

At trial, despite the evidence, Rigsby was acquitted.

He pleaded self-defense.

Rigsby emptied his weapon into JF at close range.

Shot six times. Missed once, but put four into JF's body and one into his head as he lay already dead.

John Fallis was unarmed.

Self defense?

Rigsby had a good attorney. An establishment attorney. Polk South.

Rigsby walked.

Someone, or some several ones—pillars of the establishment, City Hall functionaries—some combination of powerful and fed-up men decide, finally, to be rid of John Fallis. Collude with his enemies on the police force to find the right assassin. Plan it. Get it done.

Is that what happened?

Do I know who?

Even if I did, nothing could be proven. Many of the people who were the movers and shakers of the community were saying good riddance anyway.

I keep asking myself why he did the things he did.

Why was he so protective of the poor and the weak? Why did he fight so hard against power and privilege? How could one person be so violent, yet so gentle? So feared and yet so loved? There was so much about him to admire. And so much to dislike.

After all these years I still have no answer.

The only answer truly may be the one Lucas kept giving me when I asked.

Because he was John Fallis.

Craw is gone.

The Bottom is gone.

The town had an attack of righteousness when the Feds opened the purse strings of Urban Renewal. Tore down all the houses. Moved out all the people whether they wanted to go or not. Built flood walls to keep the river out. Leveled the place and started putting up office buildings.

Uptown businessmen made a lot of money on those transactions, my father-in-law among them.

It's peaceful there now.

When night comes there are no shouts or laughter, no lights from upstairs windows, no people on the streets. It is clean and neat there now. Funereal. Dead.

Major James can still be had if you know the right person. The country came to its senses and repealed Prohibition and the big distilleries came back on line and put the bootleggers out of business. But the Travises kept on making Major James—for their own happy satisfaction and that of a few of their friends, of which I am one. Joe Travis is now Superintendent of Schools in Trigg County. He invites me down to Golden Pond. We go after quail and laugh remembering Lucas.

Those years. Lord, they were fine.

Tomorrow is my birthday, Sunday, the nineteenth day of May. I will be fifty-nine. The moon will be halfway to full. The full moon of May. The Flower Moon. Yancey would know what it portends.

I don't need to know.

I earned my spurs in the Kingdom of Craw.

I will deal with it.

THE END

ACKNOWLEDGEMENTS

This was a difficult book to write. There were so many unanswered questions, so much to tell, so many story lines to explore that I was often so stymied by the sheer richness of the material that I found myself staring off into space trying to decide what to write about and writing about nothing.

My dad, the late James B. Rhody, taught me the way out of that dilemma. He was managing editor of the local newspaper, The Frankfort State Journal. I worked there very early in my career. One night, on deadline, he found me sitting at my typewriter staring off into space and asked what I was doing. "Trying to find the lede for this story," I said. He shook his head and said, "There must be fifty good ledes for that story. Now pick one and write it."

So that's what I've done. I've picked one and written it. But not without substantial help from a number of very special people.

I've already noted in the dedication the very important role Joyce Hudson and Russ Hatter played in getting this story told. Joyce, an accomplished author in her own right, put her considerable creative skills to work to help edit and shape the story and bring it to print. Russ Hatter, *the* authority on matters of Frankfort's history, led me to the John Fallis story, helped me uncover the facts, tried to make sure I got them right and that I did not get too carried away with some of my assumptions. His knowledge and advice were invaluable.

I am particularly indebted to James E. Wallace. His oral history interviews for his master's thesis at the University of Kentucky, "This Sodom Land: Urban Renewal and Frankfort's Craw," provided the raw material for this book. And Douglas Boyd for his "Crawfish Bottom: Recovering a Lost Kentucky

Community," which captures the Bottom and Craw and John Richard Fallis and the time and circumstances so masterfully.

Sharon Kouns did the early and much appreciated research for the project and has my thanks as well.

Jan Bush and Jim Wallace guided me through Golden Pond. Jim, a former Trigg County Superintendent of Schools, grew up in Golden Pond. He gave me a sense of what a special place it was and how intensely those who lived there before it disappeared beneath the waters of Lake Barkley loved it then ... and still.

I need to ask the indulgence of the grammarians among you before ending this. I've tried to voice this story the way I would tell it to you if we were talking together. Pretend you're hearing this rather than reading it. That may help explain the one line paragraphs and the staccato sentences and the not entirely orthodox punctuation.

That said, for any of the failings this book may have, in facts or in conclusions, the fault is entirely mine.

The editor I mentioned in beginning this note would have been a young reporter at The State Journal at the time of the Fallis shooting. About twenty, I think. He may have covered it. He would have known John Fallis. I wish I'd had the chance to talk with him about it all.

I hope you enjoy the story.

Ron Rhody
Pinehurst, NC
November, 2016

HISTORIAL NOTES

The timeline below is the framework used in constructing this story. It is included with the thought that the reader may find it interesting and be, as I am still, intrigued by the many unanswered questions surrounding the real John Fallis.
(FK, by the way, is my shorthand for Frankfort—JF for John Fallis).

FALLIS TIME LINE

John Richard Fallis
Born April 13, 1879 - son of Benjamin and Anne Fallis in Jeffersonville, Indiana.

Shot and killed Aug. 18, 1929 in Frankfort, Kentucky.

1889—Starts carrying a knife at age 10 because people "picked on him." Got into lots of fights. Parents "whipped and scolded him and made him go to church." He seems to take to church. Starts singing in the Salvation Army choir. *Benjamin (Bixie) Fallis's biography of JF.*

1879-1892/93—All this is hazy, no real info on his first 13/14 years or on his parents. He's born in Jeffersonville, Ind., but most of the earliest references are to Louisville. No real information on his parents. Father apparently was a carpenter. Mother apparently an ardent church-goer and her brand of discipline may have had a major impact on his development. According to Bixie, "His parents moved to Frankfort when he was a small boy and he lived here until his death. Johnnie, at the age of 10, often got into scraps because he was quick tempered. Often led him into fights. It seemed in those days with Johnie (sic) people picked on him. This caused him to pack a knife. His strick (sic) parents often scolded him and even gave him whippings and made him go to church, which he learned to love early in his life. He was singing in the choir of the Salvation Army when he met the girl of his dreams, which later in life became his wife." *This is Anne Thompson Crain, daughter of Jackson and Francis Crane. Bixie says JF was 11 at the time. Assume this was in FK. Louisville Courier Journal story has him in Louisville at age 14 (see the Nov. 23, 1894 story below). So no real clarity of when he met Anne Crain or where—or where he lived in this time frame.*

1892—Goes to work at age 13. "His parents were poor." Gets a job at the Hemp Factory. (What kind of job?) This according to Bixie's bio. If Bixie is right, JF was in FK at this time because that's where the Hemp Factory was. But Courier Journal story (see next) suggests he was living in Louisville in 1892 and still there in 1894. *So when did he come to FK and what were the circumstances? Re: school, he could have made it to/through/ the 6th grade if these years are right.*

1894, Nov. 23—First press mention. Courier-Journal story reports that his mother has contacted the Louisville police chief reporting she has just received a letter from her son, John Fallis, "who is only 14 years of age, in which he said that he had just run off to Frankfort, never to return." Chief telephones ahead to Anchorage where police board the train and take the boy off, bring him back to Louisville, place him in the police station to be sent the next day to the House of Refuge in compliance with his mother's wishes. The House of Refuge is an orphanage and a reformatory. *His mother had him committed to a reformatory? Interesting marginal point: his mother must have had influence with the Louisville police to have them stop a train, collar her boy, and bring him back and put him in the reformatory/orphanage.*
Unclear about where he is or what he's doing between 1892 and 1898, except for the House of Refuge sojourn.
Bixie says "at age 13 he went to work at the Hemp Factory and several years later went to work at the O.F.C. Distillery which is now known as the Stagg Distillery. He worked there 17 years and became beer runner. His first job was in the mill room. This new job brought more money."

1898, May 6—Enters military for Spanish-American War. Serves only six months. He's injured in a fight aboard a train on which he is a guard. Is decorated and honorably discharged. He's 19.

1900, May 30—Marries Anne Thompson Craine. She's 18. He's 20. *Assume he's working at the distillery then?*

1900-1912—Unclear about what's going on during this period. Said to have worked at various jobs—carpenter, stonemason, blacksmith, logger—but principally at George T. Stagg. The dates are confusing. If he went to work at the Hemp Factory age 13/14 and worked there for two years to age 15/16, then went to the distillery and worked there for 17 years, he would have been working at the distillery from 1895 (age 16) to 1912 (age 33) but by December of 1912 he and Anne are running a grocery store. *So he's working at the distillery and running a grocery store?*

1906, April 28—Frankfort Roundabout story has him injured at work at the distillery. Hit by falling brick and taken to hospital. He's listed as "beer runner" at the distillery. *What's a 'beer runner?"*

1906, May 5—Frankfort Roundabout. He's buying a lot in Thorn Hill and is expected to begin building immediately.

1908, Feb. 1—He's attacked by two "highwaymen" on his way to the Odd Fellows Lodge. Occurs in front of Presbyterian Church on Main Street about 8 p.m. "Being wiry and very athletic, he was holding his own when one of them struck him was a slug shot on the back of the head knocking him to his knees. Recovering himself as quickly as possible, Mr. Fallis drew his gun from his overcoat pocket when the thieves broke and ran, one across the street and the other scurrying to the shelter of a tree. In the dim light, Mr. Fallis fired at both the men, who again ran, and separating, made their escape. Having exhausted his ammunition, Mr. Fallis could not pursue them any further. He reported the facts to the police as soon as he could and a search was instituted. Mr. Fallis carried a big lump on his head and was decidedly muddy, as there was a drizzling rain falling at the time of the assault." Story in the Frankfort Roundabout. He's 29.

1912, Dec. 10—The Big Disappearance. Fakes his death by dynamite explosion and disappears. Reappears Dec. 14. Anne about to collect on his insurance. Says all he remembers is coming conscious somewhere and overhearing someone talking about someone being killed in the explosion. He thinks he's killed someone and runs. Finds out later he's the supposed victim. So comes home. He's 33. Newspaper clips. Day of and follow up stories. *Bixie thinks he staged it because of a big fight with Anne. JF never offered a reason. He stuck with the "accident" story.*

1914-1917—World War I. He's 35 when it starts.

1920-1933—Prohibition. He's 41 when it starts.

1921, June 15-17—The Big Shoot-Out. Shoots 4 policemen and 2 bystanders. Is freeing son Carlos from police as the boy is being hauled off to jail for crashing a carnival performing on a lot behind the Old State House near the center of town. Mob gathers. He takes refuge in his home/grocery. Police and mob surround it and attack. Their gunfire sets the buildings on fire. The place is burned down. He escapes. He's 42.

1921, June 21—JF surrenders after the Big Shoot-Out to his cousin Will Fallis. Story in Mt. Sterling Advocate says Will Ferris, but not seen this reference anywhere else. Surrender is conditional on being taken to jail at Louisville (not FK) and is taken to jail there.

1921, June 29—JF sues insurance company for $1,600 damages to his burned out home & grocery during the Big Shoot-Out.

1921, Sept. 16—Indicted by Franklin County Grand Jury on four counts of shooting with intent to kill for shooting and wounding four policemen in June who were attempting to arrest his son. The Big Shoot-Out

1921, Dec. 28—Judge rules insurance company must pay. Company appeals. Loses. JF finally gets his judgment on May 10, 1924

1922, April 12—The Big Shoot-Out trial begins in FK. He's 43.

1922, April 14—The Big Shoot-Out trial ends. Verdict: six months in jail and a $250 fine. His attorney, Leslie Morris, immediately appeals the verdict. JF is released on bail.

1923, Jan 20—Court of Appeals upholds Big Shoot-Out trial verdict: six months in jail and a $250 fine for shooting Policeman Guy Wainscott. The court noted "the verdict was inadequate for the offense." *Wainscott was one of the policeman shot in the Big Shoot-Out. He was shot through the liver and his arm was splintered. His condition was listed as serious. Others shot were: Policeman C.E. Noonan, wounded in the face, neck, chest, and arms with buckshot. Condition serious. Policeman William Wilhelm, shot in shoulder. Policeman Jesse Colston, wounded in arm. John Foster (deputized civilian) slightly wounded. Jeff Lynn (deputized civilian) slightly wounded.*

1923, May 19—JF acquitted of shooting and wounding Policeman Charles Noonan. Jury deliberates 15 minutes. *The City Attorney must have brought a separate charge in this case. Noonan was not party to the Big Shoot-Out trial. The news story notes that the jurymen were selected from the outlying districts of the county and knew little about the case. The Fallis trial took up most of the day. Are those two judgments the full result of the Big Shoot-Out?*

1923, Nov. 22—JF and two others arrested by Probation Agents for possessing illegal still and selling intoxicating liquor. His still has a capacity of 250 gallons -- 2,050 gallons of whiskey taken in the raid. Pleads guilty & sentenced to four months.

1924—Big fight with Anne. She kicks him out. Is having an affair with Anna Mae Blackwell. Moves in with Anna Mae (date uncertain). He and Anna Mae live together until his death. They have a son.

1925, July 9—JF has warrant taken out against Jack Chinn for "cutting his daughter and her husband, Mr. & Mrs. Jessie Smith of Frankfort, Saturday, July 4 on the Frankfort Pike about two miles from Versailles." Argument over a car accident. Road rage? *Seems out of character for JF to get a warrant taken out rather than handling the matter himself.*

1927—Files for divorce from Anne, says no cohabitation for past four years. The divorce is never granted.

1929, Aug 5—Election Day shooting. Ricochet bullet from a gun fight after an argument with FK policeman Richard Glass at the Gas House voting precinct hits a friend in the leg and the friend subsequently dies from blood poisoning. The policeman and two others are slightly injured. Unclear whether JF's shot or a shot by Policeman Richard Glass was responsible. Fallis surrenders to County Judge James Polsgrove but is not held. Offers to post bond, but County Attorney declines. No warrant issued. He's 50. *Strange. What's this all about?*

1929, Aug 11—JF charged with manslaughter after warrant issued in the death of Lewis Brightwell, hit by a ricochet bullet in the Election Days shooting. Fallis released on bail. *Why the delay in issuing the warrant?*

1929, Aug. 18—Shot and killed by Everett Rigsby in Craw. He's 50.
A Sunday, at approximately 2:30 in the morning during either a poker or a craps game.
R.T. Brooks' oral history tape says it was at a card game at Fincel's place on the corner of Clinton and an alley he can't remember the name of but which goes up by Mayo-Underwood school. Howard Henderson's story in the Courier-Journal says it was a craps game in a back room of a place on Gas House Alley. Henderson's front-page story in the Courier-Journal says "the hard surface of a craps table served his as a deathbed." Very dramatic story ... sobbing Anna Mae with child in arms, three of the four boys (John, Benjamin, Carlos) standing around the body.

1929, Aug. 20—The funeral. A Tuesday.

####

ABOUT THE AUTHOR

Ron Rhody has been a reporter, a sportswriter, a broadcast newsman, and covered the Kentucky Legislature before moving on to a career as a corporate public relations executive in New York and San Francisco. He is the author of three works of non-fiction and four novels. He and his wife Patsy make their home in Pinehurst, North Carolina.

ALSO BY RON RHODY

Fiction

The Theo Trilogy

THEO's Story

"The death of Benjamin Dannan was the driver. What happened to Michael, what happened to me—Benjamin Dannan's death was at the root of it. That was thirty years ago. Lord, what I wouldn't give to be a boy again, back at that time when everything was just beginning, back when we'd never heard of Jesse Bristow."

THEO and the Mouthful of Ashes

By the time daylight came, Theo was almost to Grayson. Will was dead. The Ashes Murder was yesterday's story. He was on his way, alone, to conquer the Capital of the World.

When THEO Came Home

"There was nothing to link me to the killing, but a gray fog of depression wrapped round me. I tried to throw it off by leaving. I had no intention of returning. Yet here I am—in the cemetery overlooking the river—kneeling beside Rhae Dannan's grave and not embarrassed by the tears or the hurt in my heart."

NonFiction

Soccer: A Spectator's Guide

This book is for all those who find themselves at soccer games and not fully understanding what's going on. It clearly explains the "beautiful game" so that none of the excitement is missed. It spells out what each player at each position is supposed to do, describes the skills and talents needed to perform well, and lays out the basic offensive and defensive strategies teams employ to secure a win.

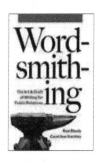

Wordsmithing: The Art & Craft of Writing for Public Relations

Here, at last, is a book that explains the how and why of writing for public relations from the perspective of a world-class professional and a ranking academic. It covers the basic forms used in writing for public relations, from news releases to white papers and op-ed pieces, and gives step-by-step instruction on how to write them. Equally important, it explains how and when to use each form.

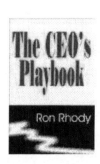

The CEO's Playbook

A concise guidebook for managers and executives on how to successfully handle the outside forces that shape success: the news media, government, activists and special interest groups, shareholders and employees -- with special emphasis on crisis management and damage control, establishing the right persona, the uses of spin, why public opinion doesn't count, and doing the right thing.

Made in the USA
Charleston, SC
19 October 2016